AFTER
GREGORY

Austin Wright was born in New York in 1922. He was a
novelist, an academic and, for many years, Professor of
English at the University of Cincinnati. He lived with his
wife and daughters in Cincinnati, and died in 2003 at the
age of eighty.

AFTER GREGORY

Austin Wright

ATLANTIC BOOKS
London

First published in the United States in 1993 by Baskerville Publishers Ltd.

Originally published in Great Britain in 1994 by Touchstone,
an imprint of Simon & Schuster Ltd.

Reissued in Great Britain in hardback and export
and airside trade paperback in 2010 by Atlantic Books,
an imprint of Atlantic Books Ltd.

This paperback edition published in Great Britain in 2017 by Atlantic Books.

1 3 5 7 9 10 8 6 4 2

A CIP catalogue record for this book is available from
the British Library.

Paperback ISBN: 978 1 78649 211 1
E-book ISBN: 978 1 78649 212 8

Printed and bound by CPI Group (UK) Ltd, Croydon, CR0 4YY

Atlantic Books
An imprint of Atlantic Books Ltd
Ormond House
26–27 Boswell Street
London WC1N 3JZ

www.atlantic-books.co.uk

For Gerry and Mary

PART ONE

The River

ONE

So here you are, writing at last. After two days in strangers' cars, listening to conversations drop into memory and out, thinking all the while what to write when you had the chance. Here's the chance. Tell where you are at this important moment: Georgia, a motel, November. Describe it, a machine noise, muffled sound of a television set, an audience laughing. Go into detail: a slamming door, a Coke can dropping into the slot, chuckle of ice, feet. Silence wraps these noises like a doughnut. You have now written a paragraph.

The story spreads out, delicious and full of woe, hungry to be written. You have told it often, but only in speech, where it disappears into other people's vanishing memories. Oral. You told parts of it to the hitchhikers and more to Jack Rome and Bonnie Brown and others, a lot of people. Your tellings narrowed it into a track which served your purposes in one situation and another, but writing is different. The story waits for you, you look forward to the words that will settle it: what it was like to swim out of the river, to hitchhike across the country without a name, to receive the fortune Jack Rome gave you and live in the mansion that fortune bought, all those surprising adventures.

Decisions to make. Where to begin—which depends on whose story you try to tell. If it's Peter Gregory's, you could start anywhere, with the Sebastian case, or Linda his wife, or Florry Gates, or his birth. *Your* birth was different. Think about you. You came into being in the crisis of drowning, alive in the body of a dying man. Discovered like a prophet in the water where he tried to submerge you, without name, only the irreducible sentient *you*, and you came into life by asserting your refusal to be drowned. You swam and crawled out on the other side of the river like the first amphibian up from the sea. If the story is about you who did that, that's the place to begin.

Writing can record and then ignore the skepticism of someone like Bonnie Brown. When you told Bonnie about drowning in the Ohio River, she thought you made it up. When you described your Long Island Sound mansion and the fortune which came to you so miraculously, she laughed. Wow, she would say, what happened to it? We could sure use a little of that around here. Why, Bonnie would ask, would Jack Rome endow a nobody like you? A nobody, she called you, a con man inventing picaresque adventures to bolster a weak ego. Her words: con man, picaresque, weak ego. There, you've written that, and now it's part of the story too.

To you reading this, whoever you are—whether you are the one you were meant to be, who has answered and followed up the personal ad with your name in the newspaper and thus returned to the world, or if you are just some stranger: apologies for the confusion of second persons. It's just one of those ambiguous linguistic things one falls into, unless you prefer it to mean that there really is not much difference between you, you, and you—the you who reads, the you who writes, the you written about. Your second person sets all of you apart from some invisible and undecipherable me, and it's through you that I exist. Looking at you, thinking through you, writing to you.

TWO

In the beginning, water. Closing over you whistling, cold and black, tasting of mud. You broke through and found air. The city lights were going by in the waves. In heavy clothes, you found yourself swimming. The current was carrying you toward the bridge. Moving downstream in the middle of the river, the stadium parking lights gliding by, the suspension bridge almost overhead. You and he. He had never been a strong swimmer, but the question was whether you in coat, pants, shoes, could make it across. Not urgent, just curious. Under the bridge, trucks rumbled in the waves. Red and green marker lights high up. The steady rhythm less tired than before. Each stroke brought you a few inches toward shore, while the current carried you parallel. The concrete pier of another bridge aimed at your head, swept by, you were surprised how fast. Now you were tired, the way he used to feel, heart swollen under a column of water. Maybe the drowning had only been postponed. You grabbed a rotten log sticking up. It had holes, a light coating of slime, remains of some old dock. From here to shore only twenty feet. Wait, catch your breath, take a look. A chain link fence enclosed a pile of coal, two floodlights on stilts, two parked trucks. Stay out of the light. Just downstream a barge with coal tied up without lights. Then trees growing out of the water's edge. You made for them. Your hands in the mud, you scrambled up. Found dry ground in the bushes, flung yourself down, rolled over, closed your eyes. Now we can drown in peace, you said, without all that racket and all that water.

You, imagine that night. An unmarked time, neither before nor after, when you became aware of place. Darkness and water flowing, lights on bridges, tiers of lights in a parking garage upriver, back there. Nearby, near the quiet slopping shore, cold and wet in heavy soaked clothing, someone was alive surviving someone who had drowned. If you were going to drown you would have done so before, not resting in a wet body on a hard shore.

That time faded into others with no before or after. A loud near automobile fart without muffler, outside of time. A parallel time when a diesel noise moved a blind spot across the opposite configuration of lights, a gliding clot, an embolism with square orange windows, then the original lights restored.

Again time changed, though still the clothing was wet, necktie, trousers, a mess of wet rags clutching your parts, with a need to pee. Light of the early morning, chilly, ambiguous, a pale white glare full of dark lead, pigiron, and coal. The river visible now, close to his feet, silver and black, a smooth current flattening left. Conveyor belts on the other side, black giraffes arching next to the highway loops into the bridge. The white sky was undifferentiated, dull, dark, tired and bored. Jesus Christ, the man said, what am I doing here?

Scramble to your feet. Shifting soppy clothes, ugh. A house with tacked-on green siding directly above, two screened windows looking down. Everything was closer than last night, the barge, the bridge almost overhead. The bushes were thin scraggly things. The people in the house could hear your pee exploding on the dirt.

A rusty play set, a swing, a slide behind the house, fifteen feet from where you had slept. You sat on a knob of earth. Across the river to the left, beyond the giraffes, houses patching a gray hill asked questions. Why don't you go home? The pale bored morning has returned, curing you. You sat plunking sticks, arguing with somebody. Go back to the car, he said. The public landing, use the bridge. But a man was coming along the barge, walking with a purpose. Better get out of here. You went back, past the bushes where you had slept and the house, up a dirt path to the road above, where you paused.

Small houses on both sides of the road, mailboxes at the edge, no sidewalks, overhanging trees. Further down it widened with signs and shops. You went that way. Though you couldn't remember why you couldn't go home, you knew there was a reason.

A post office, schoolyard, quicklunch, everything closed except the quicklunch. The sign said EAT. You saw light inside, people in back. You entered in your dark soppy business suit, muddy necktie. A long narrow room, brightly lit with an old man in white in the kitchen and waitress in yellow at the counter. Men in work clothes in the booths. A faint steamy smell in your clothing. Once you were in there was no way out.

The waitress was solid and stout, with a nice face. What would you like, honey? You still had the wallet in your pants. The money would not be hurt by wetting, and you ordered bacon, eggs, juice, coffee.

She was talking to everybody. Some people are born mean, she said. She came back with your juice and asked you, Ain't that right? She leaned her elbow against the coat rack. You can't change your basic kid. The man in the next booth spoke up, a single word. Permissiveness, he said. Naw, honey, the waitress said, you don't mean that.

7

You ate your meal and paid for it. Now what? Back to the street, busy now with school children holding hands to cross and cars trying to park. You saw a path going down between two houses. There was a little park on an embankment with a row of green benches. You sat down there to look at the river or think about this strange new life you found yourself in.

THREE

The day had cleared. The park bench was green, the sky blue, the grass around the bench green. The water close to shore brown, the middle blue, the warehouses dark red and brown. The city skyscrapers beyond the bridges were brown and tan and beige, and the hill to the left green with slabs of white houses.

You sat on the bench, clothes almost dry, a slight crusty stiffness. Up river beyond the bridges, on a slope descending into the water, was a sparkling screen of bright points, the whole slope jumping with fragments of sun: windshields. The public landing, all parked up in the morning. If Peter Gregory's car has not been discovered yet, it could go unnoticed all day.

The situation includes an imaginary or real policeman on the public landing, preparing to write a ticket for overnight parking. Tomorrow he will come back and find the same car with the same ticket still on the windshield. Then he will see what he missed before: the keys, the envelope. Policeman says, Uh-oh.

The news spreads quickly, giving little shocks as it goes. Did you say Peter Gregory? Students, colleagues, neighbors examine their memories. Did you see it coming? Mrs. Gregory will say she's not surprised. But you on the green bench, looking at the color of the river, you are surprised. You always thought suicides were different. Suicides I have known: Dr. Holman, May Glesser, Harold Hastings. Trying to understand them always too late, the split between you and the severed friend, deceiving you all your life. Now it's the same question about Gregory: did you, his intimate for thirty-five years, see it coming? Peter Gregory added to the list, defined by a word.

You looked for something to explain his suicide: Disgust, shame, intolerable frustration. Long low depression. The unbearable process of living—irritation of the senses, light on the eyes, skin, mind. Whatever was wiped out by the drowning: you couldn't remember.

Maybe you weren't trying to remember. Maybe you didn't realize there was a gap. The sun was bright. It shone warmly. You watched a motor launch—a family boat—moving up the river with children aboard. Across the river the conveyor belts moved. A string of coal cars passed slowly along the railroad track, its flanges screeching across the river. You remember that but not what you were remembering then. Maybe it's not possible to remember an act of remembering. Maybe you merely substitute what you remember now. You do remember this: the sudden fright of wondering if he had forgotten to leave the note.

> To my colleagues, children and ex-wife.
> By the time you read this

Such a fright on the bright green park bench would make you try to remember, recapitulate the night before. Recapitulate: downtown in the car, twice around blocks, past hotel lobbies where late night people waited for taxis or the airport limousines, past the square (fountain turned off for the night), naked mannequins in department store windows, waiting for traffic lights.

The public landing was a broad concrete slope descending into the river along a front of several hundred feet. In the daytime cars parked in rows, but at night it was empty and dark. Peter Gregory drove out to the middle point in the slope, turned off the engine, fastened the parking brake. Breathing more heavily with a thumping heart, waiting.

No memory, though, of how long he waited and what finally brought him to act. Such knowledge went to the bottom with him. You remember Peter Gregory blushing in the dark, a fiery burn, fiery enough to put the car into neutral, fasten his seat belt, release the brake, let it roll.

Well, the reason he didn't do that was that the letter would have been lost too. Which proves the letter was on his mind. So it must have been there, on the seat of the car as planned. Remember coming to that conclusion on the sunny morning park bench, and feeling relieved. Though he should have left the letter in the motel. You can't remember what was in it. Powerful reasons, no doubt, to explain to Linda and the world what had happened to Peter Gregory.

Well, what did happen to Peter Gregory? He walked down to the river and when he got there kept going until he slipped, fell, and drowned. He was tired when he drowned, and glad to go.

A towboat with barges was coming upstream, daytime equivalent to the blind gap in the night. You watched this one, crisp and enamel white, man standing on the deck, looking at the shore—looking at you. Since you couldn't see his face, he couldn't see yours. Engine humming, water churning at the stem. Peter Gregory would have considered it a machine, all energy and power, impersonal as rivets, but to you it was as much a blossom of life as a bird's nest in a tree.

You looked at your hands, felt your high forehead, scratched the thin curly hair on top and in back, the body that had escaped from the river. Peter Gregory's body now belonged to you.

11

There was a danger, a risk of being mistaken for him. It made you nervous. Time to go. Why? Because you can't just sit here. Why not? Move, man, move. Where? Two possibilities, back to the river or the road. The road then, but then what? To avoid Gregory, you needed to get away from here, the city, the region. You had forty dollars which Peter Gregory had left in your wallet along with credit cards. The credit cards, unusable, had his name on them. But the money was free, it would sustain you for a few days, while you figured how to get more.

The quickest way out would be to cross back over the bridge and take Gregory's car. But then you would have to mail the suicide note. They would wonder what happened to the car, and then you would no longer be a suicide but a missing person. You were on the narrow road above the river, concealed from the river by trees, headed out from town. Cars passed occasionally, going slow on this road. You could hitch rides, like the kids. You turned to face the traffic, raised your arm, put out your thumb. You acquired an identity and a name: Hitchhiker.

With inherited politeness, Hitchhiker tried to look civilized, pleasant, human, like one of you. A big car stopped, man in a business suit and bright tie. Where you going? Hitchhiker hadn't thought about that. Try East. New York, Pennsylvania.

Mister, you better get over on the other side of the road. You're headed in the wrong direction.

Hitchhiker wondered why he had said East. It was not that he wanted to go there. But he crossed over anyway and thumbed the other way. A pickup truck stopped, dirty white. A boy and a girl in jeans, both with long hair. He sat beside them in the seat. They didn't say where they were going. In a moment—how fast it was—they passed EAT where you had breakfast and the green-sided house under which you had spent a night long ago in clothes that had subsequently dried. Where to?

New York? Pennsylvania? The boy laughed. Take you through town and leave you where the Millyville road intersects the Interstate.

Across the bridge and through the city. By Long Avenue past familiar roads up the hill to the University area. Hitchhiker knew what those streets would look like now in the bright middle of the morning. Delivery trucks doing business on the hillside, wives going to the grocery store, heads of families teaching classes in the high school. Children at school, a fat boy, a skinny girl, both with glasses. Messy apartments of lonely males separated from their wives. The archetypal young separated widow had a red Volkswagen of her own and worked in a college office. One particular street went up to a group of houses, immediately obscured.

The girl with long hair said, If you cut them back, that makes them grow more thickly. You have to keep cutting them back so they'll shape up and get full. The houses were gone, they were waiting for a light on a broad industrial street between warehouses and a yellow brick factory opposite a playground. In the bleak bright sunny morning, an invisible storm was gathering.

The girl with the long hair said, I'm going to trim those lilacs in the back and give them one more chance. Another thing, I'm going to divide those peonies—

Which peonies?

The red ones next to the shed. I'm going to divide them and put some of them around the garage.

He was disgusted, he had been so careful to calculate the emotional costs. It was a big storm, high tide. The girl did not notice. I've got to get at those dandelions, though. Maybe you should do that.

I still don't know which peonies you're talking about.

The *red* peonies.

Which red peonies?

Idiot, Hitchhiker said, furious with your grief. You denied it and tried to blame Gregory, but Hitchhiker said it was you and even accused you of grieving for him. The girl noticed. Jesus Christ, are you all *right*?

Allergy, he said.

FOUR

Later, after Jack Rome made you rich, you liked to look back,
scorning people like Hitchhiker. You knew he was allergic, but
whether any brighter than Gregory—that's still to be decided.
He watched the children disappear down the Millyville road,
their white pickup truck skimming along above the flat farms
on both sides, babbling about him.

They had left him just beyond the overpass where the Millyville road crosses the Interstate. All the country was flat, fields
divided by lines of brush, with clusters of trees around groups
of farm buildings, widely scattered. He stood slightly above the
general level of the fields. Just here, where the eastbound ramp
descended to the Interstate from the Millyville road, was a
gasoline station with a high sign (TEXACO) on two white legs,
writing in the sky for motorists ahead. The wind whistled
against the pipes. Another sign said TRUCK STOP, and another,
FOOD. There was a low single-story building, sprawling back
from the asphalt lot toward a little stream at the edge of a field.
The building had orange shingles, a solid plate glass front, and
the lot was parked with tractor trucks and automobiles. Hitchhiker crossed the lot, glanced in the window (counter, souvenirs,
cash register, women in slacks), and went in.

Try lunch. He ordered a hamburger and chocolate shake, sat
in a booth, and ate slowly. Went to the men's room. Mirror
there, a shock, the exposed view of ugly Peter Gregory gaping
at him. The high balding forehead, yellow curly hair, eye bags,

bloody eyes, anyone would recognize him. It took courage to go back to the booth, but no one noticed. Sat a long time, delaying. Then out again into the sun. Noticed a poster tacked by the door:

HEAR THE WORD OF GOD
Rev. Osgood Landis
Miranda Landis
Coliseum, 8:00 pm

That would have been last night, the big windowless amphitheater over the river where Peter Gregory drowned, the believers worshiping in their lighted vault while you struggled for watery rebirth below. That too was past. Soon I must hitch rides again. Because that's what I have been born to: a hitchhiker. With all the time in the day and no place to go. Let's sit in the sun a while at that table in back. Someone will come from the kitchen and chase us away, but until then, tables for travelers tired from the road.

This particular bench, splintery and reddish brown, had a crust of dried ice cream at one corner, flies working on it. Flies all over. The discussion at the picnic table was lethargic, dazed by the sun. Questions without answers. Mainly this one: in view of the sudden allergy in the truck this morning, why can't you cross back and raise Peter Gregory from the dead?

It was the sun, bright shining at midday on the back of your head, making a sharp shadow of whoever you are on the red painted picnic table, stunning your eyes with the sharpness of contrast between sunlight and shadow. This sun was warm, but the air was cool as it came across the flat land undeflected, stirring the grasses, flapping the banners at the gas station next door, whistling on the pipes that held up TEXACO and TRUCK

STOP and FOOD. See how the land stretches away from you in all directions, miles and miles, how the sky runs away from you into that blue beyond all horizons, out of sight. On the Interstate, cars zip past, down below the bank, zip and silence and thdrumm a truck and more trucks, while nearby people you do not know drive into the lot, unload into the building with the orange roof, come out again, get into their cars, descend the ramp to zip again.

Waiting for an answer. No inside sound at all, only the whistling pipes, some live squeaking of birds in the grass. Then suddenly, Peter Gregory at the door of his house, walking into the kitchen and saying to Linda, his wife, *Linda, I've come home:* She looks at him with shocked joy and clattering plates: Oh my *dear.* Children, fat boy, skinny girl, climbing onto him in a tableau of reconciliation.

Chasm in your brain, black hole. Try again. Linda in the kitchen doorway, looking at him straight. The delicate face, pale diamond eyes. He tries to explain: I've just come back from killing myself. She stares. Stop, don't let her speak.

What a jolt. No projections could alter her direction, hastened by his falling into the river, not to be reversed by jumping out again. No allergy in a stranger's pickup truck could hide what Peter Gregory knew. Which Hitchhiker, dozing in the windy afternoon sun on the picnic table, could not remember. Warmed by the sun, watching the flies, listening to the zip and thdrumm, this man neither young nor old in the dark shapeless clothes put his elbows on the table, rested face in hands, brooding while the metamorphosis struggled to undo itself. Peter Gregory groping back to life, threatening all your joy, all the effort of the wet night and zest of the bright morning. Yet if he can't go back, you ought to know why. All you know is Peter Gregory against Peter Gregory, who had made a botch of things. Peter Gregory whose dislike of Peter Gregory arose out of Peter Gregory's own fine and finicky judgment. Piling manure on his head until it was difficult to distinguish manure from Gregory.

But you, it wasn't your disgust, your hatred, your rage. You try to remember, help him remember, because you need some excuse for being here. Some history to explain why he can't go back and start over again. But it's too hard. He took you into the river for reasons of some sort. Remember how sweetly the river washed away that crusted pile of disgust and soothed the angry disturbance. This question remained: If Peter Gregory drowned in the river, who are you? Did you plan this? Did you deliberately arrange to leave him in the river and you here?

Never mind. It was impossible to tell what was on your mind when you were Peter Gregory. He knew his weakness, inability to swim, and despair would be enough. With the water in his shoes, socks, pants, shivering and defying his natural repugnance, he slipped, fell, and was in. Head under for a second—the slosh and pressure in his nose, bubbles streaming through his ears—and then he swam. It was Peter Gregory saying I'll swim out far enough so I can't get back. So much for Peter Gregory.

For you meanwhile, something else. When you found yourself swimming better than expected. You had the struggle with the water, but also the lights on the shore. You were seeing those lights for the last time. It occurred to you it was Peter Gregory who was preventing you from seeing them again. It was Peter Gregory who was taking the night away from you, as he meant to take away also the morning and the countryside. The realization shocked you. That was a big sacrifice he was asking of you, to satisfy his ego. It woke you up, angry like a revolutionary with the possibility of a coup, kicking him out, letting him drown while you made your way back to the lights and life.

The revolution was successful. Which puts you here now, with the sky and the sun and the cool air blowing the pennants and whistling against the signs. Whoever you are has no name and no place, free to go wherever you like except back. If it proves too difficult, if you have too many fits of grief, you can say it was just an experiment. You can always go back to the river, you told him then: it will still be there.

FIVE

In the afternoon the fairweather clouds began to thicken. They passed in front of the sun and took away its warmth. The afternoon is moving on, you said, night is coming, you'd better do something. You went down the ramp to the Interstate. It was not a decision: something within said *Now* and you obeyed. Where are you going? you asked. No reply. It was not an adventure yet.

At the point where the ramp touched the highway, you turned to face the cars. For misidentification of Peter Gregory this was the most dangerous thing yet, for it was the main exit from the city to the Northeast. Come on, you said, get your ass out of here.

A car stopped, the color of apricots, driven by a woman in a copper-gold dress. I'll take you to the Cleveland turnoff, she said.

The car smelled clean and new. Windshield tinted, motor silent, it rode like a boat. She was a pretty young woman, not as young as you first thought. A coppery necklace, earrings, gold-colored bracelets. What's your name? It came high pitched out of the silence between you and the rock music on the radio. The question stunned you. You had no answer. You grabbed the first name flying by. It was Thomas Sebastian, but you checked that, looking for another. Osgood Landis, you almost said, catching that one too just in time, so that it came out Gilbert Osmond. You remembered too late the book that came from.

But the air remained silent, not shocked, and that moment it became an adventure. Your life was an adventure, you realized it suddenly, and it was totally new.

Gilbert Osmond: aesthete collector, effete snob, private in the recesses of his home, the last person in the world you would meet hitchhiking on an American highway. You felt wonderful, full of meringue and ice cream, just as you had hoped.

Most people call me Gil, Gil said.

All right, Gil. Who are you?

(Still, you would need a name more usable than Gil Osmond. You would have to think of a good one, that you could answer to without effort, that you would not forget. Names: Oscar Chapin. Stanley Trumpet. You would also need a job.)

The reason I ask, look at your clothes. What happened to you?

Better names, quick: Jack (Mississippi) Cousteau. Neanderthal (Ned) Truckee. That won't do.

Jobs: Truck driver. Postman. Reference librarian.

She watched you. You noticed what had made you think of Osgood Landis when she first asked your name. She said, why are your clothes so all gummy and stinky? Your pants are covered with mud.

That? I fell in a ditch.

How come?

It's a long story.

Forget it. She looked irritated, but since she'd asked your name you felt free to ask hers, hoping she would say Isabel, the free spirit of America turning its freshest face to the world.

No reply. Her mood settled in like weather. Suddenly she didn't want to talk. Is something wrong? You saw her shiver, hold herself in. At the next intersection she pulled off.

You get out now. There's something wrong with you.

What's wrong with me?

Get away from there. I don't like you.

You watched her drive off, afraid of you, and you felt like an escaped convict wondering what she had seen.

What you had seen was the decal on her windshield, showing a television screen with a large silver cross and shiny gleams of angel hair superimposed upon a castle with spires, all inside a legend reading LANDIS COMMUNITY. She had come from Cleveland to hear the Word of God but had found the devil in you.

Late afternoon, the sky fading. He walked (Harold Hastings) into the town and stopped at a small restaurant for his supper. Meditating over his hot beef sandwich, trying to forget her evil message. The question was where to sleep tonight. He went into the delicatessen and bought a tin of canned meat, a chunk of cheese, and a loaf of bread, along with a shopping bag to carry them in. Tomorrow, Harold Hastings said, having discovered the future. Louis Bolero could mow lawns. Gus Tulips, highway construction worker.

How to find a place to sleep? The town was very small. He passed a dentist's office (Forscht Sprinkel could dig in gardens), three gas stations, a store selling tractors and mowers (Mitchell Matchum), and a rooming house: ROOMS.

Did Hal Hastings want ROOMS? Could he afford ROOMS? A pair of elderly proprietors would call him "Son" and make him sign their guest book. They too would see something wrong in him. You had slept on the ground last night, you could do it again.

You went out of town along the road, up a hill, houses with lights in their windows. Late dusk. An open field, with a barn on the other side. Signs in the field, facing the road: Elks, chewing tobacco, a restaurant. Beyond the field, the woods came up to the edge of the road, with a grassy ditch between woods and road. The sign was small, white, posted on a tree: NO TRES-PASSING. Just beyond it, barely discernible in the thickening darkness, the barbed wire fence. The road leveled off. Not far ahead, the fields began again, with a group of farm buildings. Another sign across the ditch: NO TRESPASSING. All the woods in this area have signs, are black and full of thorns, brambles, and barbed wire.

Car lights approaching, you went down into the ditch and waited for the car to pass. Eyes getting used to the dark. Fence-posts for the barbed wire, tall shapes of the trees beyond, stars through the tops of the trees. The floor of the woods was clean, not filled with underbrush as it had been further back, and you heard running water. You argued. The sign is meant for hunt-ers—it doesn't apply to you. It applies to everyone, Hal Hastings said: NO TRESPASSING means everybody. You insisted, noth-ing on signs applies to you. Written in words for people who use names. It doesn't apply to squirrels or bears, it doesn't apply to you.

Leaving Hal Hastings behind, you crossed the ditch, in-spected the fence, discovered it was down, and went into the woods. Picked your way through the trees, crunching the leafy forest bottom, and found a grassy patch next to a rock. You sat there, quiet. Occasionally the sound of a car, for you were still near the road. Also the running water you had heard before, and a remote roar over the fields and woods from the Interstate where you had left it at the other side of town.

After a few minutes, what to do? By Gregory habits it was still early. You could go back to the movie advertised in the town. A long way to walk, just to see something Peter Gregory would have scorned. Yet no one could do anything in this darkness except sleep. Sleep then. Creatures without names who live in the woods, living by the natural light and dark.

You wondered what rituals you still needed for sleep. This compulsion to remove clothes. Off your jacket, but the air was chilly, and you put it back on. Off tie, empty pockets, wallet on the ground. Rituals of washing and brushing your teeth, but no toothbrush, no water. You lay down on your side as if you were in bed.

Thus began your second night without a name, alone on the unmediated surface of the earth. You had to get up again in a few minutes for what Peter Gregory's mother years ago used to call the Call of Nature. Find a place in the dark to squat, tear up the paper bag in which you had carried your bread, shivering, if not from disgust then from fear of disgust. Whose disgust? Gregory's, of course, his fastidious ghost.

SIX

Nameless in the morning after a night of names. After jobs, biographies, obituaries, confessional letters, amid ghostly trees and witches and terrors of the woods, you woke to the early morning light thinking you had not slept at all. The experiment has failed, you said.

Wakened by the birds. Chickadees, cardinals, a distant cock crow. A woody grove, sunlight in the tops of trees. The grove sloped downward, and through the trees you could see the green slope of an opposite field, with the sunlight penetrating the dissolving mist. Forgetting the burials and arrests of the night, you were awake now with bird songs and a pleasant morning, saying, Well here it is: you asked for it, now enjoy it.

A piece of cheese, two slices of bread. Down the slope, you kneeled and doused your mouth in the brook, fresh and cold, splashed your face, the stiff growing bristles. Wild life, junco in the leaves, small olive green birds in the branches.

Sitting on a rock, you dozed, waiting for the wildness to come back. You stood up and stretched. You noticed how settled the trees had become since the night before, fixed like stars, placed for life. You were different. If you weren't sleepy, you were bored. Though you weren't going anywhere you would have to go. Back to the road, carrying your shopping bag. You began your long day's walk.

That's what legs are for. All day for miles and miles, fields with scattered woods, country rolling with gentle hills, the road going mildly up and down. When the sun was high you sat on a rock and ate canned meat and bread and cheese. You came to a small town and took a long drink from the water fountain in the playground. You went to the General Store and bought a roll of toilet paper, a shaving set, an army canteen. You kept walking.

Winston Topsoil, window washer. Newton Oldflower, garden weeder. Dozed on a bench in a village square and woke abruptly. You had forgotten to pick up your mail, then remembered who you were. Nicholas Rostov, no-count white trash. Day turned into late afternoon, afternoon into evening, evening into night. You prepared for another night in the woods.

In the night a thunderstorm. You heard him curse the rain. Wet clothes, again, complaining. Followed by a day in a ravine by a stream where you washed your clothes and draped them on bushes to dry in the sun. Maybe now people wouldn't call you stinky and look at you strange and say, There's something wrong with you. Gerald Carstairs, naked bellhop under the open sky. In the late afternoon your clothes were dry. Jake Barnes put them on, climbed up to the road, back to the town he had passed through late the day before, and spent the fourth night of his life in a small hotel. I owe this to myself, he said.

He signed the register as Dick Diver, and ate in the restaurant across the street. Late that evening he burned his credit cards in the wastebasket of his room and washed the ashes down the toilet. He slept deeply in the soft sheets and the pillow against his cheek.

Morning in the Paradise Hotel, where the cracks in the ceiling bounded rectangular fields in a map of farm country. From your bed you saw chimney pots on a roof across the square and branches of a tree shining in the sun. You heard automobiles

26

below, cars starting, idling, going, and you heard voices, men greeting, a woman's voice, talk. Dick Diver, diver, needed to earn money. He got up and went to the window. Directly below were two men in farm clothes, talking by a parked car. A clock on the tower: 7:30. You felt the grief coming on again, for the dead who could never come back to tell the living how they had signed a hotel register as Dick Diver or ridden in a car with Isabel Archer. A letter for Linda, damn you: If you change your mind, please write to me care of this hotel.

Quit that now. You've got to learn the difference between Gregory and you. Slice him away with a clean knife.

To work. According to James Green, handyman, your job possibilities were limited. The skills and training of Peter Gregory were not transferable because you would need credentials to bring them into view. You will have to go from door to door, asking for work. Admit your lack of knowledge, but show your willingness—polite, pleasant, helpful.

Consider the little restaurant where you ate yesterday. He could wash dishes. You went in the door, sat down at the counter. The fat waitress was collecting glasses in a large bin to soak in water under the counter. Excuse me.

Just a moment honey.

Excuse me. He opened his mouth. It came out. I'm looking for work.

He's down at the garage. I saw him a half hour ago.

The expressionless cashier came over. You'll have to see the boss, she said. Tomorrow. I doubt if he can give you anything. The fat waitress caught on. You want a job? You'll have to see the boss. Tomorrow.

I already told him that.

James Green went into the hardware store next door, full of shelves up to the ceiling, the shelves full of goods. He went to the back and found a man trying to decide what to do about a large uncut sheet of glass.

This is a family operation, the man said. Myself, my sons, daughter, old man. Ever work in a hardware store? What do you know about hardware? Well, what *do* you know? What I mean is, what's *your* brand of expertise?

In the garage, James Green in his coat and tie faced a man in blue coveralls, who had white hair and a heavily lined tan face. The name *Work* was stitched in red on his pocket. I need a mechanic.

I'm not a mechanic. What can you do? I can work a gas pump. I can check the oil and the batteries. The man was chawing. I need a mechanic. Guess I'd better try someplace else. Guess so.

James Green crossed the street and went around to the back stoop of a large white house. Round-faced elderly woman with white hair and pleasant face. You're selling something I don't want it.

I was wondering if you had any odd jobs I might do.

Well I'll be. You remind me of the Great Depression. People don't come round looking for work nowadays. Why it takes me right back.

I could mow your lawn. She laughed. Her face changed. She was looking into the ugly mug of Peter Gregory, which he had forgotten in the excitement of his adventures, the bullfrog eyes, the bald front, he couldn't blame her. No telling what strangers might be in these changed times when it ain't people looking for work you got to worry about. Sorry, we don't have a thing.

A woman asked if he was an electrician. A man wondered if he had registered with the employment agency in Harristown. A dog barked at him. He turned down a side street where he saw a small stone bridge crossing a stream. He sat on the grass at the edge of the stream and watched the clear slow water. With a house on the other side of the stream and another house behind the bushes at his back.

Rustling grass, twigs—life around you, a cat coming out of the bushes—large, gray, striped. Well-fed. It came up to you, curling its tail in the air like a string attached to a balloon with gravity reversed. You asked its name and it told you.

You sat on the grass next to Murry Bree, and took the liberty of stroking behind its ears. Looked into its alien eyes, its face alert but not much surprised, the confident, cautious, slightly baffled expression you were accustomed to seeing on the faces of rabbits, antelope, cows, and mountain lions in the zoo. All the more expressive animals look like that, Murry Bree said. A robin lit on the grass a few feet away. Hopping along, listening for worms. Its round black eye had the same expression. The robin was calmly at work, while Murry Bree's tail twitched and his kinship eyes brightened with hope. Yet he wasn't sure, torn between his innate catness and the induced luxury of being stroked by his namesake. The robin clucked and flew away. Murry Bree relaxed and was glad, saved from decision. The second Murry was glad too, thinking how that robin's simple honest expression would have looked if Murry had caught him: how without visible change in the plain round eye the simple confidence would indescribably convert into terror. The same simple universal terror you would see on any other animal, including Murry Bree, in the presence of a larger animal or pain or catastrophe.

He asked the other Murry Bree, who was washing himself, What's it like in there? Much the same as you, the cat said. A little simpler. Harder to draw conclusions beyond the obvious inductions. Memory not too good, which you might consider a handicap.

Never mind the memory. Sitting there, warm and not too hungry, with still a little money in his pocket and unburdened by a serious name, Murry Bree thought he could live forever, for as long as that lasted, with no noticeable difference between forever and now.

SEVEN

A man gave the Hitchhiker a day's work putting shingles on his roof. Took him out to his house in his dusty pickup truck. The man wore overalls over a red plaid shirt, his face was thin, and his eyes overlooked his nose like a bird of prey.

What's your name? he said.

Murry Bree.

That's a funny name.

It's French, you explained. It used to be pronounced Bray, but my father anglicized it to Bree.

The man believed Murry Bree had just been released from prison. That's why you're bumming around for work, he said. I don't care. You served your time and now you're out.

Murry Bree (Ex-Convict) spent most of the afternoon on the roof of Roy Clements' house. He climbed up a tall ladder that swayed under his feet. You could see across rolling fields and patches of woods. He smashed his thumb with the hammer and bumped the box with the shingles off the roof twice. In the middle of the afternoon Roy Clements invited him down for a break.

He had coffee in a thermos jug. They sat on the ground by the saw horse. How come you never learned to hammer a nail? A man who can't hammer a nail, what kind of a man is that?

I can hammer a nail.

Sort of. The eye of Roy Clements, looking at him under thick red eyebrows, evil. Every man learns how to hammer a nail. How come you got left out?

That was a question only Peter Gregory could answer, but you faked it. I guess other things interested me more, you said.

The man's eyes narrowed, deep in their shade. That's a shitty answer. You hammer like a girl.

The man talked quiet and the look in his eye could be mistaken for friendly, but the words were not. So what did you do before you wound up in jail? Salesman, bank teller?

The question referred to Peter Gregory and was irrelevant, but you were the one who had to answer. I didn't go to jail. I worked just like everybody else.

That so? So tell me what you did. Schoolteacher? That's you, I bet.

You got it. You felt yourself blushing.

No shit? Schoolmarm, hey? It figures. You talk funny. So how come you're looking for work you can't do? How come you ain't giving the Pledge Allegiance?

I resigned.

Went to jail, you mean. Don't shit me, I know your type. You think you're better than folks. You think you're so much god damn fucking smarter than folks.

No I don't, you said, with loathing for Peter Gregory. You don't know a damn thing about me.

I don't hey? Okay professor, you tell me. You like the niggers and the Jews?

What?

You heard me.

What's that question supposed to mean? You knew what it was supposed to mean. This was a challenge to Peter Gregory politics, Peter Gregory conscience. You wanted to be innocent,

32

new in the world, untouched by the world's guilt. I don't make distinctions, you said.

You wondered who was talking for you now, while you watched this guy nudge you into the slot he had set aside for you. You know something? We don't allow niggers in this town.

Watching for your predictable reaction, waiting to pounce. Any objections?

You didn't say anything.

No objections? Come on, guy, no objections?

I don't want to argue.

What? Look at you. I gave you a job. You would of starved without me. You want your pay? You're fuckin right you do. You're gonna finish this job, and do it for me, and I'm gonna pay you, and then you get your ass out of here and never let me see you again, got it? His eyes were gray under the red brows, looking at you straight, smiling like human eyes, with no visible connection to his words.

That night Murry Bree blew your day's earnings for a room in the Crawley House in Badgerton. The room was not worth it, he slept so badly. Roy Clements was in his sleep, overlooking him, with tremors of rage and fear. To hell with Murry Bree, you said. If you don't like the adams apple man standing over you sneering, in ignorance of who you are, you know how to stop it. You did it once and you can do it again.

After breakfast, you sat on a bench in the middle of the town square. You noticed the action at the garage across the street, cars stopping for gas, one car on the lift, another with the front wheels off. The attendant parked one of the cars on the street, leaving the keys in the car. Full of rage, Murry Bree was a Criminal like Roy Clements, thinking, gun, holdup, steal that car and drive away, serve him right, Bree, Gregory, serve them all right. Then you heard a voice behind you. You heard it a second time, louder. Hey Bum!

Man with blue T-shirt and heavy belly, big, coming this way across the square. He looked like a bum and he said, Hey Bum!

To you Murry Bree said, I'm not a bum. Who, me? You! Hey Bum! You went for a walk, the other way, around the square. Keep out of our streets, hear, nobody wants you around here, Bum.

Past the white column door of the Crawley House, you turned a corner. The bum was following. No running, just walking fast. His face was thick, wet, shiny. Lots of s and k and ch. I'm not a bum. A curious old man looked up from the hood of his car, you did not stop to talk. Down a gravel alley between two close houses, if you could get to the next street before he could see you, past the garbage cans and back garages and back-yard play sets: it would not be nice to be caught back here.

So much for Roy Clements. Gravel road down a slope below the backs of houses, descending into a woody ravine. Across a bridge, a shallow vegetable field, a shed across the way, men loading branches into a pickup truck, unaware you were a bum. Beyond them, beside the road, you came to a row of cages, hooked up to each other on wheels, with wolves, foxes, a deer, a lynx, each animal in a separate one. No people around. The animals paced and looked at you, snuffling, thin, an empty food dish in each cage, floors dirty.

The road came to an end. A deeper ravine on the left, used as a dump, with plastic bags and faint white smoke and a putrid smell and below that the remains of old disintegrated stoves and pieces of chairs and junk. You turned and went into the woods. The slope climbed to your right, but to your left the forest floor was flat and clear of brush. You came to a place like a blight, where the raw bare earth bled into a crater beneath a bluff with streams of gravel, which your human mind recognized as a quarry. A wall of red soil and streams of pebbles rising beyond, an embankment for the quarry road. An animal at the foot of the embankment rooting and scratching around in the leaves, its furry tail up, white and black, a skunk. It was poking around a dull rubbery thing, a broken inner tube.

You stopped, realized your mistake, it was not an inner tube but the skin of some dead creature, quite large. It must be a big event when large animals die in the wild, yet how quiet this was with only the skunk paying attention. You came closer, carefully, not to disturb the skunk. He was gone now, and you saw your mistake again. It was the upturned hands alongside the body where it lay on its back, or the gray coon-like fingers curled up, or the little dust-coated dead eyes in the flat noseless face, or the flatness of the face itself with its matted black hair. Or the shoulders, the way the arms were attached to the body.

You approached to look at it, this dead thing like yourself. What to call it, he or she? Frailty of its shoulders and arms, for now you knew what kind of animal it was it did not seem so large. But the signs of its sex were buried under the leaves and mud, if they still existed. You wondered if the creature was still intact. You could not tell because of the mud and leaves in which it lay.

You felt no horror. You did not wonder who it was, nor how it died nor why it was there. A long time passed before you remembered what a civilized person does when discovering death. He calls the authorities, police, doctor, coroner, neighbors. You wondered if someone who has committed suicide only a couple of days before was similarly obligated. You sat on a stone, leaning against a tree, rested, looking through the open tree tops to the field across the valley, then went back to the thing in the leaves and then again to your seat against the tree.

You felt a distinct thrill, while you waited in the presence of the corpse. How the word *corpse* returned to your vocabulary, reminding you: if you reported this to the police, you would be Peter Gregory again.

No need for that. Police were for the people who had names, who put up and obeyed NO TRESPASSING signs. For you, it was only a certain curiosity, like picking up a newspaper in a strange city and getting a mild interest in the local obituaries. Only you'd better get out of here. Let's go, whatever your name is, Murry, let's go, Murry. Just quietly, as casual as you had come. You looked up the embankment, too steep to climb. You came to a place where the forest floor rose almost to the top of the embankment, and you scrambled up to the quarry road. It was full of shoe prints and tire tracks and big caterpillar tractor tracks. A long walk, the hot sun. You came in sight of farm houses across a field. A car approached from behind. It passed slowly, the men inside looking at you. You tried to ignore them. After a while the dirt road came out to a paved road, with farm houses, to the edge of another town, and you walked by the signs, the lowered speed limit, a motel, gas station, houses and another square, and you realized, from the cannon on the grass and the brick courthouse and the Crawley House, that this was the same town and same square from which you had been chased this morning by the bum in the blue T-shirt. You had come into it from the other end, and everything was merely upside down. You fought down despair because there was nothing you could do about it, and since Murry Bree had to eat you went into a lunch room and had lunch.

The stranger who accosted you in the lunch room had a big football face and a colorful shirt like a tourist, and when he sat down next to you he smiled like an insurance salesman. He was friendly until you refused to tell him your name, and then he asked what you were doing in the woods.

He must have been one of the men in the car that passed you on the quarry road. See anything unusual out there? he said. Like what? Unusual like what? Just wondering if you saw anything. All this, while you were standing by the stool with the lunch check, like a hold-up. Didn't see anything, eh?

What are you, police? The man was surprised by the question, he laughed, stopped abruptly, and said, What would you say if I was?

You thought your words out and said, What would you expect me to say?

How should I know? You tell me.

So it was excuse me, I've got to go. You paid the cashier and went out into the street across the square, thinking grab a ride out of here, can you grab a ride? For the first time since it began you seemed to have a stake, something to lose, and nothing was fun anymore, which was a surprise since you had not thought it was fun before. The man came out of the lunch room across the square, intending you harm.

You were to think often later about that stranger, wondering who he was. You assumed he was a detective, but he could have been one of a gang of killers. Or he and his companions could have discovered the body themselves and were just going back to town to report. In that case you yourself would have been a suspect.

You were destined never to know who was killed, what local passion had been acted out, who had suffered, who was bereaved. Your concern was to escape, and when you escaped, you left it behind and never heard from it again. And mostly you could forget, but there were always moments when, from the deep inner discomfort of unremembered things it would rise again into mind: the little raccoon. It reminded you of distractions in Gregory's life before his suicide: of the Hammer Man, who bludgeoned old men to death including the one who lived across the street from you, a night or two before your swim. And the detective named Sam Indigo, who interviewed you about that, asking if you had heard anything, while your mind was occupied by other matters. With that opening up, you remembered more, you remembered for a moment Gregory things no one should have to remember, like a dream you had waked from, to make you glad to be here, after all.

The man with the football face was across the square, looking at you. If you stuck out your thumb to hitchhike, he would drive up and offer you a ride. You moved on quick to where the garage attendant had parked his cars with the keys in them. You got in the Ford, which started right up, fresh and new, waxed and polished. Drove to the corner, turned right, and headed out of town on the next road. Good to be driving again. It was only Murry Bree who was shaking so hard he could hardly steer. Back roads, the Criminal said. Just keep it long enough for the escape. At the edge of town he saw two hitchhikers, standing by the sign that said RESUME NORMAL SPEED. They were a young man with a blond beard and a woman with long light brown hair in a ponytail. They carried a cardboard sign with the black letters: N Y. They were smiling at him, and he stopped to pick them up.

EIGHT

The young man and woman, whose names were Amy and Joe, went with you the rest of the way to New York. They became good friends, sharing your adventure and taking an interest in your case, though there was an awkwardness at the beginning because of the car. You said, Do you mind if I take back roads? You turned off to a well-paved road starting up a hill, which had no route sign. You may not want to drive with me. This car.

You mean it's *hot*?

I only picked it up to get out of Badgerton.

Let us out, mister. No wait, the girl said. Why do you want out of Badgerton? Natural child, no makeup, oval face, inquisitive eyes—nice looking, according to Murry Bree.

Well. Menaced by a guy who called him a bum. No money. Not a bum, too long a story, tell you sometime. He didn't intend to keep the car, only get out of Badgerton with it.

She sympathized. Murry Bree said, I'll tell them you're hitchhikers. The road curved up a hill, down, then up again, by woods and fields and occasional houses and rural mailboxes. The guy was mumbling, stupid dumb-ass, fuckin brainless. Listen mister. How come this car was sitting there with the key in it? When do they start looking? Are they chasing you now?

There was Amy slapping her hands lightly on her knees, her voice keening, excited, a soft whinny. Joe said, When they notice the missing car they call the state police, call goes out, cop looks up from his radio and there you are.

39

Murry Bree is only trying to start a new life. Not easy to make clear to strangers. From scratch. Sounds like a place, a small country town, the wrong one too, for scratch was dry and dusty whereas his beginning was a river. You had to speak their language, translate the river into scratch. You couldn't say, I rose from the river, any more than you could say, I left a dead body in the woods. You heard them looking at each other. I just got out of jail, Murry Bree said. Maybe.

Oh. That explains it. What were you in for?

I don't know. This created another silence. I forget. How could anybody forget what they were in jail for? Murry Bree explained, it was nothing serious, I mean nothing dangerous. It's all right, you don't have to tell, Amy said. What's your name?

My name is Murry Bree. Temporarily, you added. Then, hearing himself, you think I'm crazy. That's all right, we're crazy too, Amy said. We are not, Joe said. That's bullshit, that everybody's crazy including us stuff. Bullshit bullshit. What do you mean, temporarily?

Murry Bree explained, I'm trying to get rid of my old name. Amy can understand that. Can't you, Joe? No answer from Joe.

At the foot of the hill the road joined a two-lane concrete state highway. Better watch it, Joe said. Billboards and signs in the field. You had come into another valley. In a moment you came to a small amusement park. Here, you want to leave the car, leave it here, Joe said.

They left it in the parking lot of the amusement park. Keys in the glove compartment, so no one would come along and steal it. He wiped his fingerprints away with Amy's sweater, which had been wrapped around her waist. Wiped steering wheel, door panel, gear shift. Joe was shifting his weight from foot to foot as if he had to go to the bathroom. Once they were away from the car, he was more comfortable. They went into the amusement park together. Since Murry Bree had no money, they paid his way.

So there he was, following his new friends around the amusement park like a parent or a child. A merry-go-round and three circular flying rides. Pony rides. Children, fathers in colorful shirts and mothers in Bermuda shorts, groups of girls in jeans. You rode on the Ferris wheel, Joe and Amy together in one seat while you sat by yourself in the next one. Later from a bench you watched them on the circular flying things. You had this consciousness of the crowd and a secret: I am different from you. You stopped by the psychic couple who guess your name. This Lola, who wore a turban and sat in the center of the tent. Now concentrate. Think of your name and a question you want me to answer. But remember: the mind, it has a lot of garbage to put up with. Sometimes the vibrations don't get through, interference, the thoughts fall into the great Swamp of Taboo. If that happens, Lola will hear a high buzzing in her ear, and you'll be entitled to a free prize—this teddy bear, this gorgeous bride doll.

She guessed Amy's name and answered her question (it was about love). When they made her guess Murry Bree's name, she called him Murphy and said he was named for someone dear and near to the person who had named him. Then Joe, his face anxious, drew you away from Lola's tent and pointed to the parking lot beyond the fence. Two state troopers with broad rimmed hats and golden chains were looking at the white Ford. The word is out.

Don't look. What should we do? Nothing. You sat on the bench. The whole park was enclosed by a fence, and the only gate was at the parking lot. No problem unless the man at the gate connects us, Joe said. Just keep doing what we're doing.

So you did everything in the park twice. The cops went back

to their car, parked outside the lot behind a tree. Waiting out the thief, Joe said. They'll catch him when he comes out.

So here's Joe's plan. He leaned forward and talked crisply like a boy scout leader. What we do, we stroll out like it was no problem. Out to the road walking, like we came on foot. We're hitchhikers. We've got our New York sign. And *you*, you're hitchhiking too. They can't prove a thing, Amy said. He took the sign that said NY out of his pack. Buy some cotton candy before we go. Look casual.

You skipped the cotton candy yourself. You walked toward the gate, Joe and Amy dipping their mouths expertly into the big sticky white fluffs. Notice how skillfully Joe ate without getting it into his beard. He had been eating cotton candy all his life, a lifetime skill. As they went through the exit gate into the parking lot, Joe was working a spiral around the lower edge of his fluff. They passed the white Ford, bait for the trap they were slithering out of. They saw the police car waiting with its two officers just beyond the entrance. They turned the other way and walked down the highway. Nothing happened.

Don't count on it. The police car came up quietly and pulled ahead a few feet. The cop waited for them.

Hello folks. Howdy. Where you folks going? New York. Hiking. I mean, hitchhiking.

Silence. There was a question whether the police would make a fuss about hitchhiking.

Where you from?

New York. Seeing the country. Camping. You too? We met on the road. I'm going to New York too, Murry Bree said.

The policeman's partner at the wheel kept looking in the mirror—still watching the parking lot. Can I see some identification? Joe and Amy reached into their pockets, took out their wallets, and handed the policeman their driving licenses.

"Joseph Fingerton, twenty-four years old. New York. Amy Glazer. New York. Twenty-three."

Yours? You looked at him and didn't say anything. Your identification, please?

The policeman was looking at you, his eyes scared, he held you tight with diffident hooks. No driver's license? No nothing? The policeman was ugly, he had an ugly mouth, with curling lips. His cheeks were fat. What are you, a bum?

Another bum, this one in uniform. Someone was angry at how you were about to be treated, about to be knocked around for being a bum. The policeman's ugliness, however, was a practical question, not one of principle. Use your brains.

My wallet was stolen. Yeah? Where was that? You remembered a name on a sign. Dennis Ohio (pop 375). Did you report it? What's your name, Jack?

It's not Jack, Jack. The ugliness was powerful. You were forgetting something, but the brain performs only so many calculations per minute. You needed conviction if you were to convince anyone else, and you groped for the plausible.

My name is Peter Gregory. The words came naturally to mind.

Peter, eh? You wanted for anything, Peter? Ever been in trouble with the law?

Joe's aroused. Hey man, take it easy. There was also something new in you, encouraged by Joe's flurry, a feeling of being someone, heated into pressure by the insult. My name is Peter Gregory, and I'm the senior English teacher at Uptown High School, Cincinnati. You said it with all the shock and daring of a lie, after which the world would never be the same.

The policeman was startled, then puzzled, skeptical but a little frightened. It was open to him to question your story, but he did not want to. Your anger—ignited by his condescension, though it was only an outer flame after six days banked—must have shown on your face, scaring him and forcing him to believe. He glanced at his clipboard, craned his neck for a moment back to the parking lot. Can you tell me why you're not in school, sir? Is the school year over in Cincinnati?

Research project.

Right. The policeman knew all about it and was embarrassed. I hope you find your wallet. The car swung around and went back to watch the parking lot, to trap the thief who had stolen the white Ford.

NINE

You were shocked by the banished name that had uttered itself. It was hard to imagine what could be worse than being mistaken for Peter Gregory, up from the dead to undo a week's lifetime of work. All it needed was for the police to call Cincinnati. Peter Gregory not dead but fled. Wife, children, colleagues, students. No new man of the river, only Gregory the Fugitive.

Meanwhile, down the road with the two kids, silent, puzzled, with Joe's words after they drove off, Jeez that was close.

Most likely the policeman would *not* check it out. If he had wanted to, he would have detained you. You were still safe except for these kids. To persuade them Peter Gregory, high school English teacher, was a fiction like Murry Bree.

Joe looked back. We can start thumbing now. It was Amy who asked you to join them. A quick look from Joe to Amy, and Amy returning his look.

Questions while waiting for rides. Is it really a research project? Is Peter Gregory your real name? Are you really a high school teacher?

The correct answer was, not any more. You quit? Was that when you went to jail? Oh, jail. Then a car stopped to pick you up, the three of you together now.

That evening, unable to bear anonymity any more, you told everything you could manage to say about Peter Gregory for Amy and Joe. They paid for your meal in a Pennsylvania mountain town. After dinner, you walked out along the small river that went through the town. You found a grassy place where Joe set up the tent from his pack. You would sleep on the grass nearby. You sat in the twilight by the riverbank, looking at the trailer homes on the other side, the trees turning black in the fading light, the oil refinery tanks beyond the trees, partially blocking the view of the darkening ridge. It was peaceful. Joe and Amy sat side by side, smoking.

You wanted to tell, but left it to them to ask. Out of the silence, Joe: you wouldn't kid us, would you? You never went to jail. But what were you doing with that stolen car?

No I never went to jail, but I told you, I needed that car to get out of Badgerton.

But Peter Gregory is your real name? You: I gave that name up when I quit being a teacher. My name is Murry Bree. Long silence in the growing dark, while their cigarettes glow. Why did you quit being a teacher?

Why? The question elicited no words, only whistles in the head. You weren't ready for *why*, only *when* and *what*.

When, then. When did you stop being Peter Gregory?

About a week ago.

Joe thumped the ground with his fist. Just a week? What's this, you running away? Amy: Do they know you're gone?

They'll know by now.

Won't they worry? Won't they be looking? High school teachers don't just disappear.

They won't look because they think I'm dead. The words startled you, because you had not anticipated how dramatic they would sound.

Oh, murmured Amy, long and low. Joe glooming in the dark. A long pause before he asked: How did you arrange that?

You tried to answer, face buried in arms. What did you say? You repeated, cradled in your sleeves. I can't make out what you're saying. You got the words disentangled at last. It required two sentences: Peter Gregory wrote a suicide note and drowned himself in the river. I swam out on the other side.

No kidding! Joe, transformed. For real! Is that what happened? That's what happened.

Why did you do that?

Why, again. Like asking you the meaning of life in a word. Mangled by thought, you mumbled, I wasn't suited to that life.

Amy: Your poor wife. Aren't you sorry for your wife? Pointed to his wedding ring, which you had forgotten.

My wife left me two months ago and took the kids with her.

Oh. Amy, softly: Is that why you did it? The why question again. But she had suggested an easy answer, and Peter Gregory grabbed it: Yes. Because my wife left me and took the kids.

Someone complained: lots of wives leave their husbands. People don't commit suicide over that. Yes. The question now with Amy and Joe in the increasing dark, by this little river so much narrower, gentler, slower, than the original, was how to tell what you yourself were only beginning to figure out about Peter Gregory who drowned.

You poked at the ground with sticks, they made their cigarette butts glow. They waited for the facts of life like news, as if they really believed life could be fit to words, reduced to story. Challenged to remember Peter Gregory, you had to violate the habit of a week's effort to get rid of him. The world is full of suicides, Hal Hastings for instance. It was natural for Gregory to consider this among his options.

The suicidal option worried them. They were young and full of life and hated the very idea of suicide even in the abstract with all arguments that might be made on its behalf. Children,

Joe with his beard crushed on his raised knees, Amy pulling her ponytail across her nose. Looking at you, trying to nullify the suicidal passion of this man from the road, soft talking, wry, possibly ironic stick poking, twig breaking, tossing pebbles into the stream, never quite still.

What a terrible thing to do to a child, Amy said, a parent who commits suicide. If your own parent who gave you life decides life's not worth living.

Your heart clutched to reject this effort to load you with Gregory's guilt. I told you, she took the children with her. They were gone, two months ago.

Amy's sympathy, she meant no harm. As for parents, remember his gentle father full of cigars in his brown suit with the broad vest, its gold watch chain. Who staggered in the basement and crashed into his collection of fossils under illuminated glass. His mother jumped up: Stay where you are! He heard her help him mumbling up the stairs and later he went to peek in the basement. Fossils scattered on the floor amid splinters of glass from the display case. Though his father died of a heart attack, you said, there's a family tradition of suicide.

How horrible.

Two uncles killed themselves. One before Peter Gregory was born. The other, you could call it that too—in old age (in disgrace). That establishes a tradition. They looked at you, trying to see him. Refusing to be distracted, Joe asked, Why did your wife leave?

There had to be a better reason. She took a lover, you said. That's Louis the Lover, remember him, who took the place of Peter the Dull. This is easier to write than it was to say. It would have been nice to tell these kids all about Louis the Lover, who teaches Romance Languages at the University. Teaches them all, French, Spanish, Italian, Portuguese, slithering among them like an easy jelly fish with five noiseless dictionaries in his head. With a black mustache and a black curl of gallic hair and a faint French Italian and Spanish accent, and a sport car which he drives fast and a house with sliding panels and its own personal ravine and imported china pitchers and speakers in every room and a mirror over his King Louis bed to double your fun and pink-tinted windows in the west to liven up the sunset. With attractions for children, too, wicked things, a tunnel of love in the basement, a Forbidden Room with spooks and furry tails, video games and a dollar changer and a slot machine giving you gum balls for your quarters. It would have been nice to tell them that.

And say, the trouble was, Dull Peter's wife worked at the University in the office of Romance Languages. She was daily within range of the Latin magician's perfumed spell, hearing his voice resonate in the offices, his hand tapping her shoulder every time he passed reeking through. Her own husband a mere high school teacher, such a wife can get bored, mad, fed up. She took the children to live with Lover Louis. The children: the fat boy, the girl with glasses, their backs turned.

You must have said some of this, but Joe was not satisfied. What did you do to make her bored, mad, and fed up? Remember them, Amy and Joe, sitting there quietly with their mild shocked questions. People get tired of each other. You don't know the distractions of Peter Gregory. Unable to concentrate, a burden on his mind. Bitter, sarcastic with students, snappish with wife, withdrawn from children.

Mostly shadow in the dark, Joe with his upraised knees, gloomy, skeptical. Next to him Amy, cross-legged, straight-backed, and curious. They spoke at the same moment, Joe: What burden? Amy: You weren't happy with your work?

You tried her question. Was Peter Gregory happy in his work? Distinguish what you said from what you might have said. What you might have said: postulate an original Gregory, sensitive and literary, who loved explaining what he had found hard to learn, who not wanting to be a suffering lawyer like his father or a scandalous broker like his uncle, and not knowing what else to do except make love and write bad poetry, went into the pure idealism of teaching. The security, the summer vacations. The challenge of talented students. A world of writing and reading, not merely the recreation of his evenings but the profession of his life.

What you said was: It stinks.

What stinks?

Your average high school, or even your slightly better than average high school, like Uptown H.S., Cincinnati.

You mean, like switchblades and drugs?

You weren't talking switchblades and drugs. You're talking forty students in a class, one hundred papers a week, *Silas Marner* year after year.

Didn't you know that when you went into it? (I happen to like *Silas Marner*, Amy said.)

What did you know when Mr. Gregory went into it? Never much for ambition, you thought he would have time enough, with the vacations, to be eccentric and lovable and write poetry in the summers and maybe a famous book or two, though that part's optional.

You didn't like teaching? That's no reason to kill yourself. The oil tanks across the river were still visible as large black shapes against what faint light remained. Mildly Joe snarled: Half my friends would give everything for a good high school English teaching job. (What? Amy said. Name one.) The best teacher I ever had was my high school English teacher. Above in the almost dark sky a silver jet trail caught the hidden sun.

If you hated it so much, why didn't you quit and get another job?

Energy. It took all Peter Gregory's energy to find an apartment after his wife kicked him out.

It takes energy to drown yourself in the river. You sound sorry for yourself, man.

Not I. That was Peter Gregory.

Nuts to you.

You brooded, full of wondering yourself, a problem as mysterious to you as to them, but for different reasons. You're right, you said. It's not enough.

After a moment you realized they were waiting for the rest, whatever that was. But there was nothing more you could think of, fit for words to say. Joe's problem was that there are no sufficient suicide reasons. Therefore, suicide is impossible. Are you running away from something? he said.

Is that what it looks like? you said. What would I be running away from?

You tell us. Did you commit a crime or something?

What kind of a crime could I commit?

Kill someone? You tell us. Uneasy laugh, Joe not sure what he was dealing with.

Do I look like a killer? It sounded like a real question, not rhetorical but calling for an answer.

There was Joe's look, and Amy not looking, to impress on you that they hadn't known you long enough to know.

After a while you gave them this: I used to drink.

Ha, Amy said. You're an alcoholic.

You said, If I was, would that be enough?

Would it?

I used to stop at Lenny's after school, a couple of drinks each day before going home.

You're an alcoholic, running away from the consequences.

Would that be a sufficient explanation?

They thought it over. Gently, full of cliché, Amy said: You can't run away from your problems, Peter. You should join the Alcoholics Anonymous. They can do you a lot of good. There's no need to kill yourself just because you're alcoholic.

You thought it over too. You said, I did quit. I haven't had a drink in two years.

Good for you, Amy said, but you have to keep your guard up. Once an alcoholic always an alcoholic. Just because you've stopped doesn't mean you're cured.

You said, I made a vow. Never again.

Is that what broke up your family? Drinking?

You looked back over the connections. It might have been an indirect cause.

And it destroyed your teaching career?

Joe: How could it destroy his teaching career if he quit drinking two years ago?

They sat there thinking. Amy said, So if you stopped drinking two years ago, why did you wait to kill yourself until now?

We're forgetting, Joe said. He didn't kill himself.

Oh.

Joe laughed. The laughter died in the silence. You noticed stars between the treetops. Made you think of Linda Gregory and others in houses several hundred miles back, which would be under these same stars at this same time. Questions you had been thinking about all these days: Did they discover Peter Gregory's letter? Did they find the car? Did they tell the family? Did they believe he was dead?

Hell, Joe said. Come on, he said to Amy, pulling himself to his feet, let's go to bed. To Peter Gregory he said, Don't kill us while we sleep, okay?

You lay on the ground in the blanket they had given you. Nearby the tent blocked a shadow out of the sky. In the tree dark just beyond the grass under the night, brushing its tail against your hope of sleep alone under the stars. With little raccoon hands turned up under the leaves and pale white shoulders and vanished sex. Foul play in the woods, away from the towns and cities and houses, under cover of the natural world where you had taken yourself to live. Animal deaths in the woods are always violent, the naturalist said, goshawk and rabbit, fox and squirrel, no such thing as natural death out there.

Someone did it to her, if it was a her. Someone's last violent moment mulched for the new generation. Someone is missing your little raccoon, wondering what happened.

You could hear them asleep, full of normality, while you lay thinking about dead things. The night was full of crime and law, indistinguishable, you can't have one without the other. It had public death, bodies in the road, police lights steering the traffic around. And police lights across the street for hateful old Jock Hadley where the Hammer Man had bashed him. And the Hammer Man himself, killer of old men, mythologized by the newspapers with a titillating question, where will he strike next? It had lawyers and police investigators, the lawyer for Florry Gates's father with his message on Peter Gregory's answering machine, and Sam Indigo the detective snooping around for evidence. It had insults and abuse, calling you bum, the old man's attacks shouted across the street like hammer blows to make sure no one in the neighborhood would forget what Gregory did, and Florry Gates shouting back in the clear night, her clear voice loud all the way up and down the second-story windows: Shut the fuck up, you old fart.

In the clear Pennsylvania night old Gregory shocks continued to unravel, coupling erotic images of life and death: a live Jock Hadley sitting all day on the stoop in front of his bungalow chattering to everyone who went by, with his smooth bald head, white chin stubble, mean and leering eyes. And the imagined dead equivalent, eyes glazed, crumpled edges in the bald skull and punctures of the brain. With shame for the still humming Gregory thoughts that would not die. Complicity in all. You got yours, you old bastard. The little raccoon was a creature like yourself, its death conceived in a brain like yours, which had puncture holes like Jock Hadley's. You listened to the argument leaking out through the holes, the moral difference between the homicidal stop-life imposed violently by professional murderers upon old men in the woods and the inadvertent and accidental stop-life tradition in the Gregory family.

These kids had come out from civilization to protect you from foul play in the wilderness, and they wanted to understand. You owed them an explanation, but Gregory's shame interfered. You needed to think how to open yourself to them without doing irreparable damage to Murry Bree.

In the morning, Joe passed the chocolate around to you and Amy. He washed out his canteen and brushed his teeth at the edge of the water. There was cool bright fog over the river, breathing light in the trees. Let's get going, Joe said. He enjoyed the morning. As you walked out to the road, his step became jaunty, he rose on his toes, he said Good Morning to the trees and bushes and walked with his arm around Amy's waist, and you tried to keep up with their long strides.

TEN

Here's more stories for you, kids—

Prevented from telling by your first ride, salesman in a noisy car in need of shocks, who drove you half way into Jersey, where he left you in the early afternoon. The man was worried about the education of young people in the American ways, lacking an adequate understanding of the free enterprise system. It's the future that depends on the kids, he said, that's what depends on the kids.

(While you were thinking, Maybe you could satisfy their curiosity with Lenny's, in the afternoons after school, the high ceiling with fans turning. Plate glass window to the gloomy rain or guilty sunshine in the street outside, Johnson Pharmacy, the Activist Bookshop. Stools at the counter, tables with spindly chairs along the wall. Gregory's refuge when teaching was done. A hundred papers to grade tonight but not yet. Bourbon before Linda. The whiskey had a voice that worked its way down warmly into your gizzard. No, I mean gizzard, it's the correct word. It said. Your bar friends whom you saw every day at Lenny's and nowhere else. They include the dead eyed chemistry professor from the university who didn't mind talking to a high school teacher and the old retired hospital security guard who knew everything about Gregory's private life and the woman from the Activist Bookstore who stopped regularly on her way home and wore her hair tied back like a squaw. What the whiskey said. *Drink me.* It was warm, spreading out in the

gizzard and making it glow. A free country, you have my permission. Drink me, a higher law. Free enterprise, the whiskey
said.)

The question I wonder whether kids are being properly
taught these days is our free enterprise system. That's the question I have my strong doubts about. When I see kids I try to find
out what they know. I ask them what do you know about the
system on which our country was built, the greatest land on
earth. And what I always find out, none of our kids these days
knows a damn thing about the free enterprise system. You kids
too, I bet you don't, even though you are hitchhikers, which is
the perfect expression of free enterprise.

(Drink me. Forgetting that you quit two years ago: Never
Again. Try the woman from the Activist Bookstore with straight
black hair like an Indian squaw, sitting on a bar stool next to
him. T-shirt with trees and lakes, bears and moose, antlers on
her breasts. Going her own way, independent, free enterprise.
Read books, look down on Republicans, the world of Philis-
tines. Dropped out of graduate school or flunked, not clear
which. Went to Lenny's for a drink after work like a man, no
makeup, weather beaten face, who gave him permission to talk.
Validating the whiskey's permission already given, to talk about
Louis the Lover, that's Louis the Lover, kids, yes you can tell me,
talk to me, I'm discreet. Talk, talk, by all means talk, off your
chest. Languid lazy cynical speech with permission that made it
all all right. Two jaded people, disappointed in life, as she
described them, you're jaded I'm jaded, sit side by side in Lenny's for an hour every weekday afternoon, no weekends,
enjoying life as it is, too wise to change, take it as it is. For a
while he kept forgetting her name, which was Anita Long.)

The essence of the free enterprise system is if you leave
things alone everything will take care of itself. Suppose a society

needs a service performed, some product is needed. Deodorants. Nobody wants to make deodorants, you think you need a law saying somebody must make deodorants so society don't stink. But that is socialism. You don't need laws in free enterprise. If society wants deodorants in free enterprise, it gets deodorants. Do you know how? Listen kids, do you know the little stimulus, gizmo, gadget that gives society its deodorants in free enterprise? I'll bet you do and you never thought of it.

(What kind of a crime could I commit? The whiskey gave him permission which Anita Long seconded, saying any old-fashioned husband would call up his wife once in a while to tell her sorry he won't be home for dinner tonight. It's your right, like her right as a single woman to have a drink by herself and go home with whomever she liked. The permission she gave along with the whiskey's permission peeled him open to another person inside, normally silenced, censored, unacknowledged under the artificial skin of Peter Gregory, just as it peeled off her environmental T-shirt, pulled it over her head, zip, just like that. Anita Long, teaching him how to utilize permission and escape the bonds that gregorized him, as one permission led to another. In her room small and cramped and messy with books and magazines and clothes, she had nice bare little breasts permitted without bra where the pine trees had been. Which made it natural for the jeans to come off without discussion and the rest too, changing her look, and giving the erstwhile Gregory a like permission to take off himself. There was no difference between receiving permission and taking off clothes, the same thing actually. As was lying around on the messy bed with her and soon enough climbing on top and going inside while she hummed with permission. Yes indeed, it's all right, good, fine, let yourself go, come come come, go and come both, a free country, free enterprise, the capitalist system everyone for him-or-herself, why the hell not, even though she was a stranger outside the precincts of Lenny's, unknown, with her hair drawn back black like a squaw and her face weatherbeaten and unadorned, and her heart bitter about whatever she had wanted but failed to become, while she defended fiercely her permissions with her still youthful body into her lonely forties living fiercely to herself.)

I'll tell you then. It's not laws, not regulation, not some guy with a computer figuring out which of this and that society needs. None of that socialistic crap. It's profit, pure and sweet, lovely golden profit, which gives you deodorants and keeps you from making too many, distributes our labors and makes us what we are, me a tire salesman and you a hitchhiker, and brings us all together for the good of all. Don't you never allow nobody to slander profit.

(Never Again. You could drill closer to the nerve and take a chance to tell what happened after the judge, whose name was Marla Williams, behind her raised desk in her gray hair, wisps floating free around her chubby troubled face, who never looked at him, pronounced sentence and added, "I suspend this sentence on the following grounds—" Tell the quick male shout from back of the room, "Shame!" precipitating a fast rising uproar of disappointed and angry sounds, with a preponderance of *o* and then *s*, booing, the word *no* repeated, hissing and whistling, making it hard to hear what the following grounds were. In that moment of maximum unpopularity, the Gregory man tried to separate himself from the Hate Gregory noise all around, which he heard projected from himself into the whole room and thrown back to him embodied externally in strangers' leering jeering faces and voices of people he never knew, while he tried to catch what Judge Marla Williams was saying about "first offense," "law abiding citizen," "unintended harm," "contributions to the community," "no good served by locking up this harmless man," "remorse," "fully regretful," "this tragic case." Over this, Wrong! wrong! wrong! go the voices, dissatisfied with the palliative of community service, shouting for shame and give him what he deserves, and justice, and revenge, the bleeding hearts, the weakness of female liberal judges, while this female judge goes bang, bang, bang with her gavel. The letters would come afterwards.)

And you know how free enterprise regulates itself? Keeps standards up? Self interest. Your self interest and my self interest, working together for the good of all. If your product is shoddy, if it is cheap and not what you claim it to be, the society will reject it in favor of your competitor. Your self interest requires you to turn out a good product which people can trust. So don't you let nobody slander self-interest either, and don't talk about selfish because what the hell is there in the world but selfish?

(That was two years ago, they'll say, remote and irrelevant, a distraction from the truth. Come closer to our time, folks, how History Repeats. Notice how Permission and Free Enterprise come into conflict with Never Again. Principles, terrible destructive things, both of them. The student named Florry Gates gave permission in the swing on her front porch. But you're under age, The Gregory said, which goaded her to force on him with her exploring hand the irresistible permission which only she had the right to withhold. As for her father, it was not the mistake in her assumption he had gone to bed. It was her suggestion they do it a second time. That, and the shortness of the swing, which required them to get into an ungainly position whose purpose was difficult to conceal on short notice. I vow never to see you again. Short vow: on Sunday night when Life as Gregory was already drawing to a close,

Florry Gates, whom nothing could deter, picked him up in her car and drove him out to a city park. They had a fight. Peter Gregory wanted to know what her father was suing him for. She said it was a question of her age and your being a teacher of the young in a position of trust. He had a glimpse of horror: statutory rape, he said, that's a criminal charge, what did you tell him, for God's sake? I never, she said. She cried. Her father was a lawyer, with a finicky view of things, it was beyond her, the law is a mysterious thing. She wanted Peter Gregory to make love to her in the park, to show his faith in her after their troubles. He had no faith in her. He was shocked, he told her so, he should have listened to himself: never again. Never again? She wailed, how can you be so mean? This led to a discussion about whose fault it was. Thinking it obvious, he called her the seducer, reminding how he had warned her of this very danger. She was outraged. What? she said. I seduced you? She was so extremely shocked she almost shocked Peter Gregory's memory away. He apologized for overstatement, difficult when apology of any kind seems so dangerous. She pushed his cock back into his pants and asked him to get out of her car. He got out. She asked him to get back in. He declined. She drove off. After a few minutes she came back. You watched from behind the dark pavilion while she drove around the circle, looking, because there was a limit to her anger which would not make him walk all that way. But already you were changing, and you stayed out of sight until she went away. Never again, you said, all the things you had said Never Again to when it was too late.)

The trouble with free enterprise, it's never been tried. People blame the mess we're in on something that has never been tried. Take the welfare state, for example. Listen my children, do you know anything about taxes in Sweden? Everybody talks how great Sweden is, free love and all that crap. But I tell you, which country has the highest suicide rate of all? It's those long winter nights of the midnight sun. Give me free enterprise over free love anyday.

(Maybe it would be enough to give them Mr. Gregory's student endorsements.

This coarse is the most stupid boring coarse I ever had in my life.

Mr. Gregory is a very nice man. He reminds me of my Uncle but somebody ought to tell him how to teche. He doesn't know how to teche.

This coarse is a very intellectual coarse. It is all about writing and how to think. The trouble is that there isn't anything to this coarse. The teacher (I refer to Mr. Peter J. Gregory, Ph.D.) is not interested in the coarse and is bored with the students. I can understand his being bored with the students because the intellectual level of the average senior high English class is pretty low but that is no excuse for the teacher to ignore the few intelligent students in his class as well. The result is I found the class very boring and not interesting and I didn't get anything out of it at all.

This coarse would be better if Mr. Gregory made some comments on our papers along with the grade. He skips class too much.

Improvements I would suggest. Divide the class into groups and have each group talk with itself. Each group should have an equal number of boys and girls. Eliminate the individual writing of themes. Let each theme be written by a group of students, no less than three. Have the teacher change his teaching methods and ideas. He is too old fashion. He doesn't know anything about modern innovative educational practices. Choose interesting topics for themes such as the Changing Sex Morays, Input and Feedback on How People In the Class First Lost Their Virginity, Etc.

The trouble with Mr. Gregory is he is not interested in our problems. All he cares about is how we write.

I don't think the teacher should encourage his students to think about suicide. Some students are close enough to the edge already. I think the teacher should keep his pessimystical ideas to himself. It may seem funny to him but students don't consider pessimysm a laughing matter.

I prefer not comment on Mr. Gregory's shortcomings as a teacher or as a man.)

You don't really want to know why Peter Gregory committed suicide, do you? Depressing stuff, a shadow on those glorious free days when you crossed the country with new friends.

ELEVEN

Fast driver in a big car with finely tooled parts, kid who called himself Crazy James and claimed he was worth a million dollars, right hand man to the famous Jack Rome, took you the last stretch across Jersey. Drive you to your very door, he said. Talked about money. Crazy James loved money, which was better than sex, because if you had only money you could get sex, but if you had only sex, you couldn't get money.

It turned out Joe disapproved of money. He couldn't live a life of ease at the expense of others. He said every country estate was haunted by ghosts from the slums, and in every fat broad field and foresty space he saw the absence of subway and ghetto. He believed all property was evil, since anything you own is something nobody else can own, and five percent of the world was sitting on the other ninety-five percent. We live on theft, he said. We stole the land from the Indians, and we stole the blacks from their land. Now we're like the rich man with the cigar in the mansion on the hill, and everybody hates us.

Why didn't you tell that to old Free Enterprise when you had the chance? Amy said. And Crazy James: Don't hassle me about the poor, man, because I grew up in the jungle, so don't tell me about greed and envy. Hell, man, I was just like you until Jack Rome came along.

Amy said, Who's Jack Rome?

What, never heard of Jack Rome? While Joe scoffed, Crazy James explained. Rome Enterprises, man. Electronics, computers, copying machines. Rome Spacification Company: space equipment, rocket engines, missiles, nuclear warheads.

I've heard of him, Amy said. I just didn't know what he did.

Why he's your playboy in the news, patron of the arts, he makes stars in both senses of the word. Read about him in *People*. Versatile sonofabitch, flies his plane and goes mountain climbing in Tibet and Nepal. "Financier conquers Everest," you just wait. Popular guy, but the real Jack Rome is the power man, who makes the money grow and people do what he wants.

So what's your connection? Joe said.

His right hand man, like I say, he made me what I am today. Before Jack Rome I was nothing, I was dirt on the streets of New York, I was zero. Now you see me a million dollars worth, the best cars, the best clothes, talking to the best people, all the women a man could need, doing what I like.

How did you manage that?

It's called a Me Grant.

What's that?

A personal grant from Jack Rome. A grant for being me. To live my style and be myself.

How'd you get that?

I asked and he gave.

Does he give out other Me Grants?

Ask him yourself.

Meanwhile, you watched as Crazy James zipped you lane to lane in the thickened traffic. Grim hostile drivers of the speeding cars close alongside and truck drivers up in their cabs, while you crouched in your namelessness like a cage.

Crazy James: You may have heard, when Jack Rome's wife and son were kidnapped by a religious cult. I kidnapped them back. Grabbed them off the street, whisked them into the car. To deprogram them. That was me, in case you remember.

After Gregory

A john stop, where you shied away from the crowds around
the candy counter and the souvenir counters. The ride resumed
and like a wild animal captured, you watched life in the strings
of wires leaping in high tension webs across the fields. The
brutal murderous highway was six black lanes crowded with
fast trucks and tankers and the smell of diesel. Visiting animals
stared at the office plants, the long low glass buildings, the fields
of fat colored cylindrical oil tanks, the parallel roads running for
miles with used car lots and pinwheels and drive-in banks and
fast food. The city thickened all around. In the haze across the
flats you saw the zigzag of a cantilever bridge and the deck
house and lifeboats of an ocean-going ship looming over a field
of grass. You saw a blocky horizon of apartment houses on a
ridge and suddenly behind like magic the transparent blue skyscrapers of the city, carried by a trick of light over the curvature
of the earth, over what you could not yet see: the broad river in
between and the imaginary crowds and traffic around their
invisible feet. Meanwhile Crazy James still talking about Jack
Rome's money dipped you into the poisonous tunnel. He was
taking you to your fortune, though you didn't know it then.

Down under the river then up and out into plain daylight, a
city street, a traffic light, and you terrified as if you had not
climbed out of the river until now. Traffic jam, competitive driving, Crazy James and the cabdrivers trying to edge ahead, a
game of intimidation with one inhibiting rule: don't touch.
Then suddenly free and the next moment they stopped, a cross
street downtown, the middle of a block, heart of the great city.

Everybody out. What? You stood on the sidewalk, shocked,
this outcome you hadn't given enough thought to. You watched
Crazy James (see ya sometime guys) zip off down the street.
Leaving you. No wooded groves here by the stoop of this old
brown apartment building. You awkward while Joe rummaged

in his jeans for his keys. Where they live, and time for you to go. Go where? You had landed in the city like a missile on a trajectory. Now on your own with no place to go, no ideas in your head, in all your brief lifetime you had never felt so miserable and low.

Well, they took you in. Fourth floor, the hallway shabby and warm, stinky with cooking cheese, sweaty woodwork, and old laundry, with a sound of classical music. An old apartment, rooms off a corridor. Dark—only the front room and kitchen received outside light. A stereo set, a couch, cushions on the floor, posters. Amy and Joe slept in the back.

You met the others that evening. There were Hank Gummer and Lucy Angles, who lived in the middle room, and Stowe Thompson, who slept on a cot in the front. Hank Gummer was a thick young man, almost bald, who had been a medical student and was now a cab driver. Hank's depressed, they said. That's why he's so quiet. Lucy Angles, tall with black pigtails and large front teeth, was suffering through with him. She clerked in a typewriter store across the street. She would rather an arts and crafts store in the next block, but the store had failed. Stowe Thompson was short and fat and grinned like an elf. He worked in a stereo store, owned science fiction books, and wore a white shirt and red necktie.

That evening the six of you ate dinner in the kitchen, cooked by Stowe Thompson. By now you knew Joe was a free lance photographer, and Amy was returning to a job in the library. They explained you to the others. They told how you had met on the road, and how Murry Bree was not your real name, and how Peter Gregory had done it because his wife left him—everything as they knew it. They all admired your daring, talked and talked (except Hank Gummer) and agreed to help you start a new life. They set up a cot in the front room. In the morning we find you a job, Joe said.

Then the night. You lay on the cot sharing the room with Stowe Thompson, listening to the city outside the window. You heard your new friends walking up and down the hall, flushing the toilet, whispering between doors. You heard Stowe Thompson's nose whistling in his sleep. The nights on the road flowed through you like a river. You realized you had achieved something, but time stopped here at this moment in the night, and you didn't want any more, not tonight, or the morning, the next day, or any time to come. You were too tired.

TWELVE

Your friends got you a job as Murry Bree in a restaurant down the street. You went there at noon, wore a white coat, and washed dishes until ten at night. Joe said he envied you. The thing is you don't have to *be* anybody, he said. Nothing to worry about but the necessities of life. This was an interlude in your life, no more than two months, but you thought it was the future dragging on forever.

What are the necessities of life? Good question. Food, shelter, clothes. Joe took you to buy a pair of jeans, a denim jacket, another shirt, socks, some underwear. Are there other necessities? When Amy said, Don't you find it boring, washing dishes all day? you didn't want to say. As Murry Bree, you were afraid of time—not its passing, but its accumulation, its way of massing into chunks of past spilling over boundaries.

Your friends wanted to give you more versatility. You should try cab driving, Lucy Angles said, while morose Hank Gummer, who actually drove a cab, said nothing. Go everywhere, meet all kinds, never know what'll happen next. But to do that you'll need a license—which requires a birth certificate, which you ought to have anyway, for that's the key to everything: license, passport, a certified name. You'll have to change your name again, but now you'll have something to show for it. You got your birth certificate by a method Stowe Thompson had seen in a movie. First you decide when you were born. Then out with your friends to Queens to find the death records of two-year old boy children thirty-three years ago. Though you did not know how they died, you found five names.

Stanley Caruso
Gregory McHenry
Jasper Linkowitz
John Figueroa
Stephen White

You picked one. When your chosen name, wrinkled by a seal with a number and date of birth, and registrar's signature rubber stamped, came from The Bureau of Vital Statistics, they had a christening party. Your parents were Walter Jerome White and Mary Green White. Stowe Thompson thought any of the other names was more interesting, but otherwise it was a happy occasion.

Stephen White got a job in the Corner Typewriter Shop. That was the end of Murry Bree. The new job was Lucy Angles' former one when she found what she wanted in the Arts and Crafts Shop. He worked for Mr. Crestmeyer, who said, God knows I'd rather Lucy, but she says I gotta take you, so I take you. Mr. Crestmeyer had a tattooed number on his arm. They said he had lost everybody, wife, children, parents. He came to this country knowing nobody and without a language. He never mentioned it and was mild and gentle and sad.

Stephen White worked from nine to six. People came in and he said, Can I help you? He spent most of the time at the table by the door looking out the window. Business was not good because everyone was using computers. God knows you a quiet fella, Mr. Crestmeyer said. In the evenings Stephen read the newspaper in the living room and listened to the others talk. He liked to listen as if he were participating, learning how to be Stephen White. He liked Amy especially, with her natural hair and unmadeup face, knowing all his secrets. Without jealousy.

He had no wish to take her from Joe, and the threat of anything wrong between them would have alarmed him like the divorce of parents. Unfortunately, she brought him into time. She created a memory and made him look ahead. Of course Stephen White would need a memory and you would have to give him one, but you couldn't do that until there was more of him. Until then, memory could only rebuild Gregory and deplete you.

He got used to the face in the shaving mirror, mainly by not looking at it, or not looking at it whole. He hardly noticed it, but if he caught a glimpse unwarned in a store mirror or shop window, the frail body, the balding head, the baggy eyes, it still shocked him, requiring a deliberate effort to remind himself it wasn't Peter Gregory following him around. He read newspapers and magazines, but books were out because they carried over from one day to the next. Movies were out too. Too many people in them, anger, jealousy, pride. He didn't want to feel sad or grieved or guilty until he could feel them as Stephen White. No old music, either, recalling Peter Gregory's taste, that broad sunny summit where he used to lie and think how civilized he was. A boast. From here the peak of civilization was indistinguishable from the vanity in Gregory's soul. That soul loomed over the infant Stephen White like a cat waiting to eat him up. Everything was dangerous except news and the casual chatter of friends.

What else was there to do? Out of a Gregory shadow came a sexual taunt: how free you are, if you only knew. He didn't know if he knew or not. Weak and trembling, he went out. Looking. He saw the letter X, the word ADULT, and tried that, watched the rolling flesh, the magnified organs, the heavy groany sounds. So that's what they do, Stephen White said. How uncurious he had been all this time. Odd, for Gregory would have gone crazy from celibacy. This must be puberty. You became conscious of virginity, another time-bound thought, wondering how to end it, replace X with real life. He couldn't imagine real life, a live stranger's eyes, real, too close looking into his face asking his name.

The summer was heating up. On Sundays he rode on the bus to parks in far parts of the city. Days bright and full of thick strands of warm air, odor of flowers mixed with the smell of baking and trucks. On a bench looking at the harbor. It spread out, dazzling with silver shafts. The sun glared down and squinted his eyes shut. Sitting there, you thought what is he waiting for? If you give up waiting for things, you won't need them. You won't need real women, strange or not.

In the glare of the sun, shining on his face, warming and slowing his brain, the pursuit of a woman seemed like someone else's idea, not his own. Gregory's no doubt. He leaned back in the bench, shifted his hams, watching a couple of tugboats with barges. He looks again at the harbor, now in the present tense. Sharp afternoon wind choppily whipping up waves across the bay. Nothing to come and nothing behind. Stephen White lives now. Untied from the past, free of the future. With eyes dazzled almost shut and scarcely any difference at all between the felt glare and the eventual cease of the glare. Makes you wonder why you tried so hard in the river.

How small the world is now, he thinks in the present tense. How little exists in the present tense, a slight agitation of the mind, a few flapping images. How thin, like a strand of hair, is the new Stephen White, in contrast to that imaginary Gregory, whose present tense was so full of junk, such blocks of nonexistent past and future, such fictions of fantasy and memory.

Take them away and you're left with a physics and chemistry of light and convection currents that stir the air and water and make bodies circulate and move. Now in the empty white present, free of memory and hope, the only presences are Amy and some other vaguely felt, unidentified object, perhaps large. This object no doubt is himself, dim, bulky, blunt, monolithic, occupying an empty place. He locates it, the true identity, in his pants, tingling just slightly, stirring its rudimentary nerve ends. It makes a slight personality, a slight aggression into the space around.

THIRTEEN

The night before you got away (though you did not know that was coming), Hank Gummer was upset because he'd seen a man killed by a bus. This led to a conversation about death. For once, Hank Gummer talked at length, and everybody had a point of view.

He said, The thing I can't stand about life is death. Nobody seems to realize what an outrage it is.

Joe said, If it happens to all of us, it must be natural. A bird flies away from a cat, but it doesn't worry about death.

Lucy Angles said, I expect to meet my father and mother in heaven. I am confident of that.

Stowe Thompson said, Time is an illusion. But if time is an illusion, then so is change. If change is an illusion, likewise death. *Quod erat demonstrandum*.

Hank Gummer said, You're not listening to me. I'm depressed. I was reading this book which says the mind is just a computer, no center, no spirit, no self, just an illusion of software. The trouble is, I can't refute it. Any objection I make is naive. I'm a chemical accident, the whole show's a chemical accident, no way I can refute it. My mind's a moment's flickering that will vanish in the rocks and stones. That's depressing, man.

Stowe said, Depression is chemistry. You need a pill. You don't need to be depressed, because it's only chemistry making things look bad. It's not so bad except for the chemistry.

Hank Gummer said, Jesus, I got a right to be depressed. Think about entropy. You know? Everything running down, stars, galaxies, ending up in a lukewarm soup. If that don't depress you, nothing will, man.

Lucy Angles said, Don't you believe in life after death? I put my faith in God and heaven.

Joe said, My job in life is to carry my weight. We're all in it together. If there are people starving in Africa or being tortured in prisons, that's my business.

Hank Gummer said, You fill your life with achievements and crap, but when you die it will be as if you never lived. Don't give me no heaven crap or floating spirits, dead is gone, out, dirt and rocks, don't that depress you?

Amy said, My grandmother lost her memory. If you lose your memory, you won't mind dying.

Hank said, Did you ever look into the future, any of you? Some day you'll die and some day the sun will too. Any astronomer will tell you. The earth burns up, and then where's your Beethoven and your Elvis and your Baseball Hall of Fame? Don't that depress you? I'd get mad, but who can I complain to? It's like the whole world an empty barn with the wind blowing through holes which is about to fall down.

Stowe Thompson said, You're just depressed, Hank. Go see a shrink and get a pill, for Christ sake.

Death in the river lights was outrage, goading you to the opposite shore. Now as you lay in bed waiting for sleep, death seemed easy and sweet. Probably it wouldn't seem so easy in the morning: you had a strong kicking body which would put up a fight. But it seemed easier than turning into Stephen White.

Here you had done an amazing thing. You had boldly said, Enough, and by one quick act cleared out the ruined time like dead trees. Then by struggling across the open country, trying out names, you composed a new past to replace the old. Now they wanted you to stuff future into Stephen White. Add imagination to memory, fill him out a little. But if the figure of speech should fail, you'd be back where you started, stuck in the muck of Gregory's memory and discredited hopes. Without knowing what to wish for, you could make no plans. You needed a miracle.

PART TWO

Rome

FOURTEEN

The miracle: first, a messenger. You thought it was a Gregory call from the police, Sam Indigo, or a sneaking reporter, perhaps. Mr. Crestmeyer shouted, Hey White, someone to see you. A middle aged man, dressed like the royal guard or an admiral, with braid and a gold R on the peak of his cap. Arrogant eyes handing you a card and saying, You Stephen White? Scrutinizing amusement. What do you want with me? Your illegal birth certificate, the criminal question of your right to live?

Jack Rome wants to see you.

Who?

Which is a dumb question no matter how many rivers you've crossed, like asking who is John D. Rockefeller or Howard Hughes or Henry Ford. If the man had said, God wants you, you would have said, Who?

Jack Rome. You've heard of him.

So you remembered Crazy James on the road, and you thought practical jokes. Why would he play a joke on you? What does he want me for? you said.

Don't know, son, I'm only the messenger. Interview. Rome Company. Job, probably. You're a lucky man.

An engraved card. In the top center a recognizable logo, old English R twined in snakes through its loops, below that the name JANE DELAWARE and a telephone number, and in the lower corner, modest and plain, ROME ENTERPRISES, NEW YORK AND LONDON.

Believe me, you're in luck. Take this card and call this number, tonight before ten. Don't forget, you won't regret.

You saw him go out the door, grinning, and the fine rich old car he drove off in with a license plate as a registered antique.

If I was you I'd call, Mr. Crestmeyer said.

It's a joke.

Better a joke than miss out.

In the evening the name of Jack Rome sizzled through the dinner Lucy Angles cooked. She said, Who's he? Amy and Joe recapitulated Crazy James who had claimed to be his right hand man. Joe said he was one of the six richest, but they couldn't find the list in the almanac. Amy remembered him at the controls of his airplane with a black mustache and earphones. Stowe said he was a scruffy old man with a long white beard covering a syphilitic face. Joe said, That's somebody else. Hank remembered Jack Rome kidnapping his own wife and son from the Landis Community on grounds they had been brainwashed. Amy connected that to what Crazy James told about in the car. You asked, was that the same Landis who held a revival in the Coliseum the night Peter Gregory went into the river? Joe said Osgood Landis the television evangelist and his daughter the Virgin Miranda, who heals the sick and the lame with her smile. They tried to seduce Jack Rome's family. Joe said if Jack Rome was Mafia, you'd better be careful. Everybody agreed the message was a prank by Crazy James, but why would Crazy James play a prank on Stephen White whom he hardly knew?

So you called the number, which must be private since the woman's voice did not have a letterhead, she only said Hello when she answered. Stephen White? I was hoping you'd call. Mr. Rome would like to speak with you himself, could we set up an appointment? You: Mr. Rome? Mr. *Rome*? She: Mr. Rome. In person. You asked, What for? Her voice was nice, polite, easy:

You'll find it worth your while. You said, You must have the wrong person. No, she replied (laughing) we know who you are. You said, nobody knows me, it has to be a mistake. She laughed like a sweet bell. Why don't you come around and let him explain? You've nothing to lose. At the very least you can tell your friends you had coffee with Jack Rome in his office.

The appointment was for ten in the morning. You were so sure it was a joke you almost didn't go. But you couldn't resist. You wore the suit you had bought to work in Crestmeyer's store. Tried to think what you were afraid of. You enter the office in your cheap suit and say, I'm here to see Mr. Rome. Someone will say, Get out: nobody sees Mr. Rome, nobody. Or he does see you: takes one look and says, Who the hell are you? It was impossible, and your heart thumped with the gossip of alternatives.

You followed Jane Delaware's directions, subway to the Rome Building. Glass outside, carpet and dark paneling inside. Elevator to the fifteenth floor, office marked ROME INVEST-MENTS, receptionist who took your name, looked at the Delaware card, buzzed someone and asked you to wait. Now you'd find out. Office large and bright, desks and cubicles, men and women in shirt sleeves. A receptionist took you to another elevator, summoned with a key. This one was small, carpeted, with hunting pictures on the walls, unnumbered colored buttons. Press the black one, rise fast with the wind rushing through the shaft. Door opens, you are surrounded by light, a living room in the sky with thick carpet, deep chairs and tables and lamps, bookcases, glass walls on three sides looking out over the top of the city. You'd be thrown out the window when they discovered who you were. A tall young woman came silently toward you across the carpet, greeting, Mr. White? Plain white blouse and black skirt, intelligent face, directing you to that deep chair looking out at the skyscraper tops. Wait amid the named peaks: Chrysler Tower, Empire State Building, the twin towers of the World Trade Center. Beyond them, distant and almost dissolving in the haze, the tiny figure of the Statue of Liberty, and wiry bridges pinning the sides of the rivers together.

Stephen White? The man strides in, holding out his hand. I'm Jack Rome! You could see the exclamation point. And still the joke was deferred. Thin small man neat in a black suit, a tie becoming expensive while you watched. Young. Black mustache, thick, face around the mustache smooth, eyes large and black looking first at you with serene and confident humor then darting around among the skyscraper peaks at his feet incorporating them into his point of view. Sit down glad so grateful to you. (Jack Rome the Great was grateful to Stephen White.) You in one low chair, he in another, both facing out, the view. One ankle over his knee, scratching under the sock like poison ivy, a cigarette then another tapping them out in a large abalone shell on the floor. Later a girl in a skirt shorter than the fashion brought him milk on a tray, coffee for you. My view, he said, pointing not to the girl but the buildings, the view which reduced the city to its hazy essence eliminating its crowds by height like what you had seen first with truncated base from across the industrial plain.

So Stephen, tell me about yourself.

It must be a mistake, you said, thinking maybe this wasn't Jack Rome but an impostor designed to draw you in. Or it had to do with the name you had stolen, by diabolical coincidence.

Tell me anyway.

What do you want to know?

Start at the beginning. Where were you born?

Where were you born? Trap question, obviously, and it took stammering Stephen White a moment to remember, Queens.

Jack Rome laughed. Whether or not you were born in Queens, it doesn't matter. You can't guess why I invited you here, can you? Obviously not. Carefully now, enunciating clearly, Jack Rome said this: I am trying to locate someone I want to help. I hope you can help me find him and advise me what to do.

More than ever sure, you said, I really think you've made a mistake.

Do you think Jack Rome makes mistakes? I don't think Jack Rome makes mistakes.

The intelligent young woman who let you in has disappeared, likewise the short-skirted bare-legged one who brought you coffee. Whatever Jack Rome thinks he knows, you must insist he has no power over you. The blue-tinted windows color the whole city and blunt the sharp sunglints from the chrome and steel dust below. He said, I am thinking about a young man who recently drowned himself in a midwestern city.

Like falling from the window here, where the people below have no dimension, the shock of your first breath as you start to drop. This young man with all the advantages, high school teacher, father of a family though separated from his wife, must have been feeling despondent, though why he should, a young man with all the advantages like that—

Ah, you do know me. Insides rising on the way down, question whether the heart will erase before you hit. Fight back, though, don't let on yet, see how much he knows.

Jack Rome: there was also this other young man, a happier story, came from somewhere or nowhere, recently hitchhiked across the country to this very city, living here now, no one knows his name for sure.

The blue tint of the glass makes you wonder how long the view will keep its color before it fades. Jack Rome wonders if you might know one or the other of these two young men so as to help him find them as well as judge the advisability of aid to one or the other.

(Aid?) Why should I know them?

My information suggests you do.

You'd like to know what information, and he says, the Rome organization's spread is wide, its fling is far, it has operatives, a network, that sort of thing.

Your fall has been arrested by the talk of aid, this suggestion of benignity that can only be a trap, and you have this sudden desire, which you must beware, to share your secrets with Jack Rome.

I suppose your reluctance comes from fear of divulging what your friends would like to keep secret, but if you bear in mind my benevolent purpose. That is, if you think Jack Rome has the power to help. For instance, one question is, which of these two men should be helped?

Why should that be a problem, if one of them drowned?

That's the clear thinking we need, proving it was no mistake to call you in. So there is only one candidate after all, right? But the question is still significant, for here is the interesting thing. The rumor in the Rome network is that the two young men are one, the man who drowned is the man who hitchhiked, which can be explained in two possible ways: either a miraculous resurrection and possible Second Coming, or he didn't drown at all, but cast off his old identity and took on a new. Jack Rome's eyes were large and black and clear like the robin's. Now Stephen tell me, which do you think is the more plausible explanation?

Why ask me?

Jack Rome grinned. Well tell me this. Why should the hitchhike man be so anxious to deny the suicide man?

Maybe that's because if he becomes known, it won't be a suicide anymore.

Would that be bad?

I'd think if his life was bad enough for suicide, he wouldn't want to go back to it.

Jack Rome laughed again. What could he do instead?

He could start over.

Do you think he can?

He can try.

Look at the blue tinted view again, gorgeous, a mirage of distance and power and concealment. Jack Rome lights a cigarette, leans back, scratches his ankle, sneaks a look at you, blows smoke rings. He says, What's your real name?

Don't you know?

Should I help him?

You are wary still, wondering why he wants to do that, the lack of motive, the threat of benevolence, a bomb of irony, Trojan Horse.

You don't seem to trust me.

I don't understand your reasons.

Did you ever hear of anybody named Peter Gregory?

Are you asking me?

Don't fool with me any more. I need to know so there is no mistake. Do you know Peter Gregory?

I've heard of him.

Where is he now?

You stare and do not speak. You will not surrender on your own or volunteer what you have not been asked. Yet your wish seeks release. Ask me, it says, don't make me say it, and after a long pause he does: Are you Peter Gregory?

Now it is possible to reply. Back to normal, How did you know? you say.

My operatives, never you mind. Good, now we can talk.

On the question of miracle, you realized this: It would not be a miracle for Jack Rome because for him it was simply a thing to do. Nor would it be a miracle for Amy, Joe, or any other bystander, for it's always others who get the luck. The miracle was for you, and since it was a miracle, you'll never know if it really was luck and what the catch was.

One sperm in a million reaches the egg. If you are a sperm you've got one chance in a million, which means we are a society of lottery winners. The improbabilities in the case were threefold. First, the odds against Jack Rome's knowing who you were. Second, against his caring. Third, against his acting upon it. Never mind. The odds were against you, but if there are odds there's always a chance, and somebody has to win. It might as well be you.

FIFTEEN

Jack Rome in his low chair, with his pipe, legs crossed, looking down his nose over narrow pointed shoes at his view, his city without people. Turned again to look at you, the large black robin's eyes in his delicate face with the big black mustache, and you could not tell the irises from the pupils.

Looking at you, I give you assurance of my good will. I mean you no harm and may do you good. I shall not divulge your secrets. (Four things were going on here. There was the formal and institutional language. There was the message. There was the messenger's frail appearance. And there was the effect of supernal power incarnate in room, building, view, time, concentrated in that frailty.)

Thinking, there's no reason to tell him anything, though he had the blackmail power to crush you. Your curiosity about the good he promised overshadowed the sinister mystery of why he was interested.

Jack Rome: Let's get our facts straight.

He read from an open file folder. Your name was originally Peter Gregory. (Yes.) On a night in May you left your car at the public landing with an ostensible suicide note. About a week later you turned up in New York with a different name. (I suppose so.) Since then you have been living in the Village with Joe Fingerton and four others, and you are employed in Mr. Crestmeyer's typewriter shop. (That is correct.)

I have a question. Did you actually go into the river, or did you leave the note to throw people off? (I went into the river.) Did you expect to drown? (I believe I changed my mind in the river.) In the river? A genuine change of heart? Good. Then you went to New York. How did you do that? (I hitchhiked.) Right. Those are the most important facts, you see, and I want to be sure I have them straight.

May I ask? How did you find me?

That's immaterial.

Not to me, you said. It's not immaterial to me.

It wasn't any of your friends, he said. It's irrelevant. It has nothing to do with the case.

You didn't think it was irrelevant, but what could you say? Not knowing made Jack Rome look like a god, which he wasn't.

Now let's see, he said. Peter Gregory was born thirty-five years ago in Westchester County, New York, correct? (Yes.) Parents both dead. Your father was an ACLU lawyer who had an alcohol problem. (My father was a gentle kindly melancholy man. He was much loved by those who knew him.) I'm sure he was. He died of a heart attack when you were in college at the age of twenty. (Yes.)

Your mother was Pamela Muskin. She was institutionalized for a mental breakdown two or three years after your father's death. Confined a dozen years, until her death last fall. (She died of cancer, a long illness.) Yes. Did you have some fear of insanity running in the family? (No.) No? You have no brothers and sisters. (Yes.) How would you describe your relations with your parents? (Fine.)

Eventually you'll talk more openly and intimately. I have the ability to do you good. (Yes.) You had two uncles. Your uncle Bart died before you were born. He jumped out of a hotel window on the day his ex-wife remarried. Your uncle Phil was a stockbroker, who was lost at sea alone in his sailboat somewhere in the North Atlantic. (Your researchers are thorough.)

They're the best. How do you interpret Phil's death? When he died your uncle was in process of appealing a conviction for illegal trading practices. If the appeal had failed he would have gone to jail. (Are you suggesting he was running away from the law?) Not at all. But is it confirmed his boat actually sank? (My uncle was on his way around the world, sailing by himself. It was a well-publicized trip, planned with ample time to complete before the appeal came to trial.) Fine, but that's no answer to my question. (There was a storm when radio contact was lost. It was a forty foot sloop. No way that boat could have eluded discovery around the North Atlantic.)

I'll take your word he was not running away from legal embarrassments. But did he perhaps seek his death? (I can't judge that.) Your uncle was a restless man, true? (It's true he was tired of everyday life. He didn't look forward to old age. He was an adventurous spirit and didn't like the confinements that faced him.) Confinements? (I don't mean jail.) Of course you don't. You mean offices, lawns, street traffic. Age, retirement, illness. Your uncle made his living dealing in paper fortunes, but he always wanted something else. For your uncle, the real life was not indoors with people but outside in the weather. For him life was tangible when felt in the body. He didn't want to die in a hospital.

(Did you investigate him too?) I have natural insight into what people are, based on what they do. You should be glad of that. Are there other relatives? (My grandfather Muskin is in a retirement home near Chicago. He doesn't know who he is.) Your grandfather used to be a minister, liberal. Does he remember that? (When I last saw him, my grandfather remembered a liberal minister but didn't know who he was.)

Too bad. Now let me check my knowledge of you. You grew up in Westchester. In school, adequate, not brilliant, shy demeanor, considered a loner. (I never considered myself a loner.) Summers with family in Maine. (Yes, yes.) College in Chicago, graduated 1974. Graduate school. First a college teaching job in Cincinnati while you were still in graduate school. Didn't get the degree, quit graduate school, fired by the college, got a high school job instead. (Not fired, released when my term ran out.) Whatever you say, young man. Teaching high school English ever since. Career from the beginning modest, average, I won't say mediocre but call it inconspicuous. (If you say so.)

A touchy moment, a bit of a silence here, as if he had come to a switch requiring him to choose which track to follow next. You studied his face for what he might be concealing and interrupted his thought with a question of your own. Tell me, if you know so much. Is Peter Gregory really dead back there?

He brushed the smoke away from his face. That's a natural question, isn't it? Who's to say? What can a community do when someone leaves a suicide note without a body? When my researcher inquired, your case was open. Such cases generally remain open for years, no matter what people think. I wouldn't worry. Nobody has betrayed you, as far as I know. Nobody was pursuing you at the time of my inquiry. But as to what they believe—your wife, your children, your colleagues—your guess is better than mine, because you know them and I don't.

May we continue? You were separated from your wife? (Yes.) And two children, Patty and Jeff, who went with her. (Yes.) Your wife moved into the house of a Professor of Romance Languages, you moved into an apartment, and your house was rented to another family. (Yes.) The house is still jointly owned by you and your wife, and she will have to wait until you can be declared officially dead. I presume you don't want to speed that process. (What can I do?) Nothing, probably. You can't deed the house to her without revealing your failure to die.

Jack Rome closed the folder and tilted his head back to think. Now, he said. Who are the survivors? (Survivors?) People who think you are gone, whom you would rather not meet on the street. You've left an ex-wife and two children. A grandfather institutionalized in Chicago. Colleagues and students in your home town, as well as neighbors. (Yes.) I presume you would prefer to stay away from your town for that reason. (Yes.) Chicago too. (Yes.) Any place else? (I don't know, I haven't figured it out.) At any rate, unless you repeal your suicide, your freedom of movement is constricted. Does that bother you? (Not so far.)

There's one question I must ask. Is there any possibility of your going back? Here comes Peter Gregory, back to life after all these years. (I wouldn't dare.) Think again. There's a lifetime ahead of you, which may be longer than you thought when you headed into the river. Will Peter Gregory stay dead when you are sixty years old? (He'll have no choice.)

No? So you say. He looked at the ceiling like some right wing intellectual on a talk show, and said, What happened before you went into the river?

Undifferentiated circumstance and bad feeling.

My question is why you did such an extraordinary thing. I apologize for asking, but you know why I need to know.

You didn't know, and you asked, Why do you need to know?

I mean to give you a gift, as I already told you.

What kind of a gift?

That's to be decided. Your cooperation is essential.

What do you want with me? Why are you after me?

Again his harsh little laugh, and the smoke around his ears. I mean you no harm, he said. I mean you nothing but good.

But why? What am I to you? You've got everything, why me?

Curiosity, will that do? Not everybody has done the extraordinary thing you have done.

I don't want to go back, you said. It would kill me.

You've demonstrated that. You won't have to go back.

What is it you want to know?

Very simply: why did you jump into the river?

Maybe I was depressed.

Depressed people bore me. Give me something more interesting.

You remembered explaining to Amy and Joe, how your answer evaded your memory. You repeated it anyway: I was separated from my wife.

That so? Skeptical silence while he thought it over. You waited for the obvious objection. It came: an act of spite? After two and a half months?

You remembered the additional explanation you thought of in the car while listening to free enterprise, an explanation you never got a chance to give: There was another mess the last week. A student named Florry Gates.

Well, well. So what did Florry Gates do to you?

Cursory summary: how she approached you, offered sympathy, and how her father discovered you and threatened to sue. That was one week before your jump, and there was also the time she threw you out of the car and made you walk home by yourself, whenever that was.

What's that got to do with jumping in the river?

You thought it self-evident. No? The threat of criminal charges? The humiliating exposure? The public embarrassment?

What? A little scandal? Your wife had already left you, so what was at stake?

People go to jail for statutory rape.

You don't really think there was a danger of that, do you? Didn't you want to fight it out?

It wasn't just that.

What was it then? You tell me.

You were tangled in things, you tried to tell. You mentioned Jock Hadley. An old man, a vicious old man, who lived across the street.

Vicious eh? What about him?

You said, He was murdered by someone the newspapers called the Hammer Man. Who went around smashing the skulls of lonely old men.

What's this got to do with anything?

The world was falling apart. Everything was going down the drain.

What's the matter? You can't stand a little excitement?

You said you thought you were going mad.

He looked displeased, and suddenly you feared disqualification as beneficiary. The view from his sunny blue window to the floor had thickened, an unspecifiable overcast had depleted the light of its shine.

Maybe you should tell me why you changed your mind in the river.

I saw the lights in the water.

What does that mean?

I saw the lights and decided to swim out. That's what I remember: the lights, the decision, the act following the decision. I don't remember the reasoning behind the decision.

All right, then. So what did you do next?

You slept on the shore and in the morning bought breakfast and started hitchhiking.

Okay, next question. Since you had changed your mind, why didn't you simply go back to your apartment and pretend nothing had happened? Would anybody have known the difference?

It never occurred to you. Or if it did, it was forbidden.

Forbidden. You were guided by magic signs and dark taboos. They seemed like logical imperatives.

But you forget the logic. Never mind. You started hitchhiking. What was that like, hitchhiking across the country?

It was a challenge.

Exhilarating? Tell me about it.

You told him. The peony kids, sleeping in the woods, washing your clothes, making up names, the man named Roy Clements. You did not mention the body in the woods, but you told about the man who called you bum, and the car you stole, the amusement park, and the people who gave you rides.

When you told him about Crazy James, Jack Rome laughed. Right hand man, eh? I wonder who that was? You told about his Me Grant, and Rome laughed again. All during your narrative you were jostling him, looking for signs revealing his source.

He liked your adventures. Now you see why I don't believe your reasons for jumping, he said. Couldn't stand conflict, suicide because you couldn't bear the embarrassment? Bullshit, my friend. Bullshit because you swam out. You took up a new personality and tried to establish it in the world. That's a bigger challenge than anything you ducked. What you've done the last couple of months requires more energy, more effort of character, more conflict, risk of embarrassment, than any troubles you were trying to avoid. Now I want you to stop lying to me and tell me the real reasons for your jump.

Lying to you?

Not telling the truth. Not the real truth.

What am I leaving out?

You know what you're leaving out.

What do you know?

I know things you haven't told me.

This was the abyss dropping underneath. There was the whole world in what you had not told Jack Rome.

He said slyly, When that What's-her-name Florry Gates offered you sympathy, as you said, what did she offer you sympathy for?

You thought it through and realized what he knew. Yes, you said.

Is that it? Am I right?

Yes.

You had a certain notoriety, didn't you?

Yes, yes. You shuddered now, secretly, afraid of the power he had over you, and no choice but to admit, Yes.

Okay then. He was excited. That's all I need to know. We'll talk again tomorrow. I need to know more before I decide.

Decide what?

What to do with you. Come back at the same time.

I have to work then. Mr. Crestmeyer depends on me.

Mr. Crestmeyer is profiting more from your absence than he would from your presence.

What if I don't come back?

You will.

What if I don't? What's to make me?

Your curiosity. What I can do for you. I could give you a fortune. I could make you rich. If I wanted to.

Would you do that?

Come back tomorrow and see. You can't lose.

Jack Rome relaxed and became familiar. He looked at you with his black robin's eye and said, You may think I'm a tycoon, but at heart I'm a philosopher. It's true I'm a man of wealth and power, but my spirit is with the minds hidden away in third floor offices of college philosophy departments. The human condition, that's what interests me. When you swam the river, you stepped outside the human condition. Once, however, you were a high school English teacher. So you should be able to express yourself. Tell me then, what's it like outside the human world? What's it like to look on and be no part of it?

You had no words for what he wanted. Only discredited figures of speech. You told him how you sat in the harbor feeling your present getting thinner and thinner as past and future faded away.

He liked it.

He sent you home with one final warning. Don't tell your friends. Say you interviewed for a job and filled out forms.

What shall I say when they ask how you found me?

Blame it on a mysterious and well-connected customer at the typewriter shop to whom you were surprisingly helpful. That will suggest you are being considered for a research job. Low level. That will satisfy them.

SIXTEEN

Back to Crestmeyer that afternoon, with a feeling of exile running wild and exhilarated patience waiting for the good. Mixed with the nausea of blackmail in a concentration camp. In the afternoon quiet you sat at a table in the store and tried to interpret, looking for deception and hidden meanings. Your friends were curious about Jack Rome. You put them off. Night came and your sleep was full of futures.

Back to Jack Rome's office in the morning, stranger than the first time because of familiarity. An explorer the first day, now a sleeper returning to a dream.

Jack Rome was wearing a white suit. He looked smaller than you remembered. He said, Why are we meeting today?

You asked me to come back.

Why?

You wanted to continue our conversation.

What did we talk about?

Don't you remember? I'm the one who jumped into the river and swam out.

I remember. The suicide kid. Hitchhiked to New York. Why did you do that?

We talked about that.

Because your wife left you and took the kids. Because someone's father charged you with statutory rape. Baloney.

Here was a new crabby Jack Rome, a man of unreliable

97

changes, showing how silly your hopes of good from him actually were.

But then he said (as if this were part of a strategy), Let's talk about your moment of fame.

A new shock.

Your moment in the papers, your notoriety, which you neglected to mention yesterday. (But which he had discovered, like everything else, as you should have known.)

Do we have to? you said.

He waited for you to see your stupidity.

You had hoped to put it out of your life, you said.

So that's why you jumped? Why didn't you tell me?

You said nothing.

I thought so, he said. You're dumb. If it weren't for that I'd not have bothered with you. So now we're going to talk about it. You get nothing from me unless you tell me everything. The newspapers say you were drunk. Is that wrong?

You took a deep breath, defeated. It would all come out. Despite the dread of being caught, you felt relieved, and surprised by that relief, to admit this thing which you had washed out of mind in the river. You acknowledged it: No, you said, it's true.

According to the newspaper, according to the police, according to your defense at the trial, you were so sloshed, looped, whatever your favorite slang is, that you truly didn't know where you were when the accident occurred. Is that the truth or is there a catch somewhere?

It's the truth.

You were driving your car in this condition and you turned up the exit ramp of the expressway and headed into the oncoming traffic? Wrong way.

Why are you digging this up?

You know why, so shut up. You went up the exit ramp ignoring the sign that said Do Not Enter and the sign that said Wrong Way. The bright red danger color of these signs, which did not, I assume, register on your retina at that hour of the night. You had your headlights on, I presume?

The witnesses say so.

But you were too blind to notice. Do you remember the Do Not Enter signs?

I don't know what I remember. That was two years ago.

Your true memory is corrupted by your attempts to reconstruct a memory, is that what you're saying?

I suppose so.

Well, that's all right. What have you decided you can remember from that episode? You tell me.

You tried to tell it now, not knowing how much came from the source and how much from telling it before, to yourself and to the lawyers and the police and Linda and the high school principal and the children. You said you didn't know if you remembered the warning sign or not. What you remembered in this uncertain way was the plausibility of Peter Gregory's having had a thought saying, That sign says Wrong Way. And a thought saying: Drunks go through signs saying Wrong Way, so it's natural to notice it. However, since I am not going the wrong way, I must have misread the sign. On expressways where exit and entrance ramps run parallel to each other, the Wrong Way sign is often visible to the person on the ramp to which it does not apply. Peter Gregory had often experienced the shock of properly entering a ramp and seeing the Wrong Way sign on the adjacent ramp, requiring a complex series of inferences to figure out. So when he saw the Wrong Way sign, if he saw it, that could have been what he thought, which, realizing how easy it was to make such a mistake, he put quickly out of mind.

And drove right up on the highway, Jack Rome said.

Forgetting the sign if he had ever noticed it, you said. Then (to the best of your knowledge) noticing he was on a two-lane highway, he realized he had missed his turn onto the Interstate. There was a car coming toward him in the opposite lane, a single pair of headlights, that's how he knew it was a two-lane highway. The car blasted its horn as it went by, which he attributed to drunks on a spree late in the night.

Jack Rome said, You're telling me this. Are you sure there wasn't some underlying defiance in your mind, encouraging self-deception for self-destruction's sake?

That was shrewd and psychological of Jack Rome, you thought, his mind perhaps a shade more interesting than you had supposed, and you conceded yes the possibility of some hidden anger encouraging him to make mistakes and talk himself into nonsense.

Jack Rome grinned. He liked this kind of talk. What happened after the car passed in the other lane?

Well, then he saw two cars ahead, one passing the other in front of him in his own lane, against all rules.

Against all rules, yes.

Coming right at him, damfool idiot, taking his time getting back to his side, forcing Gregory to apply the brakes, and there was another blaring of horns as the cars went by, a wild crowd of reckless drivers and merry makers and drunken daredevils on the road this dangerous Friday night. You remembered (if you didn't make this up later) thinking Friday, yes, that accounts for it.

And then, exactly how did it happen?

You read the newspapers, you know the answer.

Give me your version.

No doubt there was another car behind the car that was passing the car on the left and behind that still another, all in his lane coming at him, and when it swerved—and he swerved too, because things were getting out of hand, with still another car coming and nothing he could do but make for the shoulder, with brakes jammed, causing a skid as well, and a smash and—

Does your memory include the smash?

It seems to, the back half of a car close in the headlights, bang! swiped, and bang his chin on something like the steering wheel, and his head, and flying around, skidding and swooshing and banging and bumping, not knowing where the hell anything was, realizing the car was rolling over and coming to rest down low in the dark, with lights up behind somewhere.

Then what?

His thought was Uh-oh, the realization he had had an accident, and accidents have consequences. About the same time but in a different part of the brain it occurred to him that with so many cars coming the other way all trying to pass illegally, perhaps he had been going the wrong way on a one-way highway.

Jack Rome laughed.

You said it wasn't funny. People were killed.

Right, he said. The Sebastian family. That poor man's family you wiped out, the mother and her two little girls. Mary, Jenny, and Jacky, leaving poor Thomas bereft.

Well, actually it was the car behind.

Oh yes, I forgot. You sideswiped him and sent him into a spin, then the car behind him going much too fast crashed him broadside, doing the dirty work while you went smoking into the ditch. More his fault than yours, would you say?

No no no, not his fault, no. It was mine.

Or, to be more precise, Peter Gregory's fault, not yours?

You couldn't tell what he thought, sitting there in his white suit watching the smoke circle in wisps around his head.

Afraid of his irony, you took the blame. No, it was my fault, I can't get rid of it that way.

All right, your fault. But not Stephen White's, right? Or Murry Bree's?

If you like.

We'll see. Tell you what, Stephen. To keep differences clear, let's discuss these matters in the proper names. Instead of talking about you, let's talk about Peter Gregory, what he did and didn't do—to keep things clear. Is that all right with you?

You'd already been doing that. His irony was a marshland, but you said you'd try.

You are Stephen White, and we're talking about Peter Gregory, okay?

Okay.

So I'll tell you one thing that bothers me about this story. Peter Gregory was blind drunk that night. Am I overstating it?

No sir.

Well, listen to this. I don't like drunks. I hate 'em, I find 'em disgusting. Do you follow me?

You hate drunks.

Peter Gregory must have been pretty disgusting that night.

He was, he was.

So tell me honestly, Stephen, because this is important: was this habitual for him?

Not really. He liked a drink at Lenny's before dinner, but to get as drunk as he was that night, that was unusual. I can also tell you that after the accident, he never touched another drink in his life, and that was two years ago.

Cold turkey?

Yes sir.

Why did he do that?

Why, because of the accident. A vow, Never Again.

Has Stephen White made a similar vow?

The question was a surprise. It hadn't occurred to you.

Or does he consider himself bound by Gregory's vow?

You'd have to think about that.

I'll tell you, Stephen, I don't want to throw my money away on an alcoholic who'll blow it in drink.

Peter Gregory didn't touch a drop for two years, and the notion of a drink has never occurred to Murry Bree or Stephen White, you said, lying a little.

Maybe so, but you need to tell me, if it was unusual for Peter Gregory to get so drunk, what made him do so on that particular Friday night? The papers don't explain it.

No?

They don't say why that night was different from others.

Now you wondered what else he knew that had not made it into the papers. What private sources among Peter Gregory's untrustworthy intimates had his investigators also discovered?

He reminded you: If you're still embarrassed or ashamed on Peter Gregory's behalf, then you're still Peter Gregory.

Oh.

Anita Long had not made it into the papers. Because you had been with her earlier on that fatal night, you mentioned her, though still unable not to be shamefaced, unable to escape the wince in the recollection. Nature woman in the Activist Bookstore who came in to Lenny's for a drink every weekday afternoon after five, who knew the rumors about your wife and the Professor in Romance Languages whom she named sneeringly Louis the Lover, and who, friendly to you (Gregory) invited you (Gregory) to her apartment one evening instead of going straight home as you (he) usually did. With a domestic uproar as a result, confessions and accusation, which didn't prevent a second time, which happened to be the particular Friday night we have been talking about.

So, Rome said, other events of a dramatic kind also happened on that significant day? A little sex before submersion?

A little sex, a little drink, a little talk about what to put up with and what not, moral support and whose rights, a shot in the arm, and have a nice day. Also the flight of time, and the need to explain to Linda why he was late, which caused him to postpone his return home until he'd be so late she'd have gone to bed, returning meanwhile to wait it out at Lenny's, where the whiskey said *Drink me* in a stronger voice than usual. Then it was so late and he was so drunk he decided he should work it off before going home. Too dangerous to drive, work it by a combination of exercise and coffee. Exercise meant activity, going somewhere, movement, and when he thought of movement he thought of the car, and it occurred to him, with permission, that the way to work it off was to drive the car fast out on the open road. Let the cold air stream through his lungs. So (telling Jack Rome) he went out from Lenny's to the car at midnight, afraid of driving in the city streets because he was drunk, eager to get out to the highway where he could air it out, let the blood coursing through his body restore him to sobriety. He found the Interstate without disaster, and turned up the ramp where— we're back where we started.

Jack Rome laughed again. It isn't funny, you said.

So the police came down into the ditch, and took him in an ambulance. And then the reporters and lawyers, the charges filed, and outrage, and letters in the paper and hate mail to the house, the anonymous telephone calls, and almost everyone agreeing that Peter Gregory was a slob if not a villain, and these are the kind of people we have teaching in our high schools?

On to the trial, the lawyer who hoped to mitigate it for Gregory by saying it wasn't his car but the other that killed the family, which only added to the outrage of people writing to the paper, with the kindly well-meaning woman judge who suspended the sentence, and the shouts of loathing and execration in the courtroom. And the questions raised, the long talks with the principal of the high school and the decision to return to classes quietly with as little publicity as possible, and the quiet reserve of the students who knew what had happened but dared not mention it, but be sure they talked about it to each other. And so it went for two more years.

And what did your wife and children think about all this?

So you told how Linda stood by him in public, the loyal wife. How he did his allocated community service afternoons to the offices downtown, to neighborhoods on errands, interviews with poor people like a social worker, telling himself this was atonement to wash his soul clean, only that when it was over he was still the same person, known to anyone with memory as the Gregory who had been in the news, who had done that terrible thing. Wondering how many generations of students it would take for them to forget, with new people always popping it on him.

He was stuck with Peter Gregory, that was the problem. Frantic to think better of himself, he would tell himself Never Again, a solemn vow, in hopes this would distinguish the new Peter Gregory from the old. The question was, Never Again What? Since drink had brought the worst of his troubles, try that. Never Again drink. It worked, but it did not help. By Never Again, he kept from drinking, but this did not prevent people from reminding him, nor him from remembering. He detected the silent shift in his wife's attitude from pity to contempt, the euphemism that was pity giving way to the reality that was contempt. He saw the contempt in his children too, Patty and Jeff, who looked upon him with strange alien curiosity, listened to him cautiously, held themselves in reserve, as they understood and were not allowed to forget what Daddy did, for which they had never received a sufficient alleviating explanation. This continued, while Louis the Lover became a fact of life, until two months ago when she moved out, taking the children with her. They called him Poor Daddy and did not object.

Never saw Anita Long again, either. Everybody talked about him behind his back, Peter Gregory Who. That's Peter Gregory who, you mean Peter Gregory Who? Who kept repeating, Never Again, though what he really wanted to achieve by incantation was Never Was, which was impossible. He had these views of himself, glimpses of Gregory in the eyes of others, where he would see that damned accident with its disreputable origins attached to him like a smokestack on a steamboat, or else Peter Gregory himself a kind of shell wherein he lodged like a turtle or a hermit crab, how get it off?

Actually, when Linda got fed up, she didn't move out but kicked him out, right into the voice range of Jock Hadley, who wouldn't let him forget either. Jock Hadley lived across the street from Gregory's new bachelor room, Hadley in a one-story bungalow, on his porch shouting insults across the street: that's the man who killed them kids, folks, still teaching in our schools, right over there across the street.

Jack Rome asked, Jock Hadley? Is that the old man who got killed?

By the Hammer Man. Yes.

So the Hammer Man did you a favor?

What?

You weren't relieved?

I thought they were after me.

Who's "they"?

I thought everyone was after me. Except Florry Gates. Florry Gates said, I heard about your accident Mr. Gregory. I want you to know I sympathize. I think you got a rotten deal.

She was in his class, seventeen years old, scraggly looking, and she came by to see him, he didn't ask her to. She heard old Hadley asking where she was going, and when she told him he said something and she said, Mind your own business, you old fart.

Jack Rome laughed again. You said, It's not funny.

So you couldn't take it? he said.

There was Florry's father, last straw, who called up the principal's office and accused Peter Gregory of statutorily raping his daughter and what were they going to do about it?

You wrote a suicide note and took your car down to the river and went in, Jack Rome said.

Peter Gregory, you reminded him.

Thinking you'd like to try something different for a change, having got yourself deformed, a little twisted and cramped in that shell you'd grown, named Gregory, so you'd try a different fit, a new person, is that it?

Something like that.

And it was just a coincidence that the Hammer Man happened to kill mean old Jock Hadley the night before you went into the river?

It aggravated things. Everybody was after him. Peter Gregory was afraid they would blame him for Hadley's death on top of everything else.

Why would anybody think that?

Because Hadley was such a pain in the ass.

Like they would think Gregory had paid somebody to shut him up? Peter Gregory had become so huge to Peter Gregory that he thought the whole world was as obsessed with him as he was?

It wasn't rational.

You didn't bump off the old man, did you?

Of course not.

"Of course not." Neither Gregory nor you. That's the trouble with the both of you, of course. You couldn't possibly do such a thing, to save your soul if you had one. Never mind. The whole story's fine, but there's one problem yet, my friend. When you went into the river, did you intend to drown? (Jack Rome in his white suit, looking at you with his indecipherable robin's eye above the masquerading mustache.) If you planned to swim out, it would have been safer not to go in. Swimming suggests you meant to drown. Your subsequent behavior suggests the reverse.

You: Could you have one motive concealed behind the other, discovered when faced with the consequences of the other?

Rome: Whatever it was, we are faced with a notable lack of conviction on your part. Look at your names. Hal Hastings, when you were still suicidal, when the only thing you knew about yourself was that Gregory had committed suicide, and no other you was yet conceivable. Then a series of characters in fiction, reflecting your desire to create a character for yourself in the belief created characters exist only in fiction. Though why you didn't prefer to be Aladdin or Sinbad the Sailor (or Popeye) I don't know. With Murry Bree you began to regress. Alien, inferior, deliberately innocuous, soft, for the world to shelter like a pet. As for Stephen White, you could have been Stanley Caruso or John Figueroa. What does it mean?

You didn't know.

It means Gregory is still alive and sick. Those are Gregory names, names a Gregory would think of to cover the life a

Gregory would think of for a Gregory pretending to be a non-Gregory. And you know what I think of Gregory.

Do I?

Peter Gregory was a jerk. A failure. Treacherous, cowardly at all levels: at the trivial social level, timorous and servile in gutless relationships, and in the big moral issues, where he couldn't face anything. No wonder Linda couldn't stand him. I don't blame you for wanting to get rid of him.

You were turning red, you felt it in the ears.

Quit blushing. I'm not talking about you.

You were afraid he might forget the distinction later on. You said, Peter Gregory was not treacherous.

Then how come I don't trust him? Let me tell you what makes people go, because you don't seem to know. Set aside the animal instincts, food and shelter, self preservation, sex. What compels people, the human thing? This: the *competitive ego*. Write that down. Come on, write it.

Where?

Here, here's a pad. "The competitive ego." What do mortally conscious beings want in the world? They want their difference to be recognized. What distinguishes one person from another? The competition by which one beats the other. Ergo ego, competitive ego, remember, Jack Rome told you. What is your self? It's your human part which pursues success, the drive to win. To win is to beat out somebody else. That's the human story: you ratify life by coming in ahead of somebody else.

You remembered the free enterprise man, but this was the great Jack Rome.

Jack Rome: I changed my name when I set out to make my first million, the better to represent myself. Just as you changed yours. Succeed means exceed. Outdo someone.

More Jack Rome: Everybody picks a competitive field or two in which to win. Little people pick little fields. Big people pick big ones. Athletes, financiers, professors. Husbands, fathers, lovers. Saintly mothers of children—you don't believe me? Good implies bad. If you're a good mother you're better than some other mother, that's the point.

You thought, if Jack Rome is to make a difference in your life, you should adapt to his ways of thinking.

Rome: Peter Gregory didn't understand this. His truth was obscured by righteous sentimentality and sentimental guilt. He let a stupid cowardly accident ruin his life. That's how losers express their competitiveness, by rising below themselves. Peter Gregory is a better loser than anybody else. Everything goes wrong for Peter Gregory. Suicide shows his superiority to all the hypocrites who go on living, indulging their vulgar pleasures and soon-to-be-forgotten little wins.

You listened gloomily, feeling betrayed.

You don't like this? he said. Tell me then, what exactly was your idea of Stephen White's future, there while you were working in Crestmeyer's store with your young friends?

You hadn't got that far looking ahead. You had to get used to the feel, first.

Feel of what?

Of not being Gregory any more.

Well good, that's where your hope lies. As we both agree, you're not Gregory. There's a difference between you and him. *You're* not about to allow Peter Gregory back. That, my friend, is what interests me in you.

(You wondered how Jack Rome would like the comparison between his eye and Murry Bree's.)

Do you think you can succeed as someone else?

Forced to speak: You can try.

That's the spirit.

The smoke went deep into his lungs and filtered out through his fine nostrils and delicate mouth upward into the air-conditioning system. I said I would do something for you. What do you think I should do?

I don't know. What do you have in mind?

Listen to this question and don't answer without thinking. I could do this for you. How would you like to be rich?

What?

Suppose I gave you a gift that would make you rich, easy and comfortable for the rest of your days, would you like that?

What would I have to do in return?

Nothing. No strings. Would you like it?

Sure I'd like it. What's the gimmick?

Don't be so suspicious. I'm talking about a real possibility. A gift from me to you to make you rich.

The devil and your soul. You remembered Crazy James. A grant?

All right, a grant.

Why?

Because I'd like to see what you do with it.

Why me?

Leaning back in the deep chair swinging his polished pointed shoe on the end of his toe, chain smoking, Jack Rome: Why you? Because you had the brains to realize you didn't have to be Peter Gregory and the guts to do something about it. I'd like to give you the chance to continue the experiment.

By making me rich?

You aren't going anywhere in Crestmeyer's store. Let me predict what will happen if you stay. You'll move into a place of your own. That will give you a sense of accomplishment. You'll get married, a big move. Time will pass. A kid or two, life gets better and better. Time passes, you have trouble telling better and better from worse and worse, knowing which is which. They seem about the same to you. Working in nice small dusty intellectual shops on side streets, your worry about keeping your identity secret is so habitual you won't even realize it's worry. Keeping Stephen White modest and inconspicuous as a matter of life and death, forgetting what death you mean. If you like the girl you marry, you might stick it out. If you don't, you'll go back to Gregory. It makes no difference either way: in the end you won't know the difference between White and Gregory.

Jack Rome's point: you've already reached the ceiling on which you will bump your head. Now you'll thicken and harden, you'll age, sweet and sour, doing nothing you haven't already done. Your boring new life will be less than average, not more as it was meant to be. That's why you need a gift.

Best to keep quiet, unavid, uncritical, let his will unfold.

Listen to me. Jack Rome is ready to give you, whatever your name is, a grant large enough for whatever you want. Enough to make you think you're rich, to live as you like, where you like, to travel, buy, whatever your imagination requires.

You, cautiously stunned, warily astounded, deeply grateful, still didn't understand: what's expected in return?

Develop the new Stephen, living alternative to Peter Gregory. What you could never be in Mr. Crestmeyer's store.

How do I do that? Do you have a plan?

That's the interesting part I'll leave up to you. Let me explain the conditions of this gift. No one will interfere with what you do. The interesting question is, what will that be? What choices will you make when you have the means to make them? In exchange I'll ask only that you stay away from Peter Gregory. Your divorce from him must be complete.

You need to know just what that means.

It means (Jack Rome said) there will be no return to the Gregory world. Your tie is cut. You'll do nothing to disturb the common belief Gregory is dead. No contact with any person from that time, no visit to any place. No secret messages, no solicitations for news, no anonymous donors endowing college educations for certain children. You start from scratch, without trace, never to double back. Clear?

I think so.

This applies also to your new friends. No Amy, Joe, Crestmeyer. No Stephen White, either, you'll need another name.

You remembered, this was the man who had deprogrammed his wife and son, believing they had been brainwashed by the religious guru. You said, What kind of person do you want me to become?

That's up to you.

What if I disappoint you?

The robin's eye looked straight at you, more like a crow's. Thus: you can't disappoint me, because I don't give a shit. If you want to make that an incentive, or if you want to defy Jack Rome and remain unchanged, I don't care.

Rome: Always think in dichotomies, it will expand your mind. If there is this, there must also be that. Getting out of Peter Gregory has two steps. First, the struggle to survive. To stay alive in the narrow sense. You enter—reenter—the world. You did that. Second, to form the new person. To live in the broad sense, with the means available to the privileged and fortunate in that world. First to live with nothing: can you do it? Then to live with everything: what will you do? What will you do when your imagination has the power to act, and your future the chance to become real.

You: What do you get out of this?

The pleasure of watching, he said.

You'll have your eye on me. Won't that make me less free?

There wouldn't be any point if I couldn't watch. But Jack Rome won't interfere. I want to see what you will do. Can a Gregory change? Will he want to?

How do you intend to watch?

You'll stay in touch with me, with timely updates now and then. The story of your latest adventures: tape it, write it, come in and talk, I don't care. That's all, no strings attached.

You: why would you go to such lengths for mere curiosity?

The only length was the length of my time. The money: what's big to you is a drop in Jack Rome's bucket.

Rome: Always been interested in how to remake character. I told you I was a self-made man. You grasped: Did you also disappear from a former life? Rome: It wasn't necessary in my case. I made it all myself without assistance from anyone.

He was superior to you is what he meant. I like to see what people make of themselves when they have the means, he said. It gives me satisfaction.

What if I refuse?

You won't. Go home, take a day, think it over, then if you're interested, come back, I'll give you the money.

Just like that?

Jack Rome: One other thing. Don't talk about this. Not to anyone. No Amy and Joe. No advice. If you ask for advice you ruin the experiment before you start. Anything else you want to know?

When I get the money, if I get the money, what am I supposed to do with it?

I already told you. Anything you want, man, any goddamn thing you want.

Except—

After Gregory

No secret messages to abandoned children.
And report to you.
Right. That's no big deal.

SEVENTEEN

Down in the elevator, back to the people Jack Rome's sky-scraper view eliminated, trying to think a coherent thought through the crackling electrical storm in your mind. Back to Crestmeyer trying to work against the static during the afternoon, dizzy and crazy thinking about Jack Rome. You wondered if he was setting a trap. It wasn't a joke but there could be a catch, and something was being withheld. It was impossible because there was no reason and because the odds were so great. This was the time you first thought of the millions of sperm.

You kept looking for a real and selfish reason that would explain Jack Rome. Archetypes threatened you. Jack Rome as devil, buying your soul. As spider, luring you. As inquisitor, nailing you. You needed advice: a Better Business Bureau to attest Rome's honesty. Ann Landers to scout the practical dangers. A philosopher to resolve the ethical questions.

It would not be possible to reject this gift. This knowledge was as powerful as law, leaving you as unfree as if compelled at gunpoint. All afternoon you tried to talk away your doubts so that when you accepted the gift you could think you had done it freely.

When you got home that night, police were removing a yellow tape from the front steps. A few people were standing around. You felt a guilty shock as if you had committed a crime, though you did not know what it was. You remembered another time when you had seen police tape and felt a similar ignorance of guilt. The policeman saw the question on your face. You live here? Go on in, he said. We're finished.

What is it? you asked. He turned away, probably because he didn't hear. A woman answered: Somebody jumped. Who? She shrugged her shoulders. Suicide? What else? Another shrug, her eyes full of aged criticism of everything. You live up there? Go up, find out. Already you had guessed, Hank Gummer.

Hank Gummer, depressed and unable to reconcile himself to death, solving his problem by death. With enough breath climbing the stairs to reflect puritanically that this news, if true, was the end of your hopes from Jack Rome. You came into the apartment and Amy told you. Hank Gummer it was. Found at the foot of the stairwell three flights below when Joe came home this afternoon. Police just left. She was frantic. Did *you* see it coming? Was there anything we should have done?

You were thinking: It couldn't have come at a worse time. Ashamed of the thought, but thinking it just the same. While Amy asked, as if you were the suicide expert around here, Why did he do it?

They were all there except Lucy Angles, who had gone to stay with somebody. Lucy Angles was crushed, they said. Why did he do it? Why, if he was so worried about dying, would he kill himself?

Because he was stupid, Stowe Thompson said.

Hush, Amy said. He's dead.

Doesn't make him less stupid.

All evening they talked about Hank. Poor Hank. We didn't take him seriously. What could we have done?

It's not our responsibility, Stowe Thompson said.

Should somebody get him from the morgue? Does he have any relatives?

No one asked where you had been today. A phone call came from someone setting the time for a funeral. Amy looked around and asked if the time was okay. You guessed you wouldn't be available but didn't say anything.

You were thinking, these people in their state of shock, and you in your state of shock. With your secret, which they knew nothing about. Worst possible time, screeching across your path like an accident in the road. It was an overpowering disappointment, as if you had lost everything, which you quelled by the clarifying thought that there was really no reason to lose anything. You kept repeating it: there's no reason to alter your plans. If, that is, they are your plans.

Eventually everyone went to bed, and all night long your mind went back and forth between Jack Rome and Hank Gummer. Suspicion of Jack Rome. So rich and powerful a man must have underworld connections. If he was responsible for the raccoon in the woods, accepting the gift would make you accomplice to the crime. Talk yourself out of that. Think how to spend the money, which will certainly be much less than implied and won't make you free because you'll have to clear everything with Jack Rome, despite what he said. Imagine reporting to him on your character at periodic intervals and the effect of this on your freedom. Imagine worrying how to make yourself likable to Jack Rome. Think what it really means to get rid of Gregory, whether it wouldn't be the same as killing your children and the memories of your father and mother, filling you with grief and guilt. Of course, Rome would say, you got rid of Gregory weeks ago. The gift confirms that.

And then Gummer, whose depressed stare merged in your mind with Jack Rome's sharp and crafty eyes. You thought, what is Hank to me? You had never known him other than depressed. He irritated you, for which you now felt ashamed.

But you were glad to see him gone, as you were when Jock Hadley died. It went beyond relief from petty irritation. It was as if Gummer's suicide vindicated you, past and future, and gave you liberty to take up Jack Rome's offer. You felt this at the same time you were thinking if the decorum of Hank Gummer's death required you to postpone your fortune. On the other hand, you knew that if you postponed it, Jack Rome would renege and you wouldn't get it.

Against all such questions and all old Gregory grief and guilt, you weighed the indescribable power of money. You: with a large amount of money you can do anything. Mitigate the awfulness, for the power of wealth would make possible much good you had not dreamed of. Which brings up another question you hadn't asked. What would Jack Rome do if you disobeyed his rules? Suppose you did violate the ban and made contact with the forbidden? Could Jack Rome take it back? Did he have executioners? Three o'clock in the morning, sweat on your pillow, trying to keep the squeaking cot from waking Stowe Thompson. Forgive me, Hank, you said. You never expected anything of me, and I have my life to lead. Forgive me Linda, forgive me Patty and Jeff. Forgive me, Father and Mother. The night in the window was pale when it occurred to you before you fell asleep: I shouldn't have accepted his gift. It was a fatal mistake to have done so.

The womanly voice said, Mr. White, come right over. You went, thinking I don't have to decide yet.

This time a different room. No windows, acoustic tiles, a shiny safe in the wall, a small table with two chairs facing each other. Jack Rome was in one of the chairs, in an open-collar yellow short-sleeved shirt, looking contemptuous.

Have you decided?

You said, One of my roommates killed himself last night.

He stared at you, a long moment. What about it?

I don't know.

Why are you telling me?

It was a shock.

So you don't want the money?

You almost jumped. No, I don't mean that.

You've decided then? Did you mention this to anybody?

No. You thought you should ask more questions, but you couldn't think of any.

Good. He repeated the proposal. Jack Rome will give you a grant sufficient to satisfy your needs, which you'll be free to use as you wish without interference, subject only to the stipulation you make no contact direct or indirect with any person or persons from your previous life and take pains to keep your new identity and circumstances from becoming known to any such person or persons. He would furthermore like you to report to him informally from time to time. Any questions?

Not to be ungrateful, you didn't think you should agree without knowing how big a grant it will be.

How much do you want?

Was it up to you? Dizzied, you recognized the danger of ruining yourself by naming a figure too small, or of being ridiculous by something too large. You tried to think how much would give you a comfortable income and make you secure. But the word he had used, several times, was "rich," and you had to think what that meant. A good baseball player gets five million a year.

He laughed. It adds up. Magic Johnson will get fourteen million, but his life expectancy is reduced. Tell me something to show the magnitude of your imagination.

You didn't want to. You said hopefully, What seems big to me will seem small to you.

Obviously.

Delaying, you said, if I accept a grant today, must I move out of my apartment right away?

Today. To reduce the temptation of spilling the beans. Don't say where you're going, it's private, just say good bye.

He gave you a look. What's the matter, you want to go to your friend's funeral?

There's no need.

Damn right. What was the matter with him?

He was depressed.

What kind of a reason is that?

I don't know why he did it.

How did he do it? That's a more interesting question.

He jumped down the stairwell.

How many flights?

Three.

There should have been more flights. Did he make a splash or was it more a crunch?

I wasn't there.

Good. It's none of your business, remember that. He's an idiot, and your business is here. So it's decided, right?

Is it really?

He went to the safe, took out an envelope, handed it to you. You didn't know you had already decided and were full of shock.

Open it now.

You opened it, looked inside, with surprise and unsurprise. Your trembling was palpable, and you wondered if you should faint, except you were not the fainting type. You were riven by forces of wild desire with exaltation terror anguish and rage, if those were the feelings. You said, Who's Stephen Trace?

You're Stephen Trace, Jack Rome said.

The envelope contained a check, a passport, and a birth certificate for Stephen Trace. The birth certificate was identical to Stephen White's except for his and his father's last name, altered both in the typed part and the father's signature. The passport belonged to Stephen Trace but had a picture of you. You had never seen the picture before. Where did you get that? you asked. Jack Rome did not reply.

The check was drawn on ROMEX BANK. The pay to the order of was typed, Stephen Trace. The signature was stamped in three-color ink, the name J. Finley Gowan, and printed underneath, Treasurer. The dollar amount was imprinted, a three, followed by a confusing number of zeroes. You checked the commas and counted the zeros.

Cal Ripken and Roger Clemens will catch up to you in six years, he said.

My God, you said, What do I do with it?

Whatever you like. Let me remind you: you're cutting off your connections now with every person in your past. Do you understand how important? Three reasons, don't forget. One, Jack Rome doesn't want it noised around that he does this kind of thing. Two, the new Stephen Trace will not want the public scandal of disclosure of his Gregory connection. Three, it would violate the clarity and integrity of the experiment.

Experiment?

It would offend me.

An alarm was hammering in your head: confess while you can—as if there were a crime you had not confessed to Jack Rome. What could it be, you had told him everything? You thought of the undiscovered little body rotting in the woods, somebody else's crime, and you thought of somebody unknown grieving and wondering, who would never know what happened. You thought of Jock Hadley with his head smashed in, and Hank Gummer, who couldn't stand the thought of death, and the mother and her two children in the burning car. These thoughts were sad, but there was nothing to do about them, so you did nothing.

EIGHTEEN

You'd better sign the passport, he said.

Can I borrow your pen?

My pen only writes for me.

You asked, Does Stephen Trace have a life story I should know? Make him up, he said.

The check is for thirty million. What can I do with it? Anything you like. Can I cash it? You can try.

Do I have to move out now? Today, he said, get out of there this afternoon. Where should I go? Wherever you like. Any suggestions? You're on your own. Do you have any advice? No. I don't want to see you for a month.

He opened the door, waiting for you to go. You looked at the thirty million check and wondered if it was too late to refuse. No, you wondered if you should thank him or shake his hand.

I appreciate this, you said. You held out your hand. Standing beside him, you noticed how small he was, how thin, his face emaciated, the muscles like strings in his neck to hold him together. He wiped his hand on his shirt, though he had not shaken your hand. I don't want to hear from you for a month, he said.

He shut the door behind you leaving you in a large office with cubicles, each cubicle with a computer terminal and a color picture of a family with children. You looked at the papers in your hand, flapping losely: four items, the check, the passport, the birth certificate, and the torn envelope. You stopped, put the three documents back in the envelope, and the envelope in the inside pocket of your suit.

Down in the elevator thinking, what should I do? You patted your jacket over the pocket, nervous about it. In the elevator vestibule at the bottom you stood still. The man in uniform at the desk watched you. You must think things through one at a time. You looked around for a place to sit, but there was none. You went into the lobby and looked through the glass wall to the Romex Bank on your right. You were afraid of dying before you could put the check in a safe place. Should you take it into the Romex Bank? You had to think, you didn't know, would a bank cash a check for thirty million? Would it be any safer to carry thirty million dollars cash?

Through the glass front you saw a fountain on the plaza with a row of curved stone benches forming parts of a circle around it. You went down and sat on one of the benches. There was a family of children playing around the bench on the opposite side. The fountain rose out of a pile of rectangular blocks, curtains of film hanging from the rims, with a light spray misting coolly across your face. Also the bright sun glinting in the geyser and sparkling on the window corners across the plaza. Men and women with briefcases or attaché cases, wearing suits and ties, walked in diagonal lines across the pavement. The street was beyond, two steps below, and taxis waited in a row by the signs.

All the busy people, and the tourist families with cameras, and two youths in the corner with a frisbee trying not to hit anybody. A man with balloons, an old woman on the bench eating a sandwich and reading the newspaper it was wrapped in. No bums. You: none of these people knows I am carrying a check for thirty million dollars.

You gave numbers to the things you had to do. (1) Get rid of the check. (2) Move out of the apartment. (3) Find a place to stay. (4) Eat lunch. Also (5) Apologize to Mr. Crestmeyer. You considered and moved 3 ahead of 2, then you could move your things from 2 to 3 in a taxi. You thought maybe you could do 4 before 2. You felt nervous about 1, what would happen when you went into a bank and presented the check. Thirty million dollars, you ought to turn that into securities or something, but you'd need advice and for that you'd have to talk in somebody's office. You weren't ready for that, in your cheap suit and dull shoes, conscious on the bench of your feet in your socks and your shirt over your sweaty arms and chest, along with your millions. You had to go to the bathroom too, you had to pee.

You looked around, no bathrooms, no silhouette figures of men in pants or women in skirts. Nothing in the Rome Building either, and you didn't want to go to a restaurant just for that. Now to pee replaced 1 on the list as first priority. You went down to the sidewalk, looking for men-women signs. You walked a block or two, straying out into the world, vulnerable to attack and kidnapping.

You saw a subway station. Down the greasy steps, two seedy men watching you shove through the filthy door, stepping around the puddles on the floor to the urinal, your shoulders hunched against being mugged with thirty million dollars on your person. The room was empty thank god, your relief quick, then out quickly past the seedy men and up to the bright sunlight and briskly home to the plaza in front of the Rome Building. Thirty million dollars had turned the Rome Building into home.

You went into the Romex Bank, since the check was drawn on it. To one of the tellers, behind a glass shield, you said I would like to deposit this, and showed her the check.

She said, You must fill out a deposit slip, and then saw the check. She looked at it a long time. She said, Do you have an account here Mr. Trace? You: No, I would like to open one. In that case you'd better talk to Mr. Maglee. She handed the check back to you, went over to the buzz door at the side and took you to Mr. Maglee's desk behind the tellers' desks under a high glass window reaching up beyond two balconies. Mr. Maglee was a young man with tight curly yellow hair.

Mr. Maglee, Mr. Trace would like to open an account here. Maglee: How do you do, Mr. Trace? He saw the check. He too looked at it a long time, sitting down gradually while looking. He turned it over to look at the back but there was nothing there. After a while he said, May I see some identification, Mr. Trace?

You showed him the passport. He looked at that awhile, compared you with the picture, and said, The passport is not signed.

I'm sorry, may I borrow your pen? You took his pen, signed the passport, and gave the pen and passport back to him. He looked at them some more. He picked up the phone on his desk but set it down before dialing, said, Excuse me, got up and took the check with him across the room. Hey come back with that, you kept yourself from saying, wondering if you would ever see the check again, but he stayed in sight, went to the telephone on the file cabinet in back, picked it up and dialed.

It took a long time. You saw him talking and waiting and looking at the check and at you across the room as he talked. You thought of the police coming to get you, charging Stephen Trace with forgery or a dead raccoon in the woods. You wondered if you should get up and run before his call was finished, if Peter Gregory was about to be jailed for accepting a bribe. When he came back, finally, he was smiling, and you saw the money spread out for you in his smile. Yes indeed, Mr. Trace, we'll be glad to set up an account, what kind would you like?

Oh you didn't know, just an ordinary checking account would be fine for a start.

Thirty million in a checking account? Don't you think much of it should be—how about a certificate of deposit? Yes, you'd want advice later on how to invest it, but just for the start, you need time. Well of course we'll be happy to, and if you would like to apply for a credit card.

You filled out forms. Mr. Maglee mentioned the IRS. He gave you a checkbook with blank checks and a card and a faded pink stamped copy of a deposit slip showing thirty million dollars. You: Can I get a more definite looking receipt? He seemed surprised but went to the woman at the typewriter in back and came back with a typed statement on fine paper announcing that Stephen Trace had deposited thirty million dollars to start account number such and such. You put Stephen Trace's official signature on file. Mr. Maglee shook your hand, you drew your first check for a couple of hundred dollars in cash, took it to the teller, and left the bank thinking I'm a millionaire.

What next? You went out to the plaza again, trying to think. Thought: 11:30, too early for lunch, you could start looking for a place to stay so you could move out of Amy and Joe's this afternoon. This would be a hotel until you find something more permanent. But what kind of hotel, and where would you find one? With so many millions, you could go to any hotel you liked—unless it wasn't really true you could go anywhere with thirty million. You tried to remember hotels. Not the one where Gregory and family once stayed. You remembered names vaguely, Algonquin, Biltmore, not knowing which were old or extinct or how many stars, trying to think which might be expensive, Ritz Carlton, St. Regis, Plaza, Waldorf Astoria. You realized it wasn't necessary to stay in an expensive hotel this first night. The immediate problem was to find any hotel at all. Telephone.

Not from home, though, your dying friends must not hear. It would have to be one of the open pay phones, in the lobby of the Rome Building by the elevators.

Phone book on a swivel, awkward. You looked up hotels in the yellow pages. Don't take too long, you were conscious of people going by. There were too many hotel ads, bewildering. Pick one near the beginning of the alphabet: there was the one across the street from where Peter Gregory had stayed with his family, which at that time looked bigger and classier than the one he was in. It was called the Arthur, and you made a reservation for one, name of Stephen Trace, two nights starting tonight, check-in middle of the afternoon. The woman on the phone was Bronx and efficient.

That's two things done. Next comes lunch. Across the street to a cafeteria, through the line, roast beef, mashed potatoes, roll, pie, coffee, the meal heavy, no taste, hard to get down. You felt sleepy. Back to the street, the sun blazed on your eyes, shut them tight, you waited for life to come back.

Subway to your old apartment. Climbed the cheese-smelling dark stairs for the last time, shocked by the sudden memory of Hank Gummer's plunge, the place on the tile where he fell. Your feelings were suspended, you didn't know what they were. Only Amy was at home, looking at you puzzled. Aren't you working today?

Stephen Trace now, prepared to be hard-hearted, said, I have to move out. I have to move out this afternoon.

She was shocked. Before Joe comes home?

You moved around collecting Stephen White while Amy watched. All you had were the clothes bought after coming to New York, a couple of towels, and toilet things. She gave you a shopping bag to put them in. You ran across the street to Crestmeyer, who said, I always knew you a funny fella. You come back tomorrow I give you your pay. Forget the pay, you said, it was the least you could do for leaving him like that. Forget your pay, you're crazy. Okay, you said, give it to Amy.

Back in the apartment, you called a taxi. All the time thinking I am seeing all this for the last time, telling Amy how grateful you were for all she and Joe, you would never forget it. She said, What's going on? Are you giving up? Are you going back?

No no, Stephen Trace said, though she did not know and was intended never to know the name of Trace. Not that.

Aren't you going to Hank's funeral?

Can't do that either. I'm sorry.

God damn it Murry, Stephen, where are you going? It's no fair not to tell after all we've been through. You make me mad, honest to God.

You waved out the back window of the taxi where she stood in the street, sad to tears but with something fake about the sadness like something fake about your love for Amy, and knowing already how quickly these good people would disappear and drop out of mind.

Then (in the taxi) in the whole world you had no acquaintances except Mr. Jack Rome and (slightly) Mr. Maglee of the bank, and how horrible they were. So new and forlorn and empty you had to remind yourself you had done it all before, the difference this time being you had thirty million dollars, which should make a difference. The taxi took you to the Arthur hotel, and you went inside to the registration desk with your shopping bag.

The hotel was old and not so big as you expected. It had stubby dirty marble columns around the staircase and dirty pink walls. You thought, Is this my home? Not for long, not for long. The clerk didn't look at you. She gave you a registration form. Home address. You wrote a fictitious number on the Ohio street where Peter Gregory used to live. How do you intend to pay, Mr. Trace? She asked for identification, you showed the passport, and she said Mr. Hessian would have to authorize your check when the time came.

She called the bellman. I don't need him, you said. The man was an old hunchback with white hair and shaky hands who carried your shopping bag up the elevator to room 818, saying nothing. He and the desk clerk both thought you a bum, skeptical of your ability to pay and afraid you would skip out or your check would bounce. Their thoughts annoyed you, thirty million dollars' worth, while he unlocked your room and showed you the bathroom, the lights, the TV, and you tipped him more than he was expecting.

The room was small. Its window looked to the other wing of the hotel, yellow brick across the areaway. There was a familiar hunting print on the wall, a single chair and a dresser whose drawers stuck. It was 3:30 in the afternoon.

You went to the window to look out, but all you could see were the walls and the blank windows. It was hot and stuffy, you opened the window, you smelled bread and garbage. You sat on the chair, stretched out on the bed, said, Home, by God, and fell asleep.

NINETEEN

Newborn Stephen Trace awoke to the shadow of late afternoon on the opposite brick wall, with a horrible afternoon nap feeling, of the world going on too long without him, thinking he was Peter Gregory. No better to realize he was not Peter Gregory, worse in fact, waking up alone in no world but a space ship leaving behind forever the bluewhite crystal where life was.

Then he remembered thirty million dollars, looking at the drab wallpaper and the trite hunting picture (every hotel has one), wondering if the memory was true. Deciding it was, he made an attempt to cheer himself saying, thirty million dollars should set things straight.

His suit rumpled from having been slept in, and this massive feeling of neglect, the whole world had moved off in a shipload during his absence. He stared at the ceiling and said, Calm down, Stephen. One thing at a time. You can pay for the hotel room and everything after that, so the only thing to worry about now is dinner. You can eat dinner in the hotel dining room. Then it will be evening. You can sleep here tonight. Then comes tomorrow, which will be tomorrow.

Dinner in the hotel dining room then, despite your crumpled suit, no proper clothes. You washed up, pressed the wrinkles with your hands, no effect. Never mind, since the people in the dining room didn't know about your money it didn't matter how you looked. You went down in the elevator. The restaurant was mostly empty. It had paper place mats. You sat in a booth by the window, ordered a drink and then a meal. In the center of the table was a card describing special concoctions from the bar. You could read that. You could also look at the street through the slats in the blinds, but you wished you had a newspaper. Thinking there is no pleasure in a restaurant alone, even with a lot of money.

After dinner, the late summer twilight, again the question what to do? On your first night in the woods you had refused to go back into the village to see a movie Peter Gregory would have avoided. This time you would go. Kill the evening, that was the point, knock it dead. Anxiety was stammering in your bloodstream, how to get out of here, with nothing possible until tomorrow. You bought a paper, took it to your room, picked a movie, went by taxi: detective thriller, minimum emotional demand. All through the movie you were distracted by money. It wove through the shots of city streets and highways and green buildings like lines of music. It grew through the excitement of the movie into a clamor, so that by the time you came out, you were wild with exhilaration, swollen with thrill, how gorgeous, how full, how rich I am. Your heart was a dynamo humming with power, your soul was full of ice cream and swagger, thinking the stories you could tell.

You skipped the bar with jazz across the street, so as to go back to your room and play with your wealth. Buy a notebook, make plans, figure things out.

From the standpoint of exhilaration, you thought how ugly, drab, miserable and lonely this hotel room is. Ideas of the rich twisted through your mind like music, up from Gregory depths. You mingled with them, saw yourself at a country club playing golf (Peter Gregory had never played golf). Stood on the grass with sporty young men wearing white pants talking to young women holding cocktail glasses outdoors. Idled on the dock in white shorts with other bright people in shorts, their suntans, the colors of their T-shirts, by the sailboats tied up, gleaming with brass and teak, with coils of rope and comfortable people on the decks talking to those on shore. Through the city streets and out to the towns in a chauffeured limousine, insulated from the crowds by glass and your driver to houses in the country, estates on hills or overlooking the sea, castles with turrets, stone houses with porches and towers, great shingled sea houses, in Bar Harbor, Newport, or the Cape. Sat deep in the wide seats of first class in the airplane, rode first class in European trains. Fine clothes wherever you went, with healthy looking young people also wearing fine clothes. Gatsby parties on Long Island lawns. Voices high and fat, boasting and criticizing, though the dim faces were all looking at you a little askance, which made you feel shy, and there was something a shade unpleasant about the pictures in your mind. You will have to decide what to do with your money, that's the point, you will have to make decisions.

First the question of a place to live, a center, a place of return. The word for this was home. After all your departures, there was a kind of thrill in that: you would have a home, and it would belong not to someone else but to you. Now think: what kind of home would a rich man like you be expected to have? A house behind a great lawn with a view of the ocean. A deluxe top floor apartment with a view of Central Park. Not yet, though. It would take time to find a suitable place, and in the meantime you could only stay in a hotel. Not this one, though. What kind of hotel would a rich man like yourself live in? You must find out, then move as fast as you can.

A rich man like Stephen Trace would have to do something about the money itself, sitting like rat bait in the Romex checking account. Wondering how much it really was. With all these resources, you ought to know what they could do, what they couldn't. You tried to calculate what you would have available to live on. Estimating conservatively with hefty taxes and taking care to plow back enough to protect against inflation, you came up with a spendable income for yourself of zero dollars per year. That can't be right. Loosening your estimates gave you about as much as Peter Gregory made as a teacher. Further revision brought you a life of luxury, but now your estimates were probably too wishful. You warned yourself to restrain expectations, felt the threat of disappointment, and were ashamed of that disappointment.

You turned out the light, lay down to sleep, with a dim red glow outside on the opposite wall, and then it crashed. Like Hank Gummer down the stairwell. Everything down. Falling, down down down, a drop with no end, you could see it out below drawing away from you. Wrenching miserable loneliness. You without name or soul, exile from life in life, bereft, a space traveler forgotten on Mars. Metaphors trying to do justice to bleak pain. It was not exactly new. Though you had never felt anything like it, you felt as if you had never felt anything else, reaching back, loss and grief and horror, underneath not only this evening's phony exhilaration but long ago before your wealth, before your death, your real soul groaning in despair and loneliness under all the papier mâché disguises you had created for it. Yet it was worse in the hotel than before, worse than the woods, whose nights in this retrospect seemed so benign, healthy, natural. You wondered if other human beings endured such grief, and thought not, because others' griefs were human but yours was grief for grief itself, mourning not any loss but loss as such—or humanity, or life.

For self-preservation, such a feeling was dangerous. So: argue yourself out of it. The argument: such loneliness is not unique,

Austin Wright

history is full of exiles, many transitional to noble effects. The origins and growth of this country, families crossing oceans they would never cross again, young men and women leaving families in Ireland and Italy and Sweden and Russia to create a new national heritage. Crusaders, explorers, pioneers: only in the modern world can an exile be canceled by a few hours' flight. Say this: every rebirth requires first a death. Revolutions destroy before they build. The new world rises on the corpse of the old. You: a revolutionary of the soul, whose pain proves the integrity of the change. If there were no pain, then you should worry. Such arguments calmed you until you could sleep.

Awake in the morning, in the drab light on the opposite wall, the same misery returned, and now it was all dungeon and slave ship and land waste, bones in the desert. You had to argue all over again, this time by recalling your money, thirty million dollars you had forgotten about. You drew your money around you like a blanket, it soothed the raw burn. Think of money when the black thoughts threaten, it will keep them out of sight.

Think of the relief to be Gregory never again. The deep relief of Never Again, which the money assured, the things that would never torture you henceforth. You heard the sound of Gregory's accidents and mistakes receding into history, dropping out of your life. The name Sebastian, Mary, Jacky, Jenny, the little family they said Gregory had destroyed, disappeared in the noise of the hotel air-conditioner. You were free at last. Sebastian had nothing to do with you. Gates had nothing to do with you. Long and Hadley had nothing to do with you. Hank Gummer, in his deep and permanent chemical sadness, had nothing to do with you. It was a matter of making your feelings believe what your mind says. What you don't feel can't hurt you.

A fat breakfast in the empty hotel dining room and you felt better, in spite of the sullen silent waitress arguing with some-

136

body in the kitchen. You advised yourself to feel like a million-aire. You called the bank for investment advice. They gave you an appointment with Mr. Campbell at eleven. He was soothing and reassuring, not fat but his cheeks hung down the sides of his chin and he had a resonant church bass voice. Also a potted green plant on a stand by his desk. You told him vaguely about Jack Rome. He did not ask why Mr. Rome had given you so much, nor did he try to penetrate your vagueness. He sketched out ideas on a large pad of lined legal paper in big figures sprawled across five or six lines. Talk about a balanced portfolio, growth and security and income, hedge against inflation and keeping your tax obligation down. Whether to put it in a trust fund managed by yourself or through Rome Investors, the Rome organization's answer to Merrill Lynch. His own recom-mendation was, frankly between you and me, and since you wanted to start right away, he sent you up to Mr. Peck in his tenth floor office.

Mr. Peck was a young man with a red mustache and an over-bite. Model airplane on his desk next to a picture of a young woman and three kids. I'll be your account executive, he said, and then the same conversation as with Mr. Campbell, leading to a program of specific purchases which you paid for with a check drawn for an incredible amount on your thirty million checking account. Mr. Peck had advice on how much to keep in the checking account, and what spendable monthly income you could expect, and he recommended the Roman Arch Cafeteria in the Rome Building for lunch.

Mr. Peck walked you out to the elevator, and said, Call me anytime. Now you felt like a real person, a man of substance, in a world where people cared about you and walked you to the elevator. You had lunch in the Roman Arch Cafeteria amid tables full of young brokers and bankers male and female, and it was a pleasure to think in their midst, I'm richer than I look.

In the afternoon you shopped for clothes. Bought two suits, shirts and neckties, underwear and socks and shoes, in everything choosing the more expensive of the items you saw. You had some bad moments when you tried things on, looking at the mirror and seeing ugly Peter Gregory where you wanted to see Stephen Trace. Never mind, you'd get used to it. You carried everything in a shopping bag, except the suits, which you would come back for after alterations. Since your credit cards weren't available yet, you paid by check supported by your passport or sometimes a call to the bank.

Then you bought a suitcase. You put everything in it, there in the luggage store, and took a taxi back to the hotel. Now that you had a suitcase, you could check into a hotel worthy of your money, but it had been a long day and you postponed that.

TWENTY

In the morning, after solitary breakfast in the coffee shop, Stephen Trace scouted the better hotels. He got his new suits in the afternoon, checked out of the Arthur, and took a taxi with the new suitcase carrying everything to the Park Central, noted for its view of Central Park.

The respectful bellman took him to his suite, two big rooms, broad windows, deep chairs, a hunting picture on the wall. He unpacked the suitcase, hung things in the closet, put them in the drawers, and settled in.

Home. A view: the avenue below, the horse buggies taking children and couples into the park, the hazy towers over the tops of the trees beyond the park to the left. You stood in the window a long time and sat long on one of the golden sofas. All afternoon while the light changed, the brightness faded, and past nibbled into present. No need to hitchhike now. With only one catch: the secret which required you to lead a low profile life. That was all right, but then you noticed a second catch. Your freedom wasn't total, because you had a job to do. Jack Rome had given it to you, shackling while he unshackled: create Stephen Trace. The price of Jack Rome's gift, a clearly understood exchange. The old figure of speech by which you renamed yourself and catapulted into new life was legal language, now. The point where language deviated from reality, making it into a figure of speech, had now turned into a tough practical question, which you would have to figure out. Namely this, if you separate Stephen Trace from Peter Gregory, where do you draw the cutting line? Where does Gregory end, where could Trace begin? Looking down at the horse carriages for the romanticizing tourists, you thought hard about it. You used more images. A peach has a pit, flesh, and a skin. If Peter Gregory is the skin, you could peel him off and grow Stephen Trace as a new skin. But if he extends into the flesh, where do you cut? What if the flesh is Gregory all the way down to the pit? Could you grow a new peach around that pit to make a Stephen Trace? And suppose you could: would you recognize the peach equivalents in your own particular case?

The question, big and philosophical—What is a person, anyway?—forced you from window to sofa again, where you could lean back and see how the gold glints in the chandelier shift as you move your head. If you're expected to re-form your character, what is character? If having peeled Gregory away, you start with the remaining living core, flesh or pit, just what is it? Your body: reflexes, heartbeat, pain. Add some portion of the busy activity of your brain. Language. Whatever it is you keep addressing as "you" rather than by name. But what about the rest of your memory? You can't clean out what's filled your head in thirty-five years of life, you can't deliberately unremember—which means you can't create Trace without a portion of Gregory. What you can do is repudiate: I disclaim the remembered person, I reject his behavior, I renounce his emotions.

No doubt you had two Peter Gregories. The Gregory Jack Rome didn't like was a collection of habits, preferences, antipathies. A certain predictability. But when you sat by the harbor and felt past and future disappearing, Gregory was an impression of life, an accumulation of experience and imagination. Peter Gregory from outside and Peter Gregory from inside. To change Gregory into Trace, then, was that an outer operation, or did it require inner surgery too?

And in either case, how? How do ordinary people change themselves? Family nurture. Education. Training. Kids go through school seeking to define themselves. Now I am no longer a kid, I am a lawyer. Pharmacist. Cabdriver. Hitchhiker. If you want to know who I am, ask what I do. But Stephen Trace won't need an occupation, Jack Rome took care of that. In a story characters are revealed by the choices they make. If not pharmacist, pharmakos. Should Stephen Trace choose something? Ugh. Occupation depressed him. Character depressed him. Give him time. Get used to being alone with lots of money.

Take a walk in what's left of the afternoon. Dinner in a French restaurant and back to the hotel. Music in the evening. He stayed that night, then another, then another. He stayed on. Each morning in his airconditioned room, wearing his new rose and gold robe. Looking out the window at the Park. Shower in the glittering Park Central bathroom, down in the sleek elevator to the gold draped dining room. Then the city. Going places, any place will do. Walking, riding, looking, to create substantiality for Stephen Trace. Lunch and dinner, good restaurants, day after day, learning the pleasure of a good restaurant without company. The hotel his home, coming and going, past stacks of luggage and travelers waiting under the chandeliers, by the rent-a-car and sightseeing tour desks, the information desk with mail cubicles, the Hawaiian and French dining rooms, plaster Greek statuary, the elevator banks. No longer afraid of time or old emotions, he went to plays and movies and nightclubs like a tourist. Stayed home too, to read or watch television or sometimes even write a little, a little poetry, just like home.

He began to buy things, to build Stephen Trace into the money habit. You took him into stores to look at merchandise,

141

what some people make for others to keep. Goods to weight him down, the tangible substance which the figures in the bank attributed to him. Unfortunately, he had no space in the hotel room for what he wanted to buy. Mahogany furniture. Table settings, candlesticks, lamps. Prints and paintings with no walls to hang them on. Fine jewelry with no woman. You bought some books. More clothes, hats, ties, sporty jackets. A trunk.

You bought a car but denied your ostentatious impulse, settling for a Toyota, which you drove through the city streets to the hotel, and went driving every day thereafter.

You noticed yourself performing a certain mental exercise, probably insane, deliberate yet habitual and almost without volition, though it seemed to be an exercise of will. Derived from that fictitious difference between Gregory and Trace, which rational skepticism couldn't destroy since your fortune depended on it. Its goal was to transfer the structures and furnishings of your mind from one name to the other. To create experience belonging specifically to Stephen Trace. To do this, you would in an act of imagination gather knowledge belonging to Peter Gregory and deliberately re-encounter it in the person of Stephen Trace. You did this first with the city, physically, literally, by taking him with you (going as Stephen Trace, explicitly conscious, *Now I am Stephen Trace*) on foot, by cab, subway, and bus, showing him things, deliberately shoring him up with a stock of sights and sounds and knowledge. Out to the end of the line and back, incorporating all, whereby Stephen Trace became the world in which he lived: the city on its long thin island, its bridges pulling the great populations on all sides into himself like food. Appropriating Jack Rome's hazy view with its millions of meticulously fitted tiny parts, he added streets and crowds, dirty and hot and dangerous, filling up Stephen Trace as he moved around in the middle of them.

Everything turned into Stephen Trace. The ornamental greenery, botanical walks with liberated peacocks, yellow cats in a cage, sleek creatures with whiskered noses surfacing in a green swirl. The motionless spaced birds hanging from wires with widespread wings, green and black, against a painted forest behind glass with children's voices in the corridor. The human shapes in stone and plaster, transfixed, mutilated, loading the Trace memory bank with primitive and classical history. Civilizing him as much in moments as Peter Gregory had been in thirty-five years. He watched the world orbit the sun on the end of a wire.

Soon it was no longer necessary to go anywhere to take possession. By transferring Peter Gregory's memory to Stephen Trace's imagination he could forecast the changes of the seasons. Predict winter agony, bitter air, ice on the streets, but don't despair, for he could also predict the return of light, the smell of mud lacing the cool air in little streams, with bits of bright green on twigs and shrubby trees blossoming. All Peter Gregory's history and geography, nature and culture, passed through the city's disorderly streets and insulated museum rooms, libraries, shops, and parks into Stephen Trace, transferred like the tap of a fingertip at each new entrance. Behind it all was Jack Rome.

Sometimes he forgot the lonely horrors and was amazed to think how fortunate he was. He sat in his hotel room on a late August evening looking at the sky turn from purple to black, while the city lights began to dazzle. With music on his radio no longer sickened by Gregory, all of a sudden you heard the old question right out of childhood, fresh past the intervening years, asking, *Why me?* The sperm in a million question, for when you are feeling good. Peter Gregory as a child on the beach, squinting at the bluewhite breakers, thinking how fortunate he was. Why *me*? How amazing, that of all the kinds of life you might have been, cat, frog, or shark in the sea, here you were, a human being. Living not in the cave ages nor among the barbarians but on the crest of history in the richest country in the history of the earth. Nor slum, nor broken home, nor blind or crippled, but loving family, bright and comfortable: why should all this good luck happen to me? That was then, but now again, listening to Stephen Trace's pulse in the Park Central Hotel, enriched by Rome's gift, you heard the same question with the same astonishment: *Why me?* If in fact you were still alive, and this was not some golden after-death wish.

It was a fragile sort of boast, collapsible in the whiff of an unsmug thought. Peter Gregory's childhood wonder reminded you of the intolerable Gregory. There was abysmal loneliness in the Park Central Hotel. In bed that August night, you heard complaints. This man who had abandoned his family and friends in a fake suicide and accepted great sums of money in exchange for cutting them off: what kind of man would do a thing like that?

Then it was back to the river, the water flushing your sinuses, lights washed away in the flood. When you woke and found yourself dry, the diffused light of the city quiet in the window, you settled back and asked again, my God, Why me?

TWENTY ONE

A mind full of rich snobs, judging. Yacht club boys in white pants, discussing right and wrong. The right clothes, right sports, right clubs, golf, how to live. Sniffing out vulgarity and ignorance of class like hound dogs. The right towns and right people and right way to spend your evening. You didn't know these sniffing snobs, but you could hear them murmuring about responsibility to your money. Whether your suit was expensive enough and your hotel room worthy of your means.

Your days of riches were adding up. The second week, half as long as the first, and then the third whizzed by. It made you anxious about time and slacking on the job. This growing idleness while you continued driving around the city, practicing mental exercises for character implants. Your forthcoming meeting with Jack Rome paralyzed you, anticipating. You wanted to get out of this hotel and start your life, but you dared nothing without permission.

You made your appointment using the Jane Delaware number. The womanly voice sounded like Peter Gregory's Linda. You went, nestled like a child inside Stephen Trace, wearing one of his new suits. Swaggered through the Rome lobby, conspicuously pretending to be another inconspicuous financier among your financially secure fellow passengers on the elevator by thinking loudly of your millions (I belong here as much as you). Up the second private elevator to the carpeted suite and the tall dark-haired woman with the smile who led you to the back with the glass view to the floor. The day was rainy. Fog, streams of distortion ran in lines down the glass, you could not see the skyscraper tops. Jack Rome came in, wearing white shorts and a white T-shirt with a monogram and carrying a tennis racket.

Sit down, he said, pointing you to a chair so deep your knees popped up when you sat in it. The south end of the city was spread below, but it was invisible. He sat behind rather than beside you, your great analyst in the sky.

So, he said, tell me about yourself.

You told him everything so far. The creation of Stephen Trace, decisions you had postponed until you could consult him. Don't consult me, tell me, he said. You had been thinking what to do with your money. Frivolous things. Learn to fly. Take a voyage around the world. Serious things. Enroll in medical school. What? Not yet. Maybe a year or two, or four or five.

Or ten twenty or fifty. Doctor Trace? Don't make me laugh.

Embarrassed, you aimed for more depth: The important thing was to make Stephen Trace good. (Rome, mocking: Do good, leave the world a little better than it was?) Or at any rate be the kind of man you would respect if you were somebody else and he died. The edgy lying feeling was residue static. His scrutinizing watchful judging eye kept forcing you to retreat. Perhaps you would be content to let Stephen Trace be a man of dignity.

Stop trying to figure me out, Jack Rome said.

What do you mean, sir?

Stop trying to please me.

You sat silent. After a while he started things up again. Money is power, he said. What kind of power do you want?

You thought about power, what's available to Stephen Trace. Power suggests politics, using wealth to become a senator or governor. Not with your background, though, not a chance of that for you. Personal power can make somebody else hang up your clothes. Say something: Perhaps he could start a newspaper or a political magazine. Endow a university. What did you say?

You sound like a high school student choosing careers. I didn't notice any sex in this tale of yours. Where do sex and loneliness fit in Stephen Trace's new life?

You had thought a lot about this meeting, but you hadn't prepared for that question.

What about a wife?

Nor that.

Why not? Rome laughed. I just got a wife. My third. Jane Delaware, did you read about that?

Jane Delaware? She was the womanly telephone voice who arranged your appointments with Jack Rome. He showed you a picture. Expensive hair, bracelets, elegant like a First Lady. She looked like Linda except Linda did not look like a First Lady.

There are real advantages to having a wife. Would you like one too?

The way he said that, it sounded like an offer. He was mocking you, everything he said today sounded like mockery. He wasn't interested and didn't care what you did. Something was amusing him, though. Full of secret mirth, he went with you to the elevator. Don't wait so long for the next update, he said. When the elevator came: You're kind of a jerk, Trace, do you know? He punched you in the ribs like a school boy.

Outside on the sidewalk the rain had stopped. You saw this girl approaching, with a mop of brown hair reminding you of the former student Nancy Nolan. Then recognizing you before you recognized her, she spoke, for she was Nancy Nolan. "Hello," she said with surprise and pleasure, and you said, "Hi," and passed on. A moment later you looked back. She had stopped (for it would be natural to ask, What are *you* doing here?), and now she laughed, but something warned you, and you waved and went on, leaving her behind with regret and self-reproach.

Then the realization: All is lost, the game is up. Fatalistic, maybe a touch of relief, too late now—that kind of thought. You could guess the consequences and wait for them.

One obvious thing: when she saw you she did not know Gregory had died. It was no ghost she greeted in that friendly way, the surprise was about running into you in New York. Perhaps later she would remember Gregory's death. That would puzzle her. She would ask someone to confirm it, because she was sure she saw him in New York. Her friend would say, You couldn't have. But I did. Well then, do we know something, or don't we? After that, two possibilities: they tell and the news spreads, or they don't tell and forget it. In the latter case, eventually Nancy Nolan may decide it was not you she had seen but a stranger, who must have been puzzled by her greeting.

Or else she never did know of Gregory's death. If, having graduated, she were so oblivious to local news. She might or might not say to a friend, Guess who I saw in New York. After that, again the same possibilities. The days passed. You got used to it and realized there was no need to know what she did or did not do.

You told Jack Rome at your next meeting. You were afraid of his reaction to the threat of disclosure. You were resigned to it, yourself. There was always a chance Gregory's escape would be found out. It could be discovered without your knowing. It might even be known already, or suspected. The great advantage of your fortune, it could protect you from anything. If Florry Gates's father pursued his suit, your lawyer would fix it. The Sebastian case was closed, the only consequence would be a fuss in the papers. If your identity were revealed, you would calmly acknowledge it. The only threat would be if Peter Gregory had committed a crime. You didn't have to worry about that, as far as you knew.

Rome wanted to know what was so special about Nancy Nolan. Nothing, you said, except this one thing. She was perfectly average, inconspicuous among the other students, looking just like them, but when they met on the sidewalk she consistently noticed him before he noticed her. This happened so often he began to anticipate it, and still she surprised him. He would be walking against the crowd flow, wondering if he would see her, and there she was, saying hello before he recognized her.

So she found you out again, Rome said. You should wear sunglasses when you go into a crowd.

TWENTY TWO

As Stephen Trace you found a fine big apartment overlooking the East River, near a girdered bridge. Later Mrs. Koin the real estate agent found you a house, forty or fifty miles from the city on Long Island Sound. This gave you two residences. The house occupied a small island with garden and a few trees, separated from the shore by a ten-foot wide channel with a wooden bridge. There was a broad porch all the way around with pillars of piled boulders, wooden balconies, high ceilings, a path to the dock. Overgrown and weedy. Mrs. Koin said you could hire gardeners and turn it into a beauty spot. Stephen Trace, eyes trusting like the robin, waited to be filled up. By now it was September.

The next job was to occupy the house and apartment. He went to antique stores, department stores. Furniture vans drove up to the island, easing their heavy wheels across the wooden bridge. Fat men carried valuable pieces of mahogany up the steps past the newly trimmed bushes. Carpets, lamps, prints and decorative screens. He hired Mrs. Heckel as housekeeper and Mr. Jollop to take care of the grounds. In October he moved in. Curtains, pillows, soup dishes, furnishings for Stephen Trace.

You walked around the house, windows looking at the water, up the central staircase with its curved railing, out onto the balconies, reveling in astonishment. Mrs. Heckel made useful suggestions. It would look nicer if you had a little carpet in the dining room passage. How about an automatic washer in the laundry room?

You wanted an audience for the house and friends for Stephen Trace, to visit and sit in chairs on his porch and look at his view of the Sound. He sought groups to join and met some real people. Mr. and Mrs. McIntosh across the inlet invited him over for drinks. They showed Stephen their formal garden, with a rose-covered trellis, birdbaths, a statue of a nude woman, a gazebo. Inside, a collection of old musical instruments. Stephen studied how they spent their money, looking for ideas, while Mrs. McIntosh lectured him on the importance of a wife. Carson Grant invited him to dinner. He had hanging carpets on the walls and offered Stephen tickets to the World Series, the Superbowl, the opera, anything you want, just call me a day in advance. He also strongly advised Stephen to join the Episcopalian Church. The wine cost $300 a bottle, and you wondered how long it would take Stephen to learn to recognize the value in the taste.

The most impressive neighbor was George Bristaff, whose mansion had an awning and valet parking, like a fine hotel. Bristaff's wife wore a tiara, and he took you aside to advise you about the importance of spending your money wisely. Ordinary people are watching us, he said. They look to us for guidance, which puts a great responsibility on us, not only to show how we utilize our resources, but to impress on them the value of money by displaying clearly and unequivocally what, to put it brutally, they simply cannot afford. To serve humanity, he said, he had contributed a CAT scan machine to the local hospital: if you use it, he said, you'll see my name on a name plate above your nose just before you enter the tunnel. He had a model railway through his garden, disappearing behind the bushes and trees, and he was making plans to build a working replica of one of the classic steamboats that traveled the waters of the Sound sixty years ago, carrying passengers by this very point in the night.

Stephen Trace returned these invitations and invited other people as well. Mrs. Heckel hired a staff and served dinner. People like Carol Muldane and Professor and Elena Gorsky, new friends. They made him nervous with their questions. Genevieve Desmond on the porch by one of the stone pillars, heavily wrapped against the cold while waiting for her father's car, looked at him in an interesting way. She believed in skiing and ice skating. He told her he was a former teacher retired because of an inheritance from his aunt, his wife dead, no children.

Uneasy, he asked Mr. Peck if he was spending too much. Calculating the income from his fortune modestly, he figured he could spend annually an amount about forty times that of Gregory's salary as a teacher. This meant that for any item, such as a car or a restaurant dinner or a vacation, he could afford to spend forty times what Gregory would have spent. Of course, some things won't cost that much, which would give him leeway.

One day in November you saw Peter Gregory's children in the Park. You never did find out why they were in New York at that time of year. You were at the entrance of the Park Central Hotel waiting for Jack Rome, who wanted you to meet Luigi Pardon, an old and important friend. You saw the children across the street looking at one of the horses attached to a carriage. You saw first the boy, fat with glasses, dressed up for the city, patting the horse on its forehead. The horse had its nose in a feed bag and a red ribbon tied to its bridle. You thought, That looks like Jeff. Then Patty stepped into sight, also dressed for the city, trying to pat the horse on its cheek. Patty and Jeff, the resemblance was remarkable. Then from behind the horse you saw

Louis the Lover. Wearing a tan trenchcoat, perfect fit, and a hat, his face flushed around his black mustache. For a moment you thought he was Jack Rome, whose resemblance to Louis the Lover you had never noticed. The next moment they all disappeared behind the horse and a moment later reappeared, climbing one by one—first Jeff, then Patty, then Louis the Lover, and no one else—into the carriage. You watched. Now Patty was looking at you, then Jeff too. They were staring at you, across the street, no expressions on their faces. You stared back. They did not say anything to Louis the Lover, who was leaning forward talking to the driver. You couldn't make up your mind to wave. At that moment the limousine drove up. The back door opened and Jack Rome called, Get in. The carriage was starting up and the kids kept their heads turned looking at you as it moved. You thought, if I wave now it's all over.

Get in.

You got into the limousine, still looking at the kids while they twisted their necks watching you, and then you were in, thinking, You should have waved. Just waved, it would have been enough. You should have waved.

Instead, Luigi Pardon. I want you to meet my old friend, my right hand man. You've heard of Luigi Pardon, of course.

It was hard to concentrate on Luigi Pardon just then. This was the famous singer, who Mrs. Heckel a few days ago said was as good as Perry Como, though he had put on weight since his television days. He sat behind you in the limousine next to Jack Rome, an oldfashioned baritone singer from long ago with slick black hair that had never needed to be dyed waving over his forehead. His face was shiny and artificially tanned, with a preserved youthful look like a polished apple. Thick lips and eyes baggy from enforced smiling. His hand, trained to shake everything it meets, went out to shake yours. He was dressed elegantly in a good dark suit with a handkerchief in his breast pocket. You hadn't known he was Jack's right hand man.

The limousine wasn't going anywhere, just driving around. Jack Rome was talking to Luigi Pardon about you. I fished this guy from the Ohio River. He tried to commit suicide and I dragged him out. (You don't say.) So I gave him one of my grants and now he is trying his hand at being somebody else. (How much did you give him?) Thirty.

Luigi in his great baritone voice: You're a lucky fella, son. You musta heard me sing when I came to Cincinnati 1955.

Well no, in 1955 you were two years old and living in Westchester, New York.

Westchester? Sang a lot in Westchester in those days, White Plains, but most people came to New York to hear me. You saw me on television, I had my own program, you remember that, seven years. His head always nodding, yeah yeah. Decades later, his voice still leaned into a microphone full of this funny thing called love plus saxophones and trumpets.

Stephen here has recently bought himself a house on Long Island Sound.

Yes you are a lucky fellow young man. Not everybody gets to start life with a bundle like that. I started in the ghetto. My papa was a garbage collector, imagine that, and I grew up on the street ducking the rotten melons. But between my native talent and me, we made a go of it and look at me now.

Stephen, I want you to look at Luigi carefully here. Luigi is a good example of what you can do if you manage your money wisely. Luigi is going to use his money to extend his life span. Tell him, Luigi.

Gladly. You know I got this voice, one in a million, by which I don't mean it's necessarily the only voice in the land, but still one in a million is nothing to snooze at, and I have this talent for giving pleasure, so I figured I owe it to future generations as well as my own.

Luigi is going to have himself embalmed.

Not yet. No sense rushing into it because there is a certain risk. It might not work.

He's going to wait until he's old and falls ill with a fatal disease. That will be time enough.

Embalmed's the wrong word. Embalmed's for mummies.

He's going to have himself frozen. That way he can have his life prolonged in a frozen state until the time is ripe.

I'm gonna leave instructions to wait until they get a cure for whatever I have. Then they thaw me out and fix me up, so I can go on giving my art to future generations just like the past.

Luigi is particularly deserving of this because he has something to give.

I bring joy into hearts. But eventually this will be available to everybody. Even you can get yourself frozen so you can be cured later. If you got the money, I mean. It takes dough. You gonna do it, Jack?

I'm young yet. I think I'll take my time on that one.

There's always a risk, you know. What I like to think about is when I wake up many years from now and everybody I know is dead. Think of that, I got to start out all new friends. You ever think about that, Jack? I want to be sure to say my goodbyes before they put me in the freezer, otherwise I may never get the chance.

It's important not to forget your friends, Jack Rome agreed.

But when the limousine brought you back to the Park Central, the children were gone. That night you decided to grow a beard.

★

155

During the winter the bearded Stephen Trace got to know Edgewood Baker, stock broker, Milo Press, editor, Gamble Terhune, swimming teacher, Bink and Bonnie Pepper, youth counselors. The names add up when you make a list. He took flying lessons in a rented Piper Cub from Gordon Knott. Sent for medical school catalogues, but he didn't read them. He had a feeling there was a natural vocation for Stephen Trace and until he found it his mind would keep wandering. To soften his conscience he made contributions. He gave to the United Appeal, the Metropolitan Opera, the Negro College Fund, Cornell, Grinnell, Earlham, the ACLU, cancer, and muscular dystrophy. Also Sister Theresa and Bishop Tutu and the Policeman's Ball. He gave Christmas presents to Mrs. Heckel and Mr. Jollop.

He invented conversations. It looked just like him. It couldn't have been a ghost, would a ghost ride in a limousine? If it wasn't him why did he stare at us? If it was him why didn't he say something? Ghosts don't speak, idiot. That's a big wide street, how could you tell what he looked like across the street? If it was him, he would have waved. If it was him, he didn't want to wave.

TWENTY THREE

Having created you—poured you into the open mold of Stephen Trace—Jack Rome wanted to check you out. He wanted to see this old mansion by the water where you had settled, and one night in late January he came to take a look. He came to dinner, bringing Mrs. Rome (who still called herself Jane Delaware) and Luigi Pardon. He came spectacularly in a helicopter, settling down with a shrieking rattle on the frozen grass between the house and the Sound. Just the four of them around a small table, an intimate dinner of newborn wealth, with Mrs. Heckel serving. Jane Delaware was beautiful, with gold hair, smiling ice-blue eyes, a rich brown dress, and well-bred manner. She reminded you of Gregory's wife though it was hard to determine the point of resemblance.

Jack Rome was fidgety. He squirmed in his chair. He got up from the table, looked out the window, studied the sideboard, the pewter, the pictures, came back and resumed eating. You would have thought he was displeased with you or Mrs. Heckel's food except for his compliments. Great cook you got there, Trace, you're a regular little host with the best. Relax, Jack, Jane Delaware would say, with no urgency, as if she were used to it. Luigi Pardon laughed.

So, Jack Rome would say, this is your notion of Stephen Trace. An oasis in the midst of Metropolis. Little island mansion by the industrial waterway, garden tucked in a protected corner from the great urban suburbs and heavy traffic flow. Your old house, with great stone walls, boulders in them, sturdy pillars, Victorian ceilings, they don't make them like that no more. Stability, permanence. I get your point. No more hiking around the country for you. Solidity, security.

You wondered if he was mocking. You were never sure. He talked about hitchhiking. He had a fantasy of doing it himself, taking to the road in cheap clothes, hitching rides, to see where he could go, what it would be like. Traveling with people who didn't know who he was, who would be amazed to find out later, who could tell their friends, I actually picked up Jack Rome on the road in Arizona last year. He would collect their names and addresses, send them a few thousand bucks later on as proof, a Christmas present, what a surprise, so that's who it was.

Another possibility was to go out on the ocean like your Uncle Phil—he remembered Uncle Phil—alone on a boat, while all the world supposed him dead. Forgotten by mankind, his existence unknown to all but a few intimates, sailing from port to port around the world. Jane Delaware and Luigi Pardon listened indulgently. His voice turned urgent, as if he were lecturing you, some lesson he wanted you to learn. It wasn't clear what.

His zest, restlessness, enthusiasm turned edgy as he talked, testy, finally angry. What was he angry about? Never clear, like something other than what he said. He talked about terrorists. Why terrorists? You wondered what they stood for in his picture of the world. He raved against the arrogance of terrorists. All terrorists should be shot and countries supporting them bombed. His security men had caught a man with a bomb in the lobby of the Rome Building. They were keeping him in a cell, dealing with him in their own way. The police didn't know. Don't tell anyone.

After Gregory

After dinner Jack Rome went to the television set and turned it on. I must see my old friend Osgood Landis, he said. Not tonight, Jane Delaware said. Luigi Pardon chortled, Here we go again. Stephen must see this, Rome said. Stephen must see my old friend Osgood Landis, let it be a lesson to him. Jack, you deliberately stir yourself up, Delaware said.

Does Stephen Trace have a religion? Rome asked. Have you equipped him with one? You had neglected Stephen Trace's religious education. You remembered the neighbor who suggested you join the Episcopalian Church, but you hadn't given it any thought. Nor had Peter Gregory any religion to speak of, except to fear the voice in his head that hammered his shames.

Take a look, Rome said. Osgood Landis, I set him up in business. Damn fool me. Street corner preacher, gave him a grant like you, intended as a joke, and look what he is now, the son of a·bitch.

You remembered the name: Osgood Landis and his daughter Miranda, who had occupied the Coliseum by the river when Gregory died. Now on television: a fanfare of trumpets with flags, then a symphony orchestra and choir in a cathedral of silver columns. The music skidded from violins into jazz, with gospel singers and dancers, a medley of hymns and music from television commercials whose words were altered to fit God:

Come Listen to God Here,
This Word's For You.

Two figures came together down the carpet to the pulpit: Osgood Landis and his daughter Miranda. He wore a white doctoral robe with gold crosses, she a pale blue robe, walking with hands clasped.

Listen to this crap.

Folks, Osgood Landis said. God's folks, listen to God speaking through me and my daughter the Virgin Miranda. I received a letter from a child who said, Reverend Landis, you speak of faith, how those who believe humbly with their hearts shall go to heaven, and yet in my heart I feel ashamed of myself, all doubt and fear and ridden by guilt. Reverend Landis, am I damned already when I am only seventeen? So I ask you, folks, is he, is he damned when he is only seventeen? Therefore tonight, folks, I speak of shame, for truly, some shame is good, God's very own shame, shame for Jesus who died for us, that brings us together and makes us a church.

Landis, you ungrateful bastard.

Pan from Osgood Landis's glistening spectacles to the smiling closed eyes of the daughter to members of the audience, middle aged and various, hopefully watching with wet eyes, incredulous of their fortune to be there, on camera, witnessing.

My good people, you know what I have said about God's bounty, not to be ashamed of what you have. Not to be ashamed of what you are, of being middle class, folks, for what God loves he creates in abundance and he loves the middle class best because there are more of you than any other, loves you best as he loves all moderation, all middleness, the golden mean in all things. Feed the poor, but don't be ashamed that ye are not poor yourselves, and don't let the hypocrites twist the Lord's words to exclude you. (If it wasn't for me, Jack Rome said.) Look into your hearts, where God is. It's not what you have or do or intend that makes you godly but what's in your heart, for all God asks is to believe in Him and in Jesus who died for you, and if you believe, you'll enter the Kingdom and if you don't, you'll burn, simple as that. And if your rebellious mind resists, then you must practice it in speech, and repeat the words, I believe in Jesus, my Lord, so that true faith will respond, for words shall create belief where all else fails.

But this child in his letter has discovered the truth of shame, which is another thing. For Jesus knows what lies deep in the heart of every person who loves him, and there he finds shame, a deep perilous grievous feeling. None of you is so pure not to have felt it, and woe if you deny it. (Keep your woe to yourself, Brother Landis, Rome said.)

Delaware: Look at the Virgin Miranda. Later she'll go down and take the crutches away from the people in the wheel chairs. They'll roll the crutches away on a hospital cart.

Each of you, good people, has known a time when shame rises like a devil, torturing and making you cry out: "I can't stand myself!" Even I have had such thoughts. (No kidding? Rome said. You should have listened.) And if you are intolerable to yourself, how much more intolerable you must be to God. But folks, listen to God on this matter: the very moment you feel most miserable and repulsive, that's the moment God's grace is shining in you. For at that moment you have humbled yourself to judgment. Rejoice in that aboriginal shame, for what is it but God's own consciousness of sin and hence of God, speaking in you? What is it but pity and gratitude disguised, pity for the sacrifice of our Lord on the cross and gratitude of our souls in shame for requiring such sacrifice? This aboriginal shame, what is it but the origin of our coming together, our church?

How come I never felt like that? Luigi Pardon said.

You got no shame, Rome said. Never did, never will. You're not going to heaven. You're going to freeze and live forever.

Delaware: You shouldn't poke fun. It comforts people, and they take it seriously. If it weren't for the hokum.

Shut up.

Folks, how terrible to have the Lord within you and not to follow Him.

You'll have to guess the rest because Jack Rome switched him off. Shoot, Luigi said, now we won't see The Miranda Miracles.

According to Jane Delaware, the real reason Jack turned on the television was to look for his former wife and son in the audience. Four years ago they left him to join the Landis Community, a cult in a silver palace in the Adirondack Mountains. This was galling because of what Jack had originally done for Landis—in fact, there would have been no Landis or Landis Community without him. His response was a military operation to kidnap them back, a front page scandal with abductions and brainwashing and professional deprogrammers. Later it was made into a movie called *Salvaging God*, by the Rome Studios, starring Henry Francis. Unfortunately (though fortunately for Jane Delaware) the deprogramming didn't take, for Alex and Helen went back to the Community, and now Osgood Landis is suing Jack Rome for kidnapping, libel, and slander. Jack turns on the program when he wants to stir himself up, and he always looks for them in the audience but hasn't spotted them yet.

She told you this while you were showing her around the grounds, down beyond the porch through the frozen garden to the white gazebo above the shore, while Rome and Pardon conducted long distance business on your telephone. She knew the relationship between Stephen Trace and Peter Gregory. This suggested trust, and you heard yourself confessing how you had seen Gregory's children in the park. How sad, she said, defining your emotion as grief. She spoke as if your life were tragic, which was a flattering way to look at things, and you thought therefore she must be your friend.

*

Every night your insomnia was full of the wisdom of the ancient world, celebrated and lamented in myth and poetry. It said the past lives ever in the present, crime and guilt will not be left behind, nemesis bides her time without sleep, prophets speak truth. Beware, you know nothing, wisdom said. Those you think wrong may be right, those you think right may be wrong.

Eventually insomnia reminded you of old murdered Jock Hadley, whose memory you had shoved aside because it made you uncomfortable. Idle old man tilted back on his chair on the front stoop of his bungalow across the street calling at you: Hey mister, come over here. What happened to your wife?

She left me.

Serve you right, you son a bitch. Ought to be in jail.

The ghost of Hadley resuscitated the pale Sebastian ghosts, victims victimizing. Shadows from Gregory, chilling sleep, obscuring the boundary between what was yours and his. Memories so vivid—crash and floodlights and bodies lifted in a stretcher, bodies you (no, he) had killed, and prosecutor and judge and the vow of Never Again—it was hard to remember that Peter Gregory was gone. The voice of Jock Hadley hammered still, Child killer. I know your type.

Followed by the Hammer Man himself, hammering holes in Hadley's skull, paying him out with Gregory's wish. Police lights a second time, floodlight and circular flashers across the second stories on both sides of the street, and yellow police lines marking off the old man's house, while Gregory coming home from his walk wondered what had happened. He did not know, not yet. Not until Sam Indigo told him the next morning. Remember that. Stephen Trace was afraid of what thinking and unrelated fear could do to a clear memory. A possible danger occurred to you which Stephen Trace's wealth and new name could not save him from. Only clear and unobstructed memory could do that, and he needed to guard that memory like wealth, even though it was Gregory's memory, not his.

TWENTY FOUR

One bright sloppy day in early March, with melting ice folded into the mud foretelling spring and the ground soaked, in the afternoon a Volkswagen crossed the bridge. Mrs. Heckel called up the stairwell, Lady to see you Steve.

Lady was a young woman with loose black hair over her coat, studying the stained glass panels beside the front door. She was tall with round and healthy face, brown eyes large like the robin you knew so well. Holding out her hand, Hi Steve, knowing you. You knew her too, after a moment. She was the one at the top of the Rome Building who led you to the deep chair where she asked you please to wait Mr. Rome'll be right in. Now in your own house under the big curving stairway, saying, Hi there, my name's Sharon Trace.

Trace. Like you. Sharon Trace. We're related.

I doubt it. She giggled.

I like your house. I like those stained glass panels. Mr. Rome thought you might have a job for me.

A job? I don't have any jobs.

Sharon Trace in her brown coat in the middle of the hall. You, irritated by Rome's officiousness, though you liked her looks, her eager big bird eyes, unadorned natural face, as if she had gifts for you. What's wrong with your present job?

It's all right. Can I take off my coat?

Sure, sorry, come sit down. You went into the living room with its big windows and upholstered Victorian chairs. In

Rome's office she wore black and white dresses; now jeans and a furry blue sweater. Slim.

Jack Rome said you wanted a wife.

Such a thing has to be said twice before it can be heard.

Jack Rome said you wanted a wife.

Is that the job you're applying for? Joke. No joke. He suggested I suggest it, she said.

Sharon Trace. If Stephen Trace marries Sharon Trace, her name will still be Sharon Trace. No one said anything for a while. She, looking at the fireplace, the new antique andirons. You, looking at her untinted lips, eyelashes, loose black hair. Forehead and brain, pale cheek, long fingers, jeans and sweater, intelligence, flesh, skin, and fingernails.

If you would be interested in a wife or, specifically, me. Looked at him now, the genuine robin's eye, eye to eye, brown, but though bright and amused, she couldn't hold it, and in a moment her look slid off under the weight of civilization.

Spend your life with her. Advice and breakfast. Travel and old age. I don't know you. You and I, we're strangers.

I think that's the point. I'm to remind you how pioneers in the old west ordered their wives out of the mail order catalogues. Fathers in ancient Russia betrothed their eight-year old daughters to unknown princes and counts on distant estates. Kings gave their daughters to Persian potentates to keep the royal blood pure. I think the idea is, like everything else, we start from scratch.

Do you want to be my wife?

I don't know. What are your bad habits? Do you smoke? Neither do I. Do you drink? A little before dinner. Already we know a lot about each other. Do you find me attractive?

She became more attractive as she spoke. Attractive enough for what a husband and wife do in private? Just saying this added to her attraction. You wanted to touch her but not yet. I'm easy to get along with. I'm patient, even tempered, thoughtful. I'm simple, no hangups, good manners. People like me.

Meanwhile the living room of Stephen Trace's house had windows on three sides looking out to the glittering Sound, this room with iron fireplace, dark old woodwork, lamps and antique furniture, lavender Victorian chairs where Stephen and Sharon Trace sat, negotiating. You wondered who built it, what families lived in it, what furniture they had.

A wife is for life. Would you commit your whole life to a stranger? She: But I know you better than you know me. I know something about you no one else knows.

You heard that, it made everything quiet. What do you know? I read your dossier.

There's a dossier? The waters of the Sound, sheltered and calm, expand eastward beyond the tip of Long Island where they merge with the westward swells of the Atlantic. There's a March chill blowing off the Sound. What's in my dossier?

Your name. Do you want me to say it? If you know it, yes I want you to say it.

You heard the p and the g's and the r's. They sounded lovely in her voice. No one knows that name. It's a secret I'm supposed to keep. But you don't have to keep it from me. Love in the soft voice, sweet promise, the intimacy of knowing all.

Does Jack Rome know you know? She: I'm the one who typed it for him. He: So you're the detective who's been keeping track of me? No honey, I'm only the typist. (Honey.)

But you know where he gets his information. I don't know anything. All I ever see are scrawly notes and messy legal sheets and teletyped shreds. Her healthy outdoor face (swimming skiing horseback riding, maybe tennis) should answer all doubts.

I can't for the life of me imagine why you'd do this. (Actually you could think of two reasons. One, to spy for Jack Rome. The other, to get her sweet outdoor hands on your money.) She: I recently lost a husband. Relax, it's nothing to grieve over.

You guessed (Stephen Trace too) the breasts inside the thick blue sweater were small rather than large, the figure slim, he would enjoy the thighs when the jeans came off. He imagined emotions melting under the lucid calm of her eyes as she leaned over him. It's absolutely impossible to marry anyone without knowing you much better and longer than I do.

That's okay. I'm not suggesting you marry me now. Let me be a candidate. Let me live in the house for a while, you have plenty of rooms. Hang around, eat meals, see how we get along.

What if I have a date with Genevieve Desmond?

Tough luck for me. If you don't like me, kick me out. If I don't like you I'll leave.

It's my house. I like my privacy. Are you going to make a lot of noise? She: I don't make noise. Are you going to bring in friends? She: I can manage not to for a while. It's my house and I make the rules. She: You mean I can move in? Is that what I mean? She: I can move in today if you'd like.

Wait. Are you thinking of paying rent? She disguised her startle. To make it more regular. She: I wasn't thinking of rent. I'll pay rent if you want me to. Also board, are you expecting to eat here? She: Well I was assuming I would. Except for lunch during the week of course.

That is, you expect free room and board. I'm not sure what you are giving in return. A new tone for Stephen Trace, stern and sarcastic, a possible meanness you had not noticed before.

I'll pay if you want me to. I just assumed, in return I'd be wifely for you. Wifely? You mean, what? You expect to take Mrs. Heckel's place?

I had supposed a man of your means would not expect your wife to do what Mrs. Heckel does. Am I mistaken?

Well the fact was, until now you hadn't given a thought to what was expected of Stephen Trace's wife. Peter Gregory's wife had done all Mrs. Heckel's work, plus a full time job, and did not consider herself a slave. On the other hand, she ended up with Louis the Lover. By her question Sharon Trace defined for the first time what was not expected of Mrs. Trace. The other side of the definition remained open. He: So what do you mean by wifely, then?

I thought you would welcome company. Someone to talk to. Blah blah blah. You: I don't want to talk all the time. She: Not necessarily talk. Being there. Confidential, never to part, someone to count on, old age, pain, sickness, death.

A chartered heart's ease, a contracted turtle for your phoenix. Okay, if you could overcome this old suspicion about strangers in the house. To guarantee against her stealing, setting fires, murdering you in your sleep. You got references for Mrs. Heckel, should you get a reference for Sharon Trace? Ask Rome: would you trust Sharon in your house? You did not want to bother. If she wanted to move in today you wanted to agree before she changed her mind. All this caution was show, or Peter Gregory, or some other ass masquerading as Stephen Trace.

Still, the doubts he ought to feel. Again: *Why me?* Don't you have friends, boyfriends? Don't you consider me a bad bet?

She: Jack Rome and Delaware (Delaware too?) thought it a good idea in our circumstances. If we don't like each other, thank you, bye bye, no hard feelings.

I won't require you to pay room and board, if you're quiet and don't make a fuss.

You must be crazy. Can I move in today?

*

169

Later in the afternoon he told Mrs. Heckel Ms. Trace would be occupying the north bedroom and having meals with them beginning tonight. Ms. Trace, she said. Is that your sista?

A quick call to Rome through Delaware while Sharon was getting her things to move in. Is Sharon Trace reliable, he asked, can I trust her?

Why sure she is, he said. She's every bit as reliable as you.

That night he took a studied look at himself in the bathroom mirror and was surprised how handsome Stephen Trace was. The beard he had grown in Stephen's honor was noble, the high forehead enhanced his dignity and repose, his thoughtful intellectual eyes were full of knowledge of the world, humorous and wise. He was pleased by what he saw. No wonder Sharon Trace was attracted.

TWENTY FIVE

Stephen Trace's courtship of Sharon Trace that spring went through three steps.

The first step was sex and passion. It took a couple of days to get started. Stephen Trace occupied the big south bedroom with views of the water all around, and he put Sharon at the other end of the hall, facing the land. The hall crossed a balcony over the stairwell between their rooms. That first night after he had shut his door, brushed teeth, put on pajamas (with a fugitive memory of sleeping in the woods), he sat by his bed with the light on, the water outside with the red and green channel markers, thinking of Sharon Trace in the other room.

She thinks he is in here thinking about her body, he thought. She said Good night Mrs. Heckel, and now she is thinking nobody's in the house but us two. She thinks *he* is thinking that. She thinks he makes conventional assumptions about what happens in a house occupied by only us two.

He wondered what she thought of a man who shut himself in his room when there were just us two, man and woman, alone in the house. And the woman a candidate to be his wife. If she was lying in her bed with her clothes off, the lamp on, wondering why he didn't come. You hadn't been this sexed up since the river, creating a danger of turning Stephen Trace into a fool. If she was on her bed without clothes and he didn't come. On the other hand, if he went to her room (as you would expect of a man in such a case), and she, tucked in wool pajamas, cried

171

out, What? Or if, doing what any man not a fool would be expected etcetera, he went to her room and she said, so you've decided to marry me.

Such were the problems facing him the first night as he sat up a long time annoyed because he couldn't decide what Stephen Trace would do in such circumstances and ended up doing nothing.

In the morning he awoke uncomfortable—there's a visitor in the house—with uncomfortable responsibilities not his fault since he was under no obligation to her. Since she ought to know that, he need not worry lest she be disappointed by his lack of behavior last night. She might even appreciate his being a gentleman.

When he came down she was eating breakfast and reading the paper. Like a smart young business woman from New York, bright and fresh in a tweed business suit with a navy blue bow. Now he was annoyed, wondering what she expected of him at the breakfast table, but she greeted him cheerily, saying, You don't have to talk to me, and handing him the business section of the paper. She herself was reading the sports. She said I didn't expect you down so soon, and showed him the note she had intended to leave:

Dear ST
Have gone to work. See you tonight.
Love, ST

So off she went to New York, taking the train, while he thought of her gliding around mysteriously in Jack Rome's glass office above the world. All day "Love, ST" on her note made him feel good, though its didactic thrust irritated him.

She came home that night at six. He saw her coming on foot down the street from the station, crossing the bridge, click click her heels on the porch. She went up to change, came down in jeans, and they had drinks in an alcove looking through the porch to the red harbor buoy. Mrs. Heckel served dinner, Sharon was famished, she said it was a nice house to come home to, the train ride wasn't bad, she could tolerate such a life. He asked for her life story. She said her past was boring, and they ended up talking about Yankees and Mets. She was a fan of all the great sports. Baseball basketball football.

She kept stuffing her mouth and wiping her lips. He wondered what her nipples looked like and her navel and the rest. He guessed her hair was black. After dinner she told him he was free to read his book. You proposed chess. Okay, Sharon Trace played chess, she played fast, the game was close, she edged you out. She was amused. Any other games you want to play? Ask again: Tell me where you come from? This time she answered. Indiana, like through a screen, far away, indifferent. He was disappointed. Where in Indiana? Cowland, you never heard of it. Sounded like a made up name. They played pingpong in the cellar, and she edged him out again. She laughed and swung her paddle and reached for the ceiling and her toes. She was an athlete, lithe and restless.

That night after the muffled sounds of bathrooms and showers, Stephen Trace in his robe with a more definite idea slapped his slippers down the hall and stopped to knock at her door. Stopped by a Gregory qualm. It took a moment and a deliberate decision.

In this silence she could be shocked or scared or victorious. You heard the feet, the doorknob, the door opening. She looked out, face wet, the bright robin look in her eyes, her black hair wet and straight to her shoulders, a knee-length white puckered robe hugged across her front. He concealed himself by holding his robe out a little in front with his folded arms.

Can we talk? No games now, she looked at him straight and serious. What a sweet simple face. Sure, she said.

He sat near the bed, folding the robe to conceal his feelings, while she sat by the mirror and dried her hair. Talk above the whinny of the dryer. What do you want to know? The puckered short white robe slipped off her knee, but she put it back.

So what did you do in Cowland, Indiana? She grew up there. What was it like? Boring. Routine farm stuff. Horses and cows and pigs? Corn and wheat and clover. Silos and barns? Roads long and straight for miles between fields. Grade school, high school, college. And then you left? She came to New York. And what did you do in New York? First a restaurant, then an office, eventually Jack Rome. So how did you get such an important job, so privileged and close to The Boss? She shrugged, maybe her supervisor recommended her. Meanwhile the white robe kept slipping off her knee and exposing her thigh, and sooner or later she would put it back again. Her knee and thigh were white and pink.

How old does this make you? About thirty. Born on September 19, whatever year that was. She put the robe back in place though really too short for sitting, and turned off the dryer. She fluffed her hair. She looked great.

His chair was between her and the bed. He did not know if she had anything on beneath the robe, or if she wanted to go to the closet for pajamas or nightgown. He didn't want to do anything without her consent. He considered and said, Well I guess that's what I wanted to know, would you like me to go now?

The robin's eye flashed with intelligence. Not necessarily. Would you like to stay?

Is it all right with you?

I wouldn't be here if it wasn't.

The robe fell off by accident as she stood up. She grabbed for it, but too late, enabling him to compare her with his thoughts. Real skin and hair and light freckles on her sides and arms and belly. She came over to him in her sturdy bare feet. In case you and I get married, she said. She slipped him out of his own blue silk robe revealing you all ready to go. She laughed. They slithered onto the bed and got tangled up close and intimate. Oh ho, he roared in his millionaire house alone with her in the night, oh ho.

After that, they spent every night in one room or the other. They had a great time. The most important part of the day was when you and Sharon Trace lay on a bed or couch or floor removing clothes or already without them. She had performative zest, and seemed to come from sophisticated worlds of usage and tradition, which made Peter Gregory's experience (consisting mainly of married nights with Linda and the unforgotten memory of Anita Long) seem like forms of idiosyncrasy and solitude. There was something public about Sharon Trace, which made you avoid the word love, though it had a tendency to pop out of your unconscious like Jung, as if you had been born with it. In an instant, even while deploring it, Stephen Trace had become obsessed with dallying and horseplay, infatuated and capable of almost any sacrifice for its sake.

In the second step of the courtship, you tried to broaden their lives. You didn't want Stephen Trace to be a simple idiot with nothing on his mind but screwing his girl friend. When she was at work, you restored lost dignity by walking around his property and puffing him up with ownership. Talk to Mr. Jollop about plans for gardens and shrubbery. More flying lessons to look down on the world.

When she was home, you took walks with her in the early spring countryside, played games (scrabble, arm wrestling—whatever you played, she won), went to plays, movies, the opera. You took her with you in the plane.

The main thing in the second step was talk. At dinner, after sex, in the garden, the porch without lights. She talked about Rome's Empire, and you talked about Gregory and Trace. You told her about Linda and Louis the Lover, but you didn't mention Florry Gates or the Sebastian case.

She had been Jack Rome's Secretary for Personal Projects for three years, but she knew little about the Rome Matrix. She didn't understand Rome's dealings but was sure he meant well and did much good. She did know your gift wasn't unique, he had made similar donations to others. You mentioned Crazy James. Probably James Dziadech, petty hoodlum from Brooklyn, paroled for an armed robbery, after which Jack Rome gave him a fortune to see if it would turn him into a sober citizen. She said Jack Rome knew perfectly well who Crazy James was and agreed he was the most likely conduit from you to Rome.

You told her the Adventures of Gregory-to-Trace. You knew the story well by now, its parts had hardened in their molds. She already knew much, but you filled in details.

You mentioned Rome's theory of competitive ego. She preferred the Thomas à Becket theory of character formation. People behave according to the roles in which they are cast. Thomas à Becket was a playboy friend of the King's until the King made him Archbishop of Canterbury. This caused Becket to behave like an Archbishop, making himself such a thorn in Henry's hide that Henry finally had him killed. People strive, she said, to fit their behavior to their parts in the cast, Professor, Student, President. If they don't know their roles, they improvise like actors who have forgotten their lines. Sharon: You are learning Rich Man. You and I together are studying Man and Wife. It's not you who makes you behave as you do, it's your money.

On the porch, facing the Sound on a dark night. Your parents would not have understood Jack Rome's theory of competitive ego, nor Sharon's role theory either. Your father, the alcoholic ACLU lawyer with this severe notion of service, did half his work for no pay at all. Your mother, remembered as a religious person who believed in and taught Character, was even more severe about the Self, selfishness, selfish people. Your glamorous stockbrokering yacht-sailing Uncle Phil's mildly patronizing attitude toward his poorer brother's family was offset by their equally mild and quiet contempt for him.

As for Sharon, talk about her job and Jack Rome but not about herself. Cowland, Indiana, who cares? she said. How did she get into the Rome Corporation? It doesn't matter. How did she get so close to the top? Briefly jealous, you asked pointblank, did Jack Rome screw her? If he did I wouldn't tell you, she said.

In the golden bathtub under the overhead mirror (from the previous owner) she pointed to the little lines on her lower abdomen. Child marks.

By now she's five, she said. Her name is Melly. David's got her. David got Melly, I got the job.

The job? Jack Rome's job. More questions, then. For example, how long and how often has Sharon Trace been married? Answer, five years and just once. David who? David Trace. Which gives us another Trace in the world, two if you count Melly. Question, Who was David Trace besides your husband? First answer, a high official in the Rome Matrix. Second answer, a rich alcoholic. Third answer, Jack Rome's older brother.

Brother, hey? You do have the connections.

So it would seem.

If he's Rome's brother, how come his name is Trace?

Oh, it's an old family name.

Does that answer the question?

I don't know. Doesn't it?

You then. If you married David Trace, you had a different name in Cowland. (You don't want to know.) Tell me. Sharon Sharalike. Come on, cut it out. Sherlock? No. The name embarrassed her, she left it behind with the rest of Cowland. Stuff your ears, here it comes, don't listen. The name came out through the water she splashed in the tub.

Who wants to be Sharon Grubbs in a world like this? If you mention that name to anyone as long as you live.

Obviously you were going to marry her. The third step was to eliminate the negatives. Rule out the alternatives. You had this old notion marriage should develop accidentally. Before marrying her you had to decide if there was anyone else you knew or might meet later whom you would regret. Anita Long. Florry Gates. Nancy Nolan. Genevieve Desmond. Ephemera of past and future against the solid presence of Sharon Trace. Marry Sharon then: You got along with pretty good fun, you didn't fight, what else did you need? If Stephen Trace had come from a family, with roots and relations—but already in a month's time there was no one he knew better or who knew him better than she.

Yet he knew nothing about her parents, childhood, home. No family anecdotes. He did not know what lovers she had had, what friends, what aspirations she had abandoned. If you take that negative approach you'll never marry anybody. He asked her if she still wanted to marry him.

Sure, she said. Love to.

After Gregory

They got married at the beginning of April in the high glass office of the Rome building, attended by Jack Rome and Jane Delaware and Mrs. Heckel and a minister named Dr. Nose.

TWENTY SIX

Mr. and Mrs. Trace went on a honeymoon for two and a half months. In the joy of life together they risked death on the Interstate highway, in the wind and the engine, the vicious pavement, the teetering walls of trucks. Bridge abutments, ditches. Parallel rubber streaks veering off the road.

Ignoring death, they went out into the world and filled themselves with country. Key West. New Orleans. San Francisco. Yellowstone. From the beginning of April to the middle of June.

No one in the other cars knew their wealth. They were caught speeding in the Bible Belt. Slowed by road construction and traffic jams caused by accidents. They ignored the hitchhikers at the entry ramps. They wore jeans and bright shirts and shorts. They staggered in the lobbies at truck stops or Bob Evans, staring dazed at vending machines with key chains and combs. Their faces were shiny. They looked just like everybody else and pretended that's what they were.

They came back finally to Mr. Jollop's garden full of roses. The house had been cleaned, the furniture polished, the lamps gleamed. The lawn was rich and green, the silver globe sparkled, the irises bloomed. As Stephen Trace on the longest evening of the year you sat in a wicker chair with a drink, next to your wife. As Stephen Trace you looked at the purple waters east to a blank horizon and wondered, What next?

Here's your chance to live closer to nature and the rhythms of life. Thoreau. You got a notebook and wrote across the top of the first page: JUNE. You got up early and went outside with binoculars to look for birds. Learn the flowers, wild and tame. Name the bittern among the reeds on the inland shore. You forgot to keep your record up, forgot to get up early, with Sharon waking up there beside you and pinning you down. Too many distractions to be Thoreau.

You bought a sailboat and went cruising in the waters nearby. The sailboat made you feel guilty when you didn't use it. You joined the tennis club, where Sharon put on her sexy white shorts and beat everybody. You sat in the bar and watched her through the window. She had given up her job in town. She bought a horse and wrote a postcard to her five-year old Melly, living with the parents of David Trace. The postcard showed a tiger at the zoo. She declined an offer to keep Melly for July.

There were tense moments and peculiar impulses. You woke one morning thinking you had committed bigamy. It took a while to get rid of that. Testing the unthinkable, you allowed yourself to fly over Westchester, seeking the old house over the ravine where Peter Gregory was born. You resisted the impulse to retrace Murry Bree's route across the country.

On the porch in the wicker chair, looking at the water, lead gray on a cloudy day, watching a pair of sailboats with billowing jibs defying the forecast, while Sharon was inside polishing her tan with the sun machine, you said, I loaf too much. You couldn't postpone the question much longer. What is Stephen Trace to do with his millionaire life?

The answer appeared quietly, where it had been all along, hidden in your name. One fact distinguished Stephen Trace from what he would otherwise have been. This was his fortune, which made him Stephen Trace. Here was his occupation, the proper business of his life, designated at the start when he accepted that life: money. To hold, nourish, and use well that with which he was endowed.

The care of his wealth then. This was in the middle of July. He began to study in earnest. He consulted Mr. Peck. He brought home prospecti and announcements, newsletters, and company reports. Little by little he took charge. He threw out his Thoreau notebook and opened a new set labeled FINANCE I, FINANCE II, and FINANCE III. These were full of ledgers, graphs, plans to buy and sell. He took an office in the Rome Building, and hooked up his computer at home. He learned the companies he had shares in and made detailed studies of others. He knew stocks, bonds, and certificates of deposits, was familiar with options, intimate with ginny and fanny mae. He recognized nature's law. the only humane thing to do with a thirty million dollar fortune is take care of it like a sunflower or a puppy, so that it may fulfill its nature. His immediate goal was to double everything within the year. He named himself Stephen Trace, Financier. He became a Republican. He told Jack Rome, who laughed.

TWENTY SEVEN

You were coming out of the Rome Building late one afternoon and heard a call, Hey, Gregory, I'll be damned.

Gregory?

You recognized the face, then who he was: Archie McWare, a college friend who used to get drunk all the time.

Christ, he said, I haven't seen you in fifteen years. Come have a drink.

You played Peter Gregory like an actor. You went into a bar with him, which he settled into like an old home. You're doing well, he said. Nice suit. What brings you to the Rome Building?

His life was a tragedy (fortunately for you, since it dulled his curiosity), full of woe, and woe swam in his drinks. His wife gone, his children too, because of drink. One thing saved him, his profession, for in Boston he was still an excellent brain surgeon. Work kept him proud, when he was working he was okay, excellent concentration. It was the rest of his life that was a mess. Do his work, then go to pieces. Today for instance. He had come to New York for a consultation, should be getting the train now, but was going to get drunk first. No way to prevent it. Get drunk tonight, sleep it off, fly back tomorrow, appointments in the afternoon. An operation Thursday. He'll be all right for that. Just the rest of his life was shot to hell.

He thought Gregory was a teacher. Yes, but you gave it up. You're doing other things now. A bit of money, yes? How's

Linda? Linda? Oh? Sorry pal. So it's woe for you too, alas. Unless you found somebody new, hey? Not impossible, that. Well, I'm glad to hear at least some good coming out of woe.

The question was whether it would be wiser to take Archie McWare into your confidence. You doubted he could keep the secret. The alternative was to say nothing. Masquerade as Peter Gregory and hope the news won't spread before time can confuse the dates. The next alumni book won't be out for five years.

Of course, you could wink and say, please don't mention meeting me, I'm supposed to be in Chicago. But that would be too much of a strain on Archie. You said goodbye without telling him, leaving him in the bar with his drink, and you never heard from him again.

You had another shock one afternoon when Sam Indigo showed up at your house by the water. Sam Indigo was the police investigator who had interviewed you when Jock Hadley was killed. From the study window you saw this man coming up the walk from his car, tall, bald, familiar, frightening you with memory flapping loose from its stays. You didn't know him and then you did, right out of Gregory's past, and immediately understood he had been following you across the country for more than a year and had finally caught up with you.

Voice soft, face mild, he said, Mr. Gregory? Your answer being slow, he added quickly, I'm Sam Indigo. I used to be a police detective. You remember talking to me last year?

You: My name is Stephen Trace. He: Are you saying you're not Mr. Gregory? You: What do you want? Indigo (surprised): Why, I don't know. Friendly visit. He looked almost timid. Then, perhaps because of the look on your face: No harm, I just came to chat. Is it inconvenient?

I won't talk to you. There was screaming in your voice, though you kept it quiet. I won't allow it. I won't have you destroying my life.

Destroy your life? How could I do that?

I won't have you coming after me. I'll die first.

No, no, relax, calm down. I had no such thought.

He kept peering around at your place. I'm not with the police. I'm private, on my own.

Then why are you here?

He took a seat on the porch without being asked. He looked out at the harbor. I'm in New York on business. Nothing to do with you. No ulterior motives.

What *are* your motives?

My motives? For what? Why, nothing. Curiosity, I guess. Simple curiosity, killed the cat, hope it won't kill me, ha ha.

Curiosity about what?

You. You look pretty good. Relax. I won't tell anyone.

You served him a cold drink, and you talked together warily, trying to be casual as if past were past. Meanwhile, in the secrecy of thought, you tried to remember what made this polite and soft spoken man frightening. He was mixed up in your mind with terror, unjustified by rememberable facts. The only rememberable fact was the interview with him, innocuous enough. The morning after Hadley was killed, he just wanted to know if you as a neighbor had heard or noticed anything the night before. You remembered being agitated. There was something incomplete about it, some reason to be afraid. You were too distracted by your own problems, whatever they were, to take it in. Now, while he sat there with his mild eyes, bald head, he brought back madness from the past in an image of himself. If not police, he was personal, if not to pin you with crime, then blackmail. You saw what a fine blackmail target you were, with

185

everything that qualifies: a lot of money and a secret. You kept watching for the blackmail hint, while scrambling for how to respond.

If he makes demands, defy him. Wealth would protect you, you had figured that out before. In the woods, if things went bad your last resort was always that you could return to the river, it would still be there. That was freedom. Now you intended to live and had the means and didn't need that freedom.

You talked about house and grounds. Mr. Jollop and the garden. Sailing. You got around to asking him news from town. He didn't know anything about your wife or children. It was a long time before you could ask: how did you find me? Not hard, he said. Did anybody ask you to? Nope, I did it all by myself.

Well then (ask it), What do they think happened to Peter Gregory?

By Peter Gregory, you mean you?

I mean Peter Gregory.

Well then, it depends who you mean by "they."

Why, the people in town, the general view of things.

Sam Indigo didn't know if there was a general view. The police take no position on the question. You: They didn't buy it as suicide? Suicide? The sober blank considerate face had a glint of mischief, devilishness. Was it meant to be a suicide?

Take a moment. Was no note found?

A note was found.

I went into the river. I really did. I expected to drown.

I believe you.

Do they believe me?

How can I know what anybody "believes"? They might think others believe you are dead but doubt it themselves, or they might hear others doubting it but believe it themselves.

What about the newspapers? He: It was in the papers. Did they call it a suicide? He: The article reported the known facts. What were the known facts? He: Your disappearance, the note in the car. You: No speculations?

I don't reckon most people think about it one way or another. Shaded mirth in his eye, fun at your expense. I expect most people figure if you're not dead you wish to be thought dead.

You said, *You* had doubts. But doubts alone wouldn't have brought you here. You must have known something.

That's my business. You seem anxious to cover your tracks.

Defy him then: I can bear it if I'm found, it's not a life and death matter (implication:.I'm not vulnerable to blackmail). But it would be kinder—kinder—to keep this undisclosed.

I ain't telling.

He left without asking you anything. Thanks for the refreshment. His card, an address back home. If I can be of service. Back over the bridge, without having tried to blackmail or threaten, though you felt as if he had done both.

Afterwards you sat for a long time on the porch trying to remember why that original interview had troubled you so much. You remembered some things. You remembered that he had come back later that same morning as if to interview you again. You saw his bald head from the window above (just the way you saw him today), and you went out the back to escape him. Why did you do that? Some fright you had, something you did not want to be asked. This too came back, partially, a notion that you had told him a lie in the interview and he was going to check it out. What lie could you have told? You remembered a little more. The interview was on the morning after Florry Gates had dumped you in the park and you had come home on foot. Which happened—remembering this too—the same night as the Hadley murder, for you had seen the flashing lights and police cars in the street when you came home. You remembered that. Then a revulsion overcame you, a disgust with all things Gregory, and memory stopped.

You expected to hear from him. But like Nancy Nolan, like your children, like Archie McWare, as the days passed without consequence Sam Indigo was encysted in another memory pocket of unfinished business. You forgot about him except when the cysts broke and memories rushed back, as they sometimes did.

One day David Trace came to see you. He came to your office in the Rome Building, where you watched the waves of Dow Jones like the sea. You could watch such waves forever. The receptionist buzzed and said, Mr. Trace is here to see you.

Brown beard concealing a young face. So big, he could die of a heart attack from the enormity of himself. He had tiny blue eyes squinting through the hair on his face. He said, You're Stephen Trace, I'm David Trace.

You remembered this: Brother of Jack Rome, first husband of Sharon, nee Grubbs. High official in the Rome Matrix. Rich alcoholic. His parents (who would be Rome's parents too) keep Melly. He didn't look like Jack Rome.

How are you doing, friend, just wanted to take a look at you, another of Jack's projects. Offer support. Answer questions you might not know who else to ask. How's Sharon working out? You like her?

You liked her just fine.

Good. Have you heard from Luigi Pardon about her? Has he said anything about Sharon?

No. Why should he?

Forget it. I'm glad you and she are happy.

David Trace leaned back in the chair hands across his belly, humphing out words like Theodore Roosevelt. Tell you everything, information to light your way. Ask. What do you want to know?

Free questions? You saw an opportunity to solve the mysteries of life. Is it true you're Jack Rome's brother?

She said that, did she?

True?

What is truth? It's true enough for practical purposes.

Then why is your name Trace?

Good question, he said. You'll find several Traces in the Rome Organization. Jack's way of establishing dynasties without planting family trees. Instant genealogy. Watch for other Rome-made family names in the Company. Trace, Landis, Greenbush, Delaware—but only one Rome. Not sure what Trace means, except subordination. Residue, what's left. You are the ashes of something else. From Jack's point of view, of course.

You're subordinate too?

Jack's point of view, I said.

If you're Jack's brother, you don't look like him. (Jack small lean and dark, Italian; David big bearish and blond, Danish.)

That's because we're adopted. Then Jack changed our names: he's Rome, I'm Trace, whereby our brotherhood is sundered. Now we're associates in the organization, he the primary, I the secondary. No doubt you wonder how the younger brother could co-opt the older into his realm against everything the older believes in. But some questions you might ask can't be answered.

Delaware's a made up name? Landis, too?

Delaware, Jack's wife, created for the purpose, precisely. Landis, Osgood Landis, you've heard of him?

I heard something.

You heard about Landis and Jack's first wife?

I heard something about a feud.

You ought to know about that. Landis was Jack's mistake, regretted ever since. He was a street preacher in New Orleans when Jack picked him up. Stood on corners with his Bible and his zombie daughter and ranted. Jack saw him and gave him one of your grants: hellish playfulness, for Jack doesn't believe in God unless maybe himself, but he picked this guy off the street, and you know the rest. Cult celebrity, the Landis Community, and by way of thanks to his benefactor broke up Jack's family, as you may know. Driving Jack nutty. What else would you like to know?

Was there anything you ought to know about your own grant?

It's an attempt to corrupt you. This was said so casually it took you a moment to hear.

What do you mean by that?

Well, let me think. What do I mean? You don't think you've been corrupted?

Nobody likes to be told he's corrupt, but you checked your huff. You needed wisdom and asked, How am I corrupt?

You accepted the grant.

A banal and irritating suggestion, not to be taken seriously. Nevertheless, you asked, Why is that corrupt?

Calm down. Not suggesting you give it back, nor overlooking your situation when you got it. Just want you to recognize the moral situation Jack has put you in. The specific corruption is the impact upon your character, which you compromised.

Resist, make him explain.

Do you deny you have distorted, silenced yourself for the sake of your fortune?

Why no, you accepted the gift freely, no strings, no commitments.

In that case, where's Peter Gregory?

You felt puritanical, parental pressure. Damned if you'd give anything back.

Nobody's asking you to. Forget it. Ask another question.

You asked if there was any question David Trace thought he should ask.

That's a good one. All right. You could ask what David Trace has against Jack Rome.

So, what does he?

Some objections are ethical, some political. Politically, by conviction David Trace is a socialist. Doesn't believe in great fortunes for a few at the expense of all the rest. If he had his way there'd be redistribution and equalizing.

So why are you working for Rome?

Personal weakness.

What are your ethical objections?

Jack Rome regards himself as a sovereign principality, a state unto himself. Last month his security guards caught a man trying to plant a bomb in the Rome Building.

You heard about that. A terrorist.

You heard about it. So did everybody in Rome. But the world will never hear. "Terrorist"—Jack's word. Who was he, what did he represent? No one knows. Sovereign states take prisoners and execute spies. That man went into the Rome Building and never came out. Something to bear in mind, as you go around admiring Jack. I admire Jack too. If you think I'm biased, ask Sharon. She's a great devotee and will give you full justification for every point.

You're trying to tell me something. What should I do?

You want advice? I don't give advice. Don't do anything. No, resist a little. Don't mess with Gregory/Trace. Be yourself and resist.

The end of August. You alone on the porch, listening. You heard the late August sleep of the aging season, the still buzzing in the grass. The plopping water against the underlegs of the dock. Civilization in the air above, breath full of traffic and airliners melting into wind. You opened your eyes and saw the hazy chemical mist between you and the far city, the imaginary streets and crowds, your computerized office and Jack Rome.

You heard a nearby squawk, a real voice, resonant and hollow in a primitive throat. Sea grass in the backwater behind the island, the long gray neck sticking up like a reed, motionless as the season. You had to imagine its robin's eye because it was too far away even with binoculars. The resonance, rounded through a tube, like a child's cry, which is what you thought first before your mind corrected it to bird, frog, blowing grass. There was a playground across the channel near the McIntosh house, but it was never used, because there were no children there. Never had been since you moved in, the distant slide, rusty-piped climbing maze, concealed in the dark green foliage.

There was a book of exotic birds in the living room, left behind by the previous owner. It showed a heron in the reeds where you could see his eye clearly, just like the robin's, looking out with astonished calm at you and the universe from a position somewhere between the death he created (minnows and snails) and the death coming to him. The artist fixed him in permanent colors in the permanent reeds and leafed him in with others to create, page by page, an aviary, bittern, stork, crane, rail, long legs all.

You didn't tell Sharon. You wrapped the book yourself. You asked Mrs. Heckel if she would receive mail for you addressed to a pseudonym.

Dear Jeff and Patty,

I am an old friend of your father's. He told me once that you were interested in the birds and animals of your summer place in Maine and liked to poke around the reeds looking for crayfish and used to count the number of times a whippoorwill would repeat his call at night without taking a breath.

For old friendship's sake, I am sending the enclosed beautiful volume of paintings of exotic birds, in his memory. If you like these, I will send you another volume, birds of prey, for the book is part of a series.

You can write to me c/o Mrs. J. W. Heckel at the address on the letterhead. Please let me know quickly that you have received the book safely.

Yours,
Murry Bree

There was no reply.

PART THREE

Delaware

TWENTY EIGHT

In the middle of happiness, a request from Jack Rome: I want you to escort my wife Jane Delaware to Europe. He came in person to Stephen's office to ask you.

What is this, a favor, a command, a debt claimed? You didn't ask. Just a little errand for me, Jack Rome. You won't mind. You and Jane, to pick up a certain person in Venice and bring her home. Plus some business for Jane in our European offices. Tickets and reservations supplied, expenses paid. No more than three weeks, you'll be back end of October.

A certain person?

That was glee in Rome's eyes, a touch of devil. Her name's Miranda Landis. You've heard of her.

Miranda Landis the Virgin Healer, you had seen her hypnotic face rapt on television while Jack glowered, eyes smiling up, hands clasped, long hair down her shoulders over her blue robe.

She's coming over to us. The smug look of victory, an ecstasy of vengeance in Jack Rome's small grin. It's a secret.

(Why me?) Just get her, bring her home. Delaware will explain. She'll give you more precise directions.

You tried tactfully to determine your wife's place in this expedition, which could be a pleasant holiday. Your wife stays home, Rome said. Sharon will understand when you tell her I ask. It won't cost you a thing. You'll find it worth your while.

You waited for Jack Rome to give you another reason. In vain. You wondered what motivation he thought would make you comply, servitude, gratitude, lust, fear, which would define your place in his hierarchy. Tickets and information in the mail, he said. You and Jane Delaware and her necessary maid. Questions, call Delaware. You had no time to choose before you were chosen.

According to Sharon, if Jack wants to send you on a mission to Europe with Jane Delaware, you'd better go. Too calm, Sharon, too cool. You don't mind? You don't care? Relax, she said, it's an opportunity. With two extra games of ping pong in the cellar that night, which as usual she won. You called Jane Delaware. Do you know what your husband has asked me to do? Yes, First Lady with the lady voice. Thank you so much.

Since Jack Rome and Sharon Trace and Jane Delaware all agreed it was the right thing to do there was no reason not to go. Money would keep you safe. You had an inherited love of travel, and all you needed was to regard this as a fully authorized business mission for the man to whom you owed so much. So said Stephen Trace against you in this argument.

A fast sequence: Tickets to London for S Trace, J Delaware, H Copzik. Reservations in London, Zurich, and Venice. Separate rooms in all hotels, maid included.

So off you went to the heart of civilization, traveling in a dream with the whole world as false as you, interchangeable people, Jane Delaware for Sharon Trace. This Sharon refused sentimental good-byes. You'll be gone three weeks, no big deal. Wouldn't go to the airport. Sat on the porch railing swinging her legs in jeans over the bushes, holding the cat with one hand, the post with the other so that she could not wave, but cheerily bright in her plaid shirt, a blowing red scarf protecting her neck from the chilly sea air. In the big black car, Mr. Jollop driving, you waved for both of you.

You picked up Jane Delaware, luggage and maid. She stepped out of the brass-shining door, click clicking to the car with a uniformed man carrying her suitcases, and maid in a smart coat. Playing escort, you jumped out and opened the door, while the footman loaded baggage in the trunk, and you went to the airport riding in back with her while the maid rode in front. Plenty of space between you. She talked to the maid about what they had packed and to you about the itinerary, with suppressed hilarity, a hidden joke somewhere. The maid, indefinite age, small with a tiny chin, talked New York and said *You know* all the time.

You tipped the porter and took the tickets to the check-in like the father of a family. Waited next to her in bucket seats in the blue and silver plastic lounge, like a husband without husband knowledge. Wondered if she wanted you to sit by her and talk, or would she like to have coffee in the café, or would she prefer a drink in the bar, or walk around and look in the shops? I'll just read a bit if you don't mind, she said. So you bought a magazine and sat beside her, the maid too, all reading, and then she and the maid, whose name was Helen, talked, and you hoped you would stop feeling stupid soon.

Time to board the plane, through security and the long corridor and the bright tube to first class on the 747, and an unspoken but important question who should sit together and who behind. Settled by her—you sit with me—as was also the question who should have the window seat, who the aisle. Then the pressure click of a door sealing the capsule, severance from the terminal and your house and Sharon and your life, fatal, while life in general went on, the plane taxiing toward the runway with the shielded plastic lights above, and trying to enjoy first class as you enjoyed wealth, the space between the seats, the deep ease, to escape this still unrelieved feeling of ruin. Using male thoughts about the thrust and power of big planes to avoid being imprisoned and low while the actual plane waited for its turn and you watched the others ahead with the lights on their colorful high tail pieces move down the runway ahead.

The takeoff held your body in a vise of invisible motion, while outside a table of lights tilted and leveled and spread, grids of light in geometrical clusters which reformulated into one line and disappeared. Producing the imagined ocean while the only thing in the window was your face. Inside, Jane Delaware and the backs of the seats in front and golfball reading lights. Big geographical thoughts against imprisonment, the streets and houses which the now vanished lights represented, your country falling behind, icy October water and ocean waves and fishing boats in the dark straight below if you fell through the floor. Cast your thought forward over the great Atlantic, the latitudes of the Great Circle up the coast beyond Labrador to Greenland, the Arctic Circle, and Iceland before night was out. Geography against what was stuck in your head, the notion you had been kidnapped into an unknown where all familiar connections were broken, no mail, no telephone, nor even language to protect you.

Reluctant suspicion, Jack is setting you up to take Sharon away. Not clear why he would take her back after going to such trouble to give her to you, but your manufactured marriage seemed as fragile as the metal skins holding you up over the dark old sea. Your life compacted into passenger and baggage compartments, suspended by abstract laws of aerodynamics thousands of feet, higher than mountains, over water. You required a deliberate rhetoric: Thousands make this trip every day. A favor for Jack Rome. You had a name, money, and a home, the wife on your island was last seen on the porch rail holding the cat, etcetera.

The trip had its own rhetoric: the dignified first-class hostess brought champagne and dinner, with menu in elegant gourmet script. First class glamor, though no one to share it with, since Jane Delaware was used to it. After dinner, the movie, then a couple of hours of night intended for sleep misting by like fragments of clouds.

At 36,000 feet according to the captain, the ocean would be seven miles below. Somewhere down there, give or take a few hundred miles, the sea once caught Uncle Phil and took him in. Uncle Phil: Do you believe in God, son? In the boat at Marblehead, untying and tying, getting ready to sail, the fittings dazzling in the sun. Cussing and stomping around, more rageful than the difficulties of the moment could explain. Later he leaned back against the coaming, puffed his pipe in the deep blue air, acting the gentleman sailor in fine weather, the breeze strong, the blue and white water splitting against the bow. Hiding the cuss between his lips. This was basis for imaginatively watching him years later, days and nights alone in his perfectly fitted boat, well stocked pantry with cold meats and Campbell soup, his efficient cabin, mahogany panels, silver cleats, compass and radio, destination unannounced: I'll tell you when I get there. Guessing what he did on nights like this, setting the sail, fixing the wheel, catching sleep below in his stiff blanketed bunk. On some unknown day while you were ignorantly acting out Peter Gregory's daily calendar, he on a different calendar hunched in the cockpit and faced it, glowering in the rollers that rose gray to black, next and next, watching the sky darkening in the west. Undulating sea crest by crest blowing spray on his cheeks, and the sky turning black as it always had since before the sea's chemistry congealed into life, while he looked for the God's awe the sky was preparing for him.

But first Uncle Phil at Marblehead, bright sun glinting off the fittings, tapping his pipe, saying, Do you believe in God, son? Depends what you mean, right? Old guy in a beard, not likely. Old geezer giving orders you'd damn well better obey because I get wrathful when you don't, not likely. What does the question mean, boy? God the creator? Hell, kid, if it's God it's got to think. It don't need arms, legs, or a dick, but if it don't think, if it's only force, it ain't God, right? So tell me, boy, do you believe in a thinking God somewhere around?

Uncle Phil's Marblehead proof, who knows if it was still valid on the old gray ocean? *You* think, don't you? But if you think in a thoughtless universe then you must have invented yourself, which don't seem likely either. This don't necessarily prove God's still there, of course. He could have created the world and told it to fuck itself, or fuck by itself, whichever you prefer. Or died, while the universe spins on, like people still crossing the Brooklyn Bridge though the builder is dead. But what if he's still there thinking away, letting us have some of his thought to look at his work, you know, from a variety of angles like a bunch of eyes? You know what that makes us, don't you? God's eyes, what do you think about that? Transmitting our messages back to the collective think tank, so he can enjoy the goddamn life he created. Makes you a piece of God, boy, what do you know? And me too, by God, me too.

The sudden cold dawning sun rose over tumbles of ocean clouds, while Jane Delaware slept with her mouth open, face polished shiny by the speed of the night. Though her fine features in daylight always reminded you of somebody, the dawn had bronzed her face so that she looked like an old woman corpse without teeth. She was this and the brilliant young woman without incompatibility in the morning light where all appearances were the same.

The wake-up girls brought heavy red towels soaked in hot water to remove the bronze. Good morning, as if the two hours since the movie actually were the eight they pretended to be. Breakfast time. A change in the engine, beginning the long descent, the blank white unshaped cloud surface rising to meet you. Entry cards. It's only England, you said, a civilized country, land of ancestors, mother tongue, origins, morality, restraint. The sky disappeared into undifferentiated motionless white, requiring another deliberate rhetorical act: to assert England with its tight colonies of trim houses and gardens and roads deliberately because otherwise this would be limbo. Otherwise everything since you met Jack Rome—money, marriage, house— was merely a diversion in your projectile flight from the river. You were a missile with no control hurtled east into space by the river god, unless you could persuade yourself this white blank was not space but only an overcast over busy morning England, and the strangeness was only metaphor.

You broke out of the clouds not far from the ground. There: the patterned clusters of houses, highways, and railway lines. Now we should be safe. The plane landed and you got busy. Practical necessity: baggage and customs with Jane Delaware and Copzik. A big black left-handed taxi which Gregory could not have afforded. Hammersmith, Westminster, the logo of London Transport. With Jane Delaware to the check-in desk to register. The clerk had two rooms adjacent on the third floor and a third on the fourth. Who gets what? She picked the two rooms for herself and her maid. An old bellman up the elevator with your luggage wished you a pleasant stye in London.

She said jet lag, call me later. The drawn shades in your room subdued the morning sun to brown twilight. You peeked out at the street, the marble and brick buildings across and people in line at the bus stop. You lay down to rest, pretending day was night. When you woke you thought you had been hitchhiking.

TWENTY NINE

You stayed in London four days, then flew to Zurich. With a British intonation you had not noticed before, Jane Delaware told you each day's program day by day. Everything was pre-arranged, her duties in London and Switzerland, with no responsibilities for you before Venice.

It was easy and nice, the pre-selected small restaurants with special rooms, dark corners, and polite waiters. In afternoons when Jane Delaware visited offices and banks, you escorted Copzik, a reader of Henry James, to museums and castles. You waited to learn about your mission. In a swan boat on a chilly lake in the mountains, wrapped in heavy sweaters, Jane Delaware thought it was funny. Miranda Landis, Osgood's daughter, never named without the epithet, the Virgin Miranda. Whose healing powers, which sustained the weekly television program, depended on that virginity, guarded by God's Police Force ever since the first manifestation. She told about that: one day when her father brought her up to the stage as he always did to praise her for remaining virgin another week, she accidentally brushed the elbow of a young man in a wheel chair. Recorded on camera, the man cried out: Hey, I'm healed, a miracle. And lo, he got up from the wheel chair right there on TV. So began Miranda's Miracle Cures, thereafter a regularly scheduled feature of the program, despite the lack of interest in the press, which Landis regards as proof of an anti-God conspiracy in the corridors of power.

That was three years ago. Now, according to Jane Delaware, the poor girl is fed up with her miracles and maybe her virginity too. Pale prisoner in the Landis Palace of God, guarded in the Adirondacks like a German concentration camp. God's Police Force.

Jane Delaware shivered in the swan boat, expository. The reason Miranda's in Venice is, Landis and God's Police think she is with her angry little old mother in Paris. What they don't know is, she also has an angry little old aunt in Venice. This gives us our opportunity. Jane Delaware shapes her fingers into claws: Jack's hooks. Don't worry, she said, it's Miranda's idea, she made the first move. Help, she wrote to Jack, with tokens to show her sincerity. Spite, of course, since she knew her father and Jack had this feud, but what an opportunity for Jack, to get a daughter back for a son. Numerically he's still behind two to one because Landis has Jack's wife too, but Miranda was the star of Landis's show, which doubles her value.

This needs more explanation.

Well yes. The angry little old mother in Paris, whom Miranda is allowed to visit once a year. Why is she angry? Why is she in Paris? How did that hick from the Bible Belt happen to hook up with this Italian from Paris? How long were they hooked up? Were they in fact hooked up? Is she Italian? The anger is hypothetical. So is the littleness and the old. The only known fact is, she must be old enough to have had Miranda, who is twenty or so, provided she really is Miranda's mother. And this: the help letters from Miranda to Jack, and his replies, all had to go through the mother in Paris to avoid being intercepted by God's Police.

Poor Jack, the jerk. How hard for him when Helen his wife, in all her ease, Cadillacs, golden bathrooms, round the world cruises, announced, I'm going forth to seek God under Osgood

Landis. How humiliating. Osgood Landis, this hick from the Bible Belt whom Jack had elevated. Served him right, actually. And when Jack thundered to her, Thou shalt not go, up jumps Alec, Thou shalt not thunder against my mother, and off he goes too. Alexander, his only begotten son, did you catch his name? who never cared for money, only for drawing on a sketch pad and worrying about whales and acid rain and species of frogs: if she goes I go too. What can poor Jack do? Kidnappings, counter kidnappings, programming and deprogramming, glory what a mess.

Osgood Landis and Jack Rome as presented by Jane Delaware, pedaling vigorously the swan boat, holding down her skirt. Here's this runty little guy standing in the square in New Orleans, waving his Bible and ranting at the lunching office workers or university students about their Satanic philosophy professors, and along comes the great Jack Rome and gives him forty million. Not that Jack is religious, as you and the IRS might think. He's not even pious. Not the tax break, though of course he thinks of that. You have to get into the spirit of it, forty million dollars spent in pure irony. Only a Jack Rome is rich and powerful enough to buy forty million dollars' worth of irony.

But for Jack, it's worth more, for forty million was just priming the pump for what the public would give to the chrome and plastic Palace of God's Word, multiplying the value of the irony hundredfold. A great unconscious display, originated by Jack for the pleasure of the few, voyeurs to the mating of religious message and television commercial. Imagine his disgust when his own wife and son joined up.

You were surprised to hear Jane Delaware talk like that. It raised questions in your mind. Good, you should have questions in your mind. Why, for example, he chose you for this mission. Good question. One reason might be that God's Police don't know you. Or you are a nice looking young man, making things nicer for Miranda. Or you have a house they don't know about, where you can keep her safe for a while. Do you believe those reasons?

Did you say a house to put her in?

Until someone safely takes her off. Another question might be why Jack excluded Sharon and sent you and me out together with only our chaperone reading her book on the shore. After all, you have a wife, and I am Jack's wife.

Do you have an answer to that?

She laughed. Jack's games, what more do you want? Once again he proves his superiority to normal human weakness. By sending you out with me, he shows his contempt for suspicion and jealousy and for you and me. His lack of fear you and I will have an affair. (She was looking at you with rich blue eyes.) With a contingency fallback, she said. He is too powerful for us to dare. But if we should dare, he is far too above to care. Contempt for your wife, too, since he can make you travel around the country with another woman and knows she won't complain.

Her jewelry eyes sparkled with liberty, while you hung tremorous between excitement and shame. Shame anesthetized in the cold Swiss air. The next question came from you: if Rome's gift to Landis was full of irony, what was Stephen Trace's gift full of? The mountains were pale and pinkish, you could see through them. She thought a moment, which proved the question worth asking. You looked at the tiny figure of Copzik on a park bench on the shore. Colder and colder.

Your gift is the result of a bet between Jack and David Trace.

Stunning news, but she was so casual it took a while to realize it.

What kind of bet?

If I tell you I'll prejudice the results.

Tell me anyway.

Well sure, darling. The bet was that within two years you'd go back to Peter Gregory.

No doubt those were enormous confused feelings you should have felt (anger, insult, terror), but first you had to know who bet what.

Jack bet you wouldn't go back, David bet you would.

Why were they betting? What's the point?

Jack the Philosopher, his old obsession: can a person manufacture himself by an act of will? Jack says yes, David says no.

You listened to your amazement, not sure whether you should be outraged, or afraid, or whether it was all right to enjoy the possible power this gave you. What does it mean? Are they betting on me or on people in general? Is it whether *I* can conform to the norm, or are they deciding the norm by what I do?

She said, it's funny except to you.

What happens if I do go back?

Jack loses.

Then what? Will he punish me?

I'm not supposed to tell you any of this.

Tell me anyway.

Jack says your love of the money will keep you from going back. David says your money removes the obstacles to your going back.

What does Jack say to that?

He doesn't think you'll take the chance.

What chance?

Of jeopardizing your good fortune.

How would it be jeopardized?

That's what you want to know, isn't it? What you've always wanted to know.

What would happen to me if I went back?

Are you thinking of going back?

No. No, I'm not.

Then why ask?

I thought I ought to know the conditions of my existence.

She laughed at that. Will he punish you if you go back—in express violation of his command? How should I know? she said. He wants you to think so. Theoretically your disgust with Gregory and your success as Trace will keep you here. But you need something to lose, else there's nothing to prevent your being both Gregory and Trace.

Does David know I'm forbidden to go back?

David's betting you'll go back no matter what the cost.

You said, I left Gregory to escape horrible things.

I know, darling.

You know? What do you know?

Whatever you think I know.

Does David know? He wouldn't bet that way if he did.

David knows everything there is to know.

You thought about what would happen if you did go back. My grant had no strings attached—except that, you said. It's a gift, not a loan. Can he really take it away?

God knows what he can do. Poor Jack, she said.

What do you mean, poor Jack?

All that money, but what he wants is adulation, subjects who depend on him. Mannequins and models and automatons. Like you.

Me?

Made to order, in his image, miniature, fake. Rich and power-ful but not like him. You reiterate him, your inferiority adds to his greatness. With fake free choice.

I'm not fake.

We all are when Jack gets hold of us. Me too. Who am I? Aren't you curious? I'm Delaware because I came from Maryland, which is near enough. I'm really a very nice person. Worked my way up through the ranks, nice to high officials while I polished my manners. Even nice to the romantic Luigi Pardon, thus fulfilling according to Luigi the desires of all women in America, whom at that moment I represented. There was really no need to change my name, but Jack wanted me to for company morale.

She talked and shivered in the swan boat. Are you cold, want to go back? Enjoying this too much to notice the cold. What else would you like to know?

Is David Trace really Jack's brother? Yes. What can you tell me about Sharon? That depends how touchy you are about women with pasts. Sharon, as you may have noticed, is very high class. Not as high class as me, but not everybody gets to marry the boss.

Did you ever hear of this fellow who calls himself Crazy James?

Jimmy Dziadech, one of Jack's reclamation projects, which failed. He's back in jail. Jack wanted to prove money would cure him of his gun and robbery habits, but Jimmy decided he'd rather be his own man. Set out to demonstrate he still had his skills. Proved it by getting caught again.

Sorry to hear that.

You'd better be. You owe him. If it weren't for him, you wouldn't be here.

Is that so? I wondered.

Of course. He's the one recommended you to Jack in the first place. Found you hitchhiking, heard your story, told Jack. No one told you?

It was supposed to be a mystery. Jack's operatives, who know everything.

Jimmy told Jack, Jack had his Ohio man check it out, the news, found out who you were, which roused his interest, you with that notoriety in your case, so he looked you up. There's no secret about it.

Except from me.

She laughed. So you thought it was supernatural. That's Jack for you.

Is Sharon a reclamation project?

Ask her yourself.

All she says is Cowland, Indiana. Cowland? How nice.

That's all you remember of the outing on the lake, except at the end when you were helping Jane Delaware out, while Helen Copzik held the line. An impulse to push Jane Delaware into the lake. You didn't do it. It wasn't unfriendly or mean. As Peter Gregory you often had such impulses and never yielded to them. To drop the china plate, step on the cat, drive on the left, that kind of thing. There was no desire in them (you didn't want to dump Jane Delaware in the lake), no animus. It was curiosity of some sort, about power and the connections between brain and muscles, and it was prevented by a most powerful intervention. This intervention was not you but external to you, protecting you like a bobsled chute.

In a café overlooking a rushing river, the water green with glacial silt, you tried to tell Jane Delaware the story of your life. An outdoor table near the edge with a red and green umbrella, legs scraping in gravel. Citron pressé (diluted gradually by water to quench the sugar and slake the thirst) and the *International Herald Tribune*. Across the swirling current a grassy shore, with yellow buildings, a church, mountains beyond.

This would be the fourth time you told it. She already knew the important things, so you looked for what she didn't know. You gave anecdotes from Gregory family legend, the mythology of exile. Your father from Ireland with Uncle Phil in their teens, leaving loved ones behind and parents soon dead. Legend of old country, old days, which only bored you then. The old man saying, we'll create new roots in the suburbs, which you can take with you across the world. Father the collector, storing for display in paneled basement rooms fossils and guns, old photographs, ship models, anchors. Followed by a new generation of exiles exiled by suburban flux with no one left at home, the town full of strangers.

You wanted to tell her what led up to Peter Gregory's jump, the clear consecutive view of things you had arrived at through the continuous polishing and erosion of the memory stream on the rocks, but when you tried to tell it, it all seemed kind of disgusting. An air of falsity created by telling, which had nothing to do with the facts, maybe. You tried to correct lies where you could. It was not true that you were cold to your wife, not true you had abandoned your children. The chief falsity was the tone and unspoken interpretation of things. Like whether what you had tried was suicide or something else, false whatever you said.

The table wobbled on the gravel. She wasn't interested in that. She preferred the adventure part, your trip across the country, Amy and Joe, the free enterprise man, Crazy James. She said, it's not good to dwell on your mistakes. You're a different person now. You said you would like to know yourself, like Socrates, to understand what made you do what you did, but she, unlike Amy and Joe, Jack Rome, Sharon Trace, didn't believe in motives. She believed in the deep emotional causelessness of human acts. Jack Rome thinks you can define Stephen

Trace and teach yourself to be him, but Jane Delaware thinks you'll know only by what he does. Doing precedes knowing, she said. You won't know what you'll do until you do it and invent the reasons later.

That conversation petered out, as they all do. She spotted a small item near the bottom of the page in her *International Herald Tribune*. Uh-oh, she said. What's Jack up to now?

The notice: someone shot, gang style, outside a delicatessen in midtown Manhattan.

What's Jack got to do with that?

A company so large is into many things, they have to deal with all kinds. I wonder who got shot.

It's there in the paper, the name: Angelo Firenze.

I wonder who it really was, she said.

THIRTY

Now comes the intrigue. Not much and not really necessary, but such as it is. At 2:00 p.m., you were sitting with Jane Delaware at a café table on the Piazza San Marco, waiting to find out why you were there. Right in the middle of the famous postcard, the colonnades, the onion domes, the stars on blue, the clock, Napoleon's stolen green horses. A flare of pigeons. Jane Delaware whispered, There she is.

You saw her, walking rapidly past the table. Short bob of carelessly dyed platinum hair, big broad-brimmed Spanish hat, black sunglasses, knee-length jeans, T-shirt reading CHICAGO BEARS. She went on into the arcade.

Is that Miranda Landis? You wouldn't have recognized her. Even with the television image in front of you, the raised eyes, the long brown hair, you could not have connected her. So how do you know?

Because she described herself. Now we wait twenty minutes and then I call her at her aunt's.

Why call her?

To arrange a meeting.

Why not meet right here?

Because she doesn't want God's Police to see. There's a code. If the coast is clear, she'll go by at two o'clock in that costume. If God's Police are in town, her aunt will come instead and sit down at the next table with the *Herald Tribune* and a poodle.

Since we saw Miranda, not her aunt, it means no God's Police around. Jane Delaware looked amused.

I see holes in that plan.

It's Miranda's idea. She's been watching spy movies during her virginal leisure. It's very intricate. She skipped to Venice to elude the God's Police who are watching her mother's house in Paris, because they don't know about her Venetian aunt. She cooked this up on the chance they might follow her here. How does she know they aren't here? Why because she knows them all, she's known them since childhood.

Well now, Jane, if her going by here means God's Police are *not* in town, why can't she sit down with us?

That's because I'm a semi-public figure, and she doesn't want to risk being seen with me. When she gets home, I'll call her.

Why couldn't you have called her when we arrived in Venice?

That's because if God's Police were here the phone might be tapped.

What were we supposed to do if God's Police were around?

Then the aunt with the poodle and the *Herald Tribune* would sit at the next table, which would be a signal to pack off to Florence and try again next week.

All right, so now she's established God's Police are not in town. Why couldn't she call *us* on the telephone?

Because this is a person we are dealing with. Her name is Miranda Landis. She watches spy movies, and she's afraid of God's Police. She's making the break of her life, repudiating father, childhood, deep beliefs, and she wants everything to be just right. She wants to go by mysteriously with her dark glasses on. She may never have worn dark glasses before. She also wants to see if she likes your looks before making a final commitment. Since she's going to be living in your house for a while. To make sure your picture didn't lie.

216

What picture?

Your picture. She wanted to see what she was getting in for, so we sent her pictures, and she picked you. I hope, since you've come this far, you'll do your part.

You didn't know what your picture had to do with it. You thought all you had to do was escort Miranda back to New York. You asked, does Sharon know the house has been requisitioned? (I'm sure she does, Delaware said.) Another question was why Jane Delaware couldn't escort her by herself.

One reason might be so she won't be seen with me, because I'm too well known. We don't want to risk her being snatched out of our hands. So you and she will go on a different flight from Helen and me. Another might be to make it more pleasant for her. I hope you'll help. Make her feel good. Treat her to Venice, take her to see things. The Lido. Murano. Gondola ride. Take her to dinner. Be nice to her.

For how long?

A few days. Enough to make up her mind and get used to us.

You thought her mind was already made up. All these spy plans.

It's all tentative. She has to meet us. Negotiate the arrangements. That's why I'm here, I'm the negotiator. You're the escort. When we're ready, back to New York in our separate planes. She goes to your house until she can go on her own.

Nobody ever asked you about that. Well, I'm sure Jack cleared it with Sharon, Delaware said.

She made her call in a public phone, came back and said, She'll see us tomorrow. Come to the hotel, I want to show you something.

You went with Jane Delaware past the sights, out of San Marco by the Campanile tower and the long row of white pillars in the

Doge's palace to the waterfront, with the gondolas and motor-boats rubbing and squeaking against the pilings. A big rusty freighter from the outside world standing high and going fast out in the middle blocked the view of the church and tower across. She pushed through the brass edged hotel door, you following, and to the elevator. Come up to my room, she said.

Her room was twice as large as yours, light and full of space, high ceilings, gold fittings, soft drapes over the windows. The carpet and carved chairs and mirrors, so big and free of personal debris it looked like a public room. You scarcely noticed the bed on one side between two polished mahogany chests, covered by a smooth tan spread. She picked up the white telephone and ordered desserts, ice cream with a wafer.

To soften you up, she said.

The window looked out on a small canal. A heavy-hulled motor barge swilled through the canal rolling a wake along the pitted stone foundations. A gondola bobbed behind. When the gondola approached the second canal, the gondolier sang out a warning, what they did instead of traffic lights.

Why must I be softened up?

She was fishing in one of her bags, found an envelope, and handed you a small black and white snapshot. This. A fuzzy, badly lit photograph of a nude woman in a chair. Leaning back, head averted, long hair over her shoulder. Her navel, puff of hair, left breast. Head turned away, you could not see her face.

Miranda.

This? She took it herself, Polaroid, and sent it to us. Gesture of good faith. To show she means business. Not much of a photographer, is she?

No one would ever know that was Miranda Landis.

Do you like her? Sit down, Stephen.

Sit down means something is coming. You sat in a golden armed chair, and she in hers looked a shade uneasy, maybe. I want to soften you up. If you had to be softened up, it would be something you didn't want to do. Soften me up for what? I have to soften you before I tell you. Tell me first.

What does this picture mean to you? As you know the most famous thing about Miranda Landis is her virginity. That's her public identity. But now she wants to leave her castle and sends us this crude naked picture. What's your conclusion?

She wants to lose her virginity.

She selected your picture out of the ones we sent. See, I knew you'd need some softening.

What she meant by softening, which could equally be called hardening, and which Stephen Trace would be unable to resist. Jane Delaware in a subdued purple dress, slim and well fitting and short, was looking at you with her diamond eyes, golden hair, smiling, sure of herself again.

He's not asking for anything you wouldn't want to do. (Your marriage was universally understood as a concoction.) Just be nice to her while you show her around, be friendly, affectionate.

In other words, screw her.

Your words, not ours. Ease her out of herself, if you can manage it. If she's willing, gently. Don't frighten her. She'll be willing, the picture proves it.

And if she isn't?

Then don't. We don't want you to rape her.

Your problem was not an aversion to making love to Miranda Landis, which you might enjoy. It wasn't even your loyalty to Sharon, since this latest adventure had put your marriage into a strange light. It was trying to decide whether this was a problem. Being asked to do it for Jack Rome and Jane Delaware. The question of Stephen Trace's moral independence. A dilemma, since the newness of Stephen Trace by liberating you from inherited restraints might liberate you also from qualms about moral independence.

An Italian waiter in white coat brought the desserts she had ordered and set them on the scrolled table by the window. Well trained, silent, he left after his tip as if the ice cream had brought itself.

So how are you going to soften me up?

Now her most brilliant Delaware smile, interpreting you correctly. How would you like? Bringing you ice cream, she stood near you in her pale tight purple dress. Eat your ice cream. Italian ice cream is the best in the world. Another knock on the door. Helen Copzik, she had forgotten today is laundry. Take the afternoon off, Jane Delaware said. Go see the paintings. Helen Copzik, looking anxiously across the long room where they sat in decorum at the little table by the window.

Now. Pull the light breezy curtains to exclude the blank wall across the canal. Come. Approach gradually the astonishing prospect of Jane Delaware taking off her clothes. Arms on your shoulders, shake her hair, eyes full of joke, kiss her royalty away. A hint of déjà vu, as if you had known her elsewhere.

The light of the world was diffused by the curtains soft and white through the room. Jane Delaware sitting with you in your chair, sitting on your knees, legs, producing discovery, as if the discovery of Sharon had not been enough. She had bare shoulders with freckles, Jane Delaware. Her neck was thin, the muscles like wires. She had breasts, nipples, a bare smooth narrow belly. She had what she ought to have.

You stood up sticking out like a direction sign. Your surge like a stuck valve was full of the repealed laws, scattering blasphemy, incest, suicide, and all your past. She escorted you politely to the bed. Naked, slim and athletic, she looked more like a water nymph than a First Lady. You were conscious you were being paid, but you didn't argue. You descended into a flurry of names like Sharon and Miranda and Linda and Florry and Anita. Also Jack Rome and Louis the Lover. If Jack Rome really was above caring what his wife did and if it didn't matter in the soft sheets, bare legs still tangled letting the diluted time drain away.

After a while she came out of it. Miranda will like you, she said. You wondered if you would like Miranda. She wouldn't be easy and relaxed like Delaware. She would probably be jittery and stiff. Jane Delaware sat up by your side and looked down at you. What did you say?

Would you be willing to let a reporter interview you about Miranda, when we get home?

A reporter?

Alan Scanlon. A good journalist, working for Jack. Wants to write a profile for a national magazine, about her life, her growing up, her restlessness, her yearning, her need.

Why interview me?

Because you can describe this crucial turning point in her career. How we found her and brought her home. Insights none of the rest of us will have. And if she does give up her virginity—which she will—he'll want to ask you. Her virginity is a famous commodity, and if she sacrifices it, that's news.

You must be kidding.

Tasteful, tactful. Just a small part for you, her rescuer and initiator, telling the reporter enough to make it a step upward for her rather than just another banal affair. Ritual, deliberate sacrifice, which you can attest. You needn't fear exposure, he'll give you a fictitious name.

Lying there naked, spent, on your back, looking up at her, the ornate ceiling over her head. That's an outrage, you said.

Is that what it is? Alan's a good journalist. He won't say anything you don't like. Subject to Miranda's approval.

If he uses a fictitious name, why doesn't he just invent the whole thing?

It's got to be right with her.

You think she'll approve a thing like that?

She will if you talk her into it.

Who's going to talk me into it?

She laughed, her soft hair all over you. Straddling you, bending over, her eyes dazzling in the shadow of her hair. She sent us that picture. She didn't have to do that. She gave us hints. What do they mean? She wants to make it public, she is no longer the Virgin Miranda. I doubt she'll need persuasion.

I see now why you wanted to soften me up. Can't she just quit and let the world draw conclusions?

The individual eyelashes of Jane Delaware at close range, longer than normal, artificial superimposed upon original. Tiny pink blood vessel in the eyewhite almost invisible. You don't have to if you don't want to.

She was in this position when she suggested taking pictures of Miranda. Voice muffled against your shoulders, you tried to comprehend, blind against the nape of her neck, the light in the room cut out. Pictures? She started to move again, laughing in rhythm. Sides of Jane Delaware you had never seen.

Pictures, she said. Among my other skills I'm a pretty good photographer.

She fell over and you lay sweating in the white curtained afternoon light of the Venetian hotel. You heard the warning call of a gondolier outside the window as he approached the other canal and thought how healthy traffic is, where the only problem was to get through the canals without a collision.

Her picture suggests it. It says here's the picture I took. You take a better one. What a magnificent setting this room would be.

Nude pictures? What would you do with them?

That's up to Jack and Miranda.

Miranda?

I wouldn't dream of doing it without her consent.

But I am to suggest it to her.

Not too quickly. When you have won her confidence.

The way you did me, you mean. When we're in the thick of things, pop it on her? You had never seen her eyes at such close range, the pupils large, the little pink tearducts in the corner, looking above your face at your hair which she was twiddling with her fingers.

Nobody seems to give a damn about my marriage to Sharon.

Sharon's a nice girl, isn't she? She used to be married to David Trace. Before that she worked for Luigi Pardon. Good old Luigi. Jane Delaware swelled up her throat and bass crooned my sweet embraceable you, rollarollaroo. I too, we've both worked for Luigi Pardon.

What kind of work?

Stenographic. Is that a euphemism? I took pictures of him. I took pictures of him and gave them to Jack Rome. What kind of pictures? You know.

Without his knowledge?

Mercy no. He was very proud of how he looked in that condition. I also took pictures of Luigi and Sharon. He was very fond of Sharon. As far as I know, he still is. Perhaps you ought to know that, keep it stored in the back of your head.

Luigi and Sharon?

Sharon and I, we were Luigi's slaves. He liked Sharon better than me. I was too intelligent to be a good slave. So was Sharon, but she didn't mind so much. I hope I'm not upsetting you. You ought to know these things. There's a lot of conflict in the upper reaches of the Rome Matrix. Jack Rome and Luigi Pardon and David Trace, only the power belongs to Jack. He keeps them under control.

And you're married to Jack.

That doesn't mean I have to like him. He treats me well, I can't complain. I do good work for him.

What else do you do, besides take pictures and run errands and promote his vicious schemes?

Calm down. Most of what I do is respectable. I've answered his telephone, screened and transmitted his personal messages. I managed his benevolent projects division. I'm empowered to negotiate the arrangement with Miranda Landis. Benevolent projects. That's you, that's how I first heard about Stephen Trace.

All sorts of things I've done, she continued. Used to be an actress, okay? Actress on the bum in New York, spotted in an audition by Luigi Pardon who was looking for points. Flunked the audition but made a hit with Luigi. Oops. Lucky girl. I had class. My manners, how I held my fork. So he took me in and gave me my start. From Luigi to Jack, abilities speak for themselves. Standards of behavior, poise and enunciation. As for Jack, I have a whole apartment to myself inside his apartment in New York.

So listen my beloved, will you do this little thing for me? Her soft hair blocked your vision, her strong leg had a grip on your hip. If Miranda is willing to pose for me, as I am sure she will, would you be so kind as to find out—delicately, tactfully, when you have got her into the most receptive mood—if she would be willing to pose also with you?

You're out of your mind.

We'll conceal your face. I know you can't let pictures of you be published. No one will recognize you. The important thing is the visibility of Miranda.

The danger of being recognized as Peter Gregory through photographs of Stephen Trace had not even occurred to you. That wasn't what you meant. You didn't question where the revulsion came from or whose it was, but there it was. What are you trying to do to me? She pressed you down, smeared her face over yours while she said, Don't worry, darling, you don't have to do it if you don't want to.

Don't you think it's horrible?

She sat up. Who cares what I think?

Take a moment, take a breath. Then you do think it's horrible.

I didn't say that.

Something—the nakedness, the athleticism, the steamy mid-afternoon atmosphere, the struggle to persuade, had altered Jane Delaware's appearance. Makeup gone, face shiny, like a freckled ex-child, but a good many years beyond childhood, with some old haggard anger showing through. You're not being ironic?

If you mean I'm not telling you what Jack Rome would like you to do, then no, I'm not being ironic. Anything else I may have said is up to you.

So after a while, once more quiet, you asked: Who are you, actually? Where do you come from?

Me? I'm an orphan. I don't come from anywhere.

She put her head against your neck under your beard. An orphan child, while you stroked the fine soft gold hair. I grew up in a building. With other orphan kids. I did bad things. I stole, I told lies. I did good things too. I was kind to animals, dogs and cats. I had one great friend named Emily Lake. She was a wonderful womanly teacher at St. Kate's School who taught me everything good I know. She taught me how to be a lady. How to talk, how to hold myself. How to dress. How to think about people. How to be kind, how to love. I owe everything good to her. What else do you want to know?

Why did you marry Jack Rome?

Because he wanted me to.

Are you going back to him now?

That's my obligation. To stand by him as his loving wife. I don't necessarily like myself very much, in case you were wondering about my judgment. Will you do what you can? Jack would be grateful.

Jack.

I would be grateful, Jane Delaware said. We're only asking you to do what we have every reason to believe Miranda herself wants and expects. If it's her idea to go public with her new sexual persona, we only want to help. You can make it a little easier by anticipating her wishes, if she's too shy to tell you herself.

Jack Rome would call your resistance a recrudescence of Gregory. If so, Gregory was stronger than you realized. But as Stephen Trace you had no direction. As Stephen Trace it was hard to figure out why you should resist at all, and it would certainly be foolish to resist without reasons. You agreed to see Miranda tomorrow, but beyond that promised nothing.

You fell asleep with the Venetian afternoon light in the high windows. When you woke, the light was shadowed, time had moved on. You did not know what you were, with a woefully melancholy feeling of exile and estrangement. The sadness of the world was in the airy drapes which had lost their brightness.

In this slow waking, you heard someone crying. It sounded like a woman, sobbing deep, echoing against canal walls where a black gondola carried a movie coffin. The echo grew louder, not one woman crying but two, then three, and more, a whole crowd of criers, mourning, nor just women but children, mostly children, all children, an army of children bereaved or dead wailing off the canal walls, the old buildings, palaces, canyon walls, mountainsides, the plains of the country like hitchhikers grieving on the Interstate. Who are they, and what are they crying for? The questions brought you one step further into waking, where the noisy sorrow vanished abruptly into the silence of a room in fading afternoon. The silence was deathly because it shut the mourners in a box. Still not knowing who you were, if anybody, you saw beside you in the bed a woman, pale and white, lying on her back like a corpse, looking at the ceiling. Her face was pale and thin, a stranger, you did not recognize her. Her eyes shifted, her breath moved slightly, she was not a corpse but a priestess, a norn. Her closeness chilled you, not merely because she looked so wizened and foreign on the pillow staring at the ceiling, but because you knew she culminated miles of distance crossed since your last memory. You could not know what wastes of land you had traversed after memory failed, nor what people had gone, nor whom you had loved, only that all were replaced by the white-faced stranger who occupied this space.

A name came to you, Jane Delaware. You remembered some kindness of hers, and suddenly you wanted to speak, and as if she knew she turned her head and looked at you. But her eyes, close to, lined and shadowed with makeup, made her suddenly sexual, which was against your mood and estranged her again. You mastered that in a moment with another thrust of consciousness enabling you to speak.

What did you say? she said.

I'm remembering too much.

You'd better stop remembering, then.

I killed my children.

No you didn't.

I killed them in my drunken car. I knew they were dead because the sheets covered their faces.

Those weren't your children.

I killed my wife too. The car crushed her.

That wasn't your wife.

Who was it then?

Wake up a little. Tell me your name.

You tried to say it but stopped, remembering suddenly that it wasn't what you thought it was.

She laughed and raised herself on her elbow.

Wake up, my friend. Your name is Stephen Trace. Don't forget it.

Oh. Which brought everything back. But it was dreary, how bleak the world was. If your name was Stephen Trace, then your wife was Sharon, whom, with Delaware beside you, you had lost like the others.

Meanwhile, however, you felt Delaware's fingers down below. A surge of present-day warmth that changed everything. It woke you up at last, enabling you to forget Sharon Trace too. You realized how much your happiness depended on short term memory: on careful retention of the circumstances that named you and brought you here, and careful severance of nostalgic guilt that could only drag you back to the non-existent past.

THIRTY ONE

The next day Stephen Trace brought Miranda Landis to the hotel to negotiate with Jane Delaware. Afterwards he was supposed to seduce her.

You didn't like it. The feeling was physical, like a hole in your middle where the wind blew through. Miranda the virgin healer bored you, her implicit dishonesty irritated you. You went in the early afternoon, a back canal, a grilled gate, a flagstone courtyard, stone staircase to a corridor and a wooden door with a mailbox and a doorbell button.

Miranda herself opened the door, recognizable from yesterday, not the television image. The poorly dyed short platinum hair, without the hat and wearing clear glasses. A light green and white dress and bare legs. She was pale.

Who are you? Oh, I know you, you're Mr. Trace. You're to take me to Mrs. Delaware.

She got a hat, white with a big brim like the other. She called out back: I'm going now, Rosie.

She took your hand and led you down into a narrow street, going fast. This way. Avoiding your eyes. I recognized you from your picture. You're going to take care of me until I get settled. Nervous, her hand cold and damp.

Now you could see the television Miranda Landis, the small features, the slight overbite and narrow mouth angelic on television but anxious now. A tense forced smile. She set the pace, drawing you ahead by the hand through the pedestrian streets

229

of Venice. She said, You're going to be my guide, right? Voice out of middle America.

Escort.

And I'm to live in your house? On an island? How is it for security? They said they'd provide security.

What do they mean by that?

Bodyguards. To protect me from God's Police.

Bodyguards in my house?

I have to be protected from kidnapping, you know. Until I go public. You walked along holding hands and trying not to bump the crowds. Her pallor was unhealthy, like those who die young.

You didn't like this planned stay in your house. Probably she could use Sharon's old room. When do you plan to go public?

After I get the money.

And then you'll move out?

Don't you want me there? she said. Not that, I just want a sense of how long it will be. I'm sorry, she said, I thought you wanted me to stay with you. Yes, but some things are a little vague, and I'd like to anticipate. She said, I can move out once I know what's going to happen and get a place of my own.

To be friendly: Then what will you do?

I'm going to be a star.

Try to decide how old she was. Her movements, walk, holding your hand, suggested sixteen, but her eyes were older. Your curiosity was aroused. Did she really believe in her father's God? Was she conscious of being a fraud? What caused her to change? Could she understand such questions?

What's the matter? you said.

They will give me money, won't they?

That's Jane Delaware's department.

They said they'd give me a sizable grant. That means money, right? Do you know how much? A lot depends on that.

I'm sure Delaware will tell you all you need to know.

I hope it's enough. I couldn't do it otherwise.

How much do you need?

I'm giving up my whole life. I'm abandoning my home, my friends, my profession. If they don't compensate me, if they don't give me what I'm worth. She stopped. You were about to come into the piazza by the cathedral. Wait. She fished in her purse to exchange her clear glasses for dark ones. Public places, play safe. Better not hold hands.

You went along the water's edge past the rubbing gondolas, wind across the water, to the hotel, the gilded elevator to Jane Delaware's airy room. In the elevator, Miranda Landis frowned at the floor and clenched her fists. Jane Delaware opened the door, and they shook hands, elegant lady, nervous girl.

They sent you down to have coffee with Helen Copzik. She was an inconspicuous little woman of any age. You felt ashamed for expecting to be bored. She had been concealing a lot of excitement. For you know, she did like Venice, this might even be the high point of her life. She wanted to see more art, Titian, Tintoretto, the churches. Thrilled by the onion domes of the cathedral reaching out to Byzantium and Turkey and the infidel East. Marco Polo returning at the waterside, and Othello and Brabantio, Shylock and Portia. Byron and Wagner, who died in a palace. Rappacini's poisoned daughter (but that was Padua) and Henry James with his publishing scoundrel (that was Venice) as well as his dove with her face to the wall, and Thomas Mann dreaming of Platonic beauty and dying on the Lido beach. There was a lot you didn't know about Helen Copzik, filled with literature. The only thing that bothered her was the question of health. She wouldn't have thought of it except for Thomas Mann, who had tipped her off to the city's reputation, which she was reminded of by the hazards underfoot in the streets and the stink of the sewery canals. You could see her nostrils trying to close and her hand over her tea cup to keep out the Venetian air.

And then her curiosity about Miranda Landis. What's she really like, Stevie? Do you believe in her miracle cures? Good, neither do I. She said this, then carefully thumped the table with her fist, checking her force enough not to jar the cups. I wonder how she does it. How can you get so many people to lie? Everything Helen Copzik said had an air of surprise.

Maybe they don't realize they're lying.

That can't be. If you're pretending to be a cripple, you must know you're pretending.

You weren't so sure. It was your impression lots of fakes don't realize they're fakes. This throws the whole question of hypocrisy into an ambiguous light.

Helen Copzik discovered something: What it means is, that girl's a fraud. What a terrible thing to say. However, she *is* giving it up. Probably because she realizes she's a fraud and is tired of it. Fed up. Innate morality asserting itself against even parental force. I suppose her father forced it on her. What do you think?

It must have been her father.

Copzik was worried, she was shocked. The Virgin Miranda, it's blasphemy. It's a parody.

Not for them. They believe in her, those people.

Well, that's a shame. I don't believe in blasphemy, but it's blasphemy. I believe in the Spirit of Man, but if you believe in the Spirit of Man you respect the great religions and their symbols. That dumb girl as the living Virgin, she is absolutely vulgarizing a great religious symbol. It's disgusting, Stevie.

It's not her fault.

It's his fault, then. Don't you agree?

Stephen Trace respected her outrage.

Jane Delaware and Miranda Landis came to the café triumphant, especially Jane Delaware. All settled, Delaware said. We'll stay in Venice until Monday. See the sights, get to know each other. Then New York and a new life. A toast to Miranda.

Banal forgettable conversation (gondola rates, dirty streets, hotels) while Miranda had a limonade. I don't drink, she said. You were having bizarre connection problems. Still trying to extract the ethereal television Miranda from the uncomfortable girl. With Jane Delaware, three images: elegance of the beige dress, golden hair, diamond eyes. This was now transparent, giving a direct view to the naked sex fiend in yesterday's sunlit hotel room. The lost part was the First Lady who once inhabited the elegance.

You took Miranda back to her aunt's apartment. She said, I can't go to dinner with you tonight because I promised Aunt Rosie, but you can take me out tomorrow night.

That's all right.

I understand you got a grant from Jack Rome too. How much did he give you?

Enough.

I wonder if I capitulated too quickly. I should have bargained, more. I bet Delaware would have given more if I held out. Do you think so?

I wouldn't know.

They're giving me forty million. Is that enough?

It's more than I got.

Oh, I'm sorry, she said, as if she had been tactless. I guess I'll get a house, like you, she said. I'll hire a staff, an agent. Do you know any agents? Do you have any contacts?

Do you mean you're going into this blind?

What do you mean, blind?

Don't you have anybody to help you?

Jack Rome is helping me. You're helping me. I'm reasonably famous. When I go public, that will attract attention. I'll get offers. Won't I?

Sure you will.

Do you think my public will be disappointed? Will *you* be disappointed?

Disappointed by what?

Not to see me on the Landis show any more.

You told her. I never watched it.

You didn't?

I saw part of it once.

Oh. She was disappointed, but she adjusted. Well, there are a lot of people who love me, but I think I've done it long enough. I have my rights. What do you think? (Certainly you have your rights.) I want a bigger and more interesting career. Do you think that's gross and selfish of me?

I'm sure you know what's best for you.

I was getting too specialized. I need to branch out. I only did one thing, over and over.

You mean, curing people?

A puzzled look, and you felt sorry.

A more rounded career. I say to myself, Miranda, face the facts, I have my following, but I'm not a star. I have it in me to be one, but I'm not one now.

What kind of star do you want to be?

All round. To be a real star, you have to branch out. Movies, TV, the stage. I can't be the Virgin Miranda all my life, nobody can. I want to say I'm really grateful for this opportunity. I have Mr. Rome to thank and Mrs. Delaware, and you.

But as you say, your true fans will be disappointed.

Her face was ravaged by anxiety, which was the secular side of her televised ecstasy. If they love me, won't they follow me into my new career?

If they love you for yourself. But what about the lame and sick who depend on you?

I can't help them now, she said.

Aren't there people whose faith depends on you, bolstered by your miracles.

Miracles?

Your cures. Don't you cure people?

She frowned. Don't make fun of me. I've lost it. I haven't had it in months. I need other ways to fulfill myself. I need to act, sing, dance, get outside of myself. I need to express. Put myself forward in a disciplined shape. That's why I want to be a star. That will give me the feeling back.

At her apartment you remembered your duties. Would she like to go to the Lido this afternoon? Too cold, she said. Come in and stay awhile. Get to know you, if you're going to be my host. The apartment was small with a plainly furnished sitting room in the back. You met Aunt Rosie and the poodle.

More coffee. Miranda Landis in a sofa facing you, bare legs pulled under her, sitting as if you were a gentleman caller two generations ago.

This was the moment when according to Jack Rome and Jane Delaware you should begin seducing. You resisted, not that Miranda repelled you but the time was wrong, or the mood, or something. You were face to face with the question of difference between Trace and Gregory, if there was to be any difference. Gregory now would be full of moral resistance, guilt and shame, but would probably grab the lustful opportunity

235

anyway and feel bad while doing it, since she was there and doubtless willing. Trace, liberated with no reason to be moral, was free to do what he liked, have her and improve his place in the world, yet here he was, surly and opposed for no good reason except to prove he was Trace and was in fact free to do what he liked.

She said, Why isn't your wife going to be in the house when we get back? (What?) They told me you and I will have your house to ourselves. She noticed your look. It isn't true?

Well God damn.

What's the matter?

Nobody told me.

You're angry. I've made you angry.

Someone was angry, heating Stephen Trace, creating him out of flame. A spiteful idea occurred to you. You checked it in case you ought to think it over. But already you were saying what might rule out reconsideration: Miranda, do you know what they want me to do?

Now you didn't know whether it was spite or just the natural thing to say.

What do *who* want you to do? Jack Rome, Jane Delaware. She said, They've been very kind to me. Is there a catch?

If this was so important, you'd better stall awhile.

You'd better tell me.

Too late anyway and maybe it was just natural. Having committed yourself by accident, you were compelled to follow through: They want me to take your virginity away.

Without my knowledge?

No, not that. (You were listening to what you had just said.)

I mean, without my consent?

Not rape, seduce. I'm supposed to persuade you.

She looked puzzled. Why?

I suppose to confirm you're no longer the Virgin Miranda.

I don't know what I'm supposed to say. What am I supposed to say? Isn't it enough to announce I am no longer the Virgin Miranda? I told you, I plan to go public.

I imagine you'd prefer your own choice of ravisher.

What if I'm already not the Virgin Miranda?

Well I suppose you could tell them that. You really don't need me for that purpose at all. (So much for that, Jack.) She was looking at you, you with no idea what she was thinking or how close to disaster you might be.

They also want me to interview a New York reporter who is going to do a profile of you. I'm to give him a blow by blow account of how I took your virginity away. (It took your breath away, what you heard yourself saying, though you still did not know if it was courage.)

She stared.

They also want me to persuade you to pose for pictures in the nude. (Or idiocy?)

She still stared.

Not only that. They want to take pictures of you and me together. Do you know what they mean by that?

Her voice was faint: No.

Not family pictures. You and me, nude together. You and me doing it.

Doing what?

It, Miranda. (What Jack Rome could do to you, the various forms of ruin. And if he couldn't, was it worth anything?)

Consider the inside of the human skull, where everything is concealed except such crude signals as escape through gestures and looks and whatever deliberately chosen words issue in sequence, slow, temporal, one after another. Her eyes were dead, refusing to reveal war or peace.

In a pale voice, Why do they want all that? Do they expect me to agree?

I'm supposed to persuade you.

How are you supposed to do that? What arguments are you supposed to use?

No arguments. I'm supposed to overwhelm you with the force of my charm, what the hell, I don't know.

There must be advantages they expect me to see. If you don't know what they are, you're not a very good salesman.

Maybe I forgot.

Actually I knew about the interview. They want to do a profile. This will help when I go public. I just didn't know about the virginity part of it. I suppose their thinking is, if I'm to give up the Virgin Miranda, they want personal testimony. I don't think that's necessary, do you?

Whatever you say, Miranda, whatever you say.

As for the pictures. I suppose that's my fault. I sent them a picture of myself as a token of good faith.

Why did you do that?

Lots of famous women got a push from posing in the nude. It didn't do their careers any harm. Back home it would be shocking, but in the outside world it's another matter.

The Virgin Miranda nude in *Playboy* or *Penthouse*? That would change the Miranda image pretty quick.

Do you think it's a bad idea?

Don't you? You didn't say it, though. Having told her the worst, Stephen Trace withdrew from judgment. It depends on how you feel about it.

You were in an argument failing for lack of resistance. A meaningless display of moral energy. The resistance you'd expect from her background was not there, which left your outrage flapping in hollow space. She was coming out of her insulated world into a world she knew nothing about. She had created her idea of this world out of two things: television images and a sure realization it was different from the world she knew. She had no way to estimate how much or little that difference was.

You couldn't refrain from this: It might be a shock to those lame and sick people who rely on you to bolster their faith.

They don't read those magazines.

They'll hear about them.

She looked like crying, but pulled herself together. Well then, so I shouldn't allow nude pictures?

I'm not your adviser.

All right, I'll draw the line. And I wouldn't do the sex pictures in any case. I don't see any point in them.

Good idea.

As for my virginity, well, I really don't need you for that. Why do they want it to be you? Do I have to name somebody?

I guess they wanted me for the interview, but we've ruled that out—

We've ruled the virginity part out. There will be a profile, I'm counting on that.

So I see no need for you to name anybody.

If I named the person—no, I can't do that. It would serve him right. But then he'd only deny it, and nobody'd believe *me*.

Who is this person you're talking about?

Forget it. Are they going to be mad at me?

I doubt it. They might be mad at me. (You wondered, was Stephen Trace enough of a person to take pride in this?)

I don't want to get you into trouble. But I really don't think I need do any of those things they want.

You know why they want them, of course.

Yes. Mr. Rome wants to stick it to Daddy.

You don't mind?

I picked Mr. Rome on purpose. I thought he'd be glad to help me.

You want him to stick it to Daddy?

Henceforth I'm going to be what I am. Do you think God will be mad at me?

I can't speak for God. I'm trying to figure out what life was like growing up with your father.

It was all right. Only now I want a show of my own.

A show. You thought, a byproduct of her bizarre upbringing was that she grew up without judgment. Meanwhile she was looking you over. She said, If you really do want to seduce me—

No.

Well that's okay. We couldn't do it today anyway. I've got the curse.

What?

Don't you know what the curse is?

The curse? Oh yes, the curse.

I'll be all right Thursday. If you want to do it then.

No, but thank you very much.

THIRTY TWO

Your trajectory from the river, an eastward parabola. Its apogee, the Grand Canal of Venice. You shared a gondola with Miranda Landis, feeling great because Stephen Trace had ignored Rome and Delaware and acted on his own (though he had not told them). Alarmed too by the price he might have to pay, yet this added to the exhilaration, was necessary to it in fact. A feeling you pretended Peter Gregory never knew, reclaiming the hope in your original jump. Then everything crashed.

You were entertaining Miranda, a proper escort, with an understanding as to what that did not mean. Reclining in the gondola close to the black licking water, with another gondola coming up in a hurry, the gondolier shouting across the gap. An Italian exchange between the two gondoliers, the one calling Signor Trace are you Signor Trace? He have message, signor, the other said.

Waves in the Grand Canal as the gondolas almost crashed, motorboats and a vaporetto full of passengers intercepting the landing, with the Rialto Bridge in sight and a pink and white palace with striped poles above slimy green bastions, and at the landing Helen Copzik waving frantically.

Something's wrong, she said. Janie wants us at the hotel. You hurried after her with Miranda clinging to your hand through the narrow streets between the old buildings, avoiding dog turds. Over canal bridges, under arches, beyond the great square back to the hotel, wondering what.

In the garden café beside the hotel, Jane Delaware sat with a newspaper. Miranda was alarmed about being seen in public with Jane Delaware. Delaware looking grim shoved the paper at Stephen, the *International Herald Tribune*, the item on the left:

JACK ROME FEARED DEAD
AS PLANE DIVES IN SEA

Hard to read, the odd juxtaposition of familiar words, Jack Rome's fear of death or his fear of what the dead would do as the plane in twisted tenses dived into the sea. With Jane Delaware waiting for you to react, you had an uncomfortable feeling you had already heard this news and had not paid attention.

You grasped its meaning at once: ruin, the end. Death of Jack Rome, death of Stephen Trace, it was impossible for Trace to outlive Rome. You did not know you were grasping this—I formulate it in writing months later—but you felt it as a rumble in the earth that would grow stronger until it shook you apart, while your superficial mind relished the dazzle of shock.

The dazzle, if the news meant Jack Rome was dead, a sensation. A surge of joy, checked by the qualifying word FEARED, which meant Jack Rome was not really dead, in which case he must be alive except for Jane Delaware looking like a catastrophe.

Miranda Landis wanted to know: What does this mean?

Delaware: I saw this in the paper. No one told me.

Miranda repeat: What does it mean?

I wouldn't worry if someone had told me. But no one told me. So I called them. I called David.

What does it mean?

It means he's dead.

What does that mean?

Good question.

You were irritated by others invading your privacy. Thinking, it was not you who had considered Jack immortal but Jack himself, and it would be good for him to learn mortality like the rest of us. Loss too, magnificent and irreplaceable, you could enjoy the splendor of that. Would you grieve? Not yet. This was more like a newsbreak, a great public figure dies. With disappointment that Jack's death had made pointless whatever moral victory Stephen Trace had achieved in dealing with Miranda. (Unless of course by dying he had saved that victory from the test and preserved it in pristine uselessness.) All this was superficial, though, against the unsettling question of what would happen to the structure of Stephen Trace now that Rome was gone.

Miranda: What happens now? What happens to me?

I'm going home, Delaware said. You can do what you like.

I can't do what I like. I'm going with you.

Go get ready then. Peremptory Jane sent Miranda Landis back to her apartment, Stephen Trace to the travel agent, Helen Copzik to the hotel room, while she made calls. Flight for four to New York tomorrow morning. Later you sat with her again in the café.

She had the facts. How Jack Rome took off alone yesterday in his light plane from an airport in Westchester. Destination unknown, clearance to Hyannis but instead he headed south, over Manhattan, the Statue of Liberty, Coney Island, out to sea. There as observed by a police helicopter and watchers on the chilly beach the plane wobbled its wings a couple of times, nosed down, and dived into the ocean. Impact hard, petrifying the sea, causing the orange wing to snap in a silver veil. Search followed, small craft. Wreckage in fragments, no body. How did it happen? The newspaper hinted suicide, but that's impossible.

With time to pass, Jane Delaware, griefless but grim, no sparks now, created her private obituary for Jack. No one knew him, she certainly didn't. Sifting the legends which he created, she tried without success to see some real history. She saw the classic model, a city boy, the city reportedly New York. Stern father who ran a news store. Strong mother, goading ambition. Boy smart and aggressive, Boy Scout, doing street corner rackets at an early age, only he wasn't Jack Rome, he was What's his name, some different name which he had abandoned. This biography has no authority, Delaware said. Hearsay, rumor, all the rumors.

Jane Delaware's only history was what her imagination could guess from the anecdotal remains. The stern father with the newsshop was likely a bookmaker. The Boy Scout by another name was probably sent to jail—for he knew about jail, she had heard him rail against the human practice of ganging up on other members of the species not necessarily inferior to themselves, to put in cages like an animal.

What was the trouble he had to wipe out with another name? Mail order college degrees. Ticket scalping. Handicapped services. Stereo speakers, fine equipment cheap. Service contracts with no service. You guess too.

In Jane Delaware's obituary, Jack Rome got out of jail, vowed not to repeat his mistake, vowed also in the usual way to make his first million in so many short years. Took a name pretentious enough to suit his destiny. Started by selling school supplies. Yes, school supplies. Let the great universe of Rome Enterprises grow out of kid stuff, pads of paper, pencils and rulers, teachers' gradebooks. Next thing you know there's copying machines and computers. Then entertainment and communications and finally (no need to guess this) a company consisting of money, nothing but money, selling it, buying it, renting it out. His talent was to nurse and feed the money tree and utilize cleverly your average human being's need to take shelter under it. People worked for him for the love of it. Like any dictator he made people's lives depend on him with love. Everyone in Rome adored Rome, Delaware said.

You without grief were thinking—the deep tremors a little stronger—how exposed Stephen Trace might be without Rome to back him up. A savage world with bears. Yet you didn't want a resurrection. No body had been found, what if he parachuted out? If he wasn't on the plane at all. He would turn up in his office, call the papers and say Jack Rome here, your story is garbage. Let's have no Lazarus back from the dead. So what does this news really mean to you? Nothing at all, your money and your house belong to you. Liberation, how the world changes, new things always happening.

You were secretly annoyed with Jane Delaware. She was keeping something from you. Preoccupied, and despite her anecdotes you felt you had lost her.

So it was cut short the glorious trip and fly home. To Whitfield, Sharon, Jollop, Heckel. It didn't seem right, traveling with Jane Delaware had dislodged you. Your fine house seemed as far and cold in the past as all your other houses. All the way to the airport Miranda fidgeted nervously. The big Spanish hat and dark glasses. She said, I'm taking a chance going with you. Privately Delaware told you about another telephone call. Jack was murdered, she said. Sabotage.

How do they know?

Wreckage in the sea.

At the gate where the passengers boarded, an old woman in shabby black coat, her knotted white hair coming loose over her collar, wept. Old peasant crying son or daughter to America. You couldn't see who she was waving to, well dressed and happy down the fluorescent tube with you to the plane.

You flew all the long afternoon in the bright sun, hours and hours of unchanging day, quiet now, changed. Miranda and you, Delaware and Copzik across the aisle. Jane Delaware, rapt in problems, nothing to say. When you were settled in the plane you told Miranda Delaware's theory that Rome was murdered. She put her hand to her mouth, shocked. God's Police, she said.

What makes you think so?

God's Police. They found out about me and this is what they did. You thought it unlikely. No, it's God's Police. If not them, it's an Act of God, but I know it's God's Police. It's what they do. Oh my Lord.

She squeezed your hand so hard it hurt, her fingernails. Then clasped hers together like prayer. You have to hide me in your house. If they're not waiting for us at the airport, can we go right to your house, please? Then the question she couldn't hold back: If Mr. Rome is dead, what will happen to me?

I don't know.

You don't *know*?

I suppose you'll go ahead with your plans. Stay in my house a few days until you can settle yourself and go public (thinking already, irrationally: if you still have a house).

What I mean is, will I receive my grant? Can I assume what happened to Mr. Rome won't affect that?

Oh, I don't know anything about that.

Ask Mrs. Delaware, will you please?

You leaned across the aisle. Miranda wants to know about her money. Miranda herself leaned across you to ask: Do you know when I'll get it now?

Jane Delaware: I have no idea.

This won't be a problem, will it?

Jane Delaware looked at Miranda with frozen eyes. I don't know anything about how you can get your money.

Well who does know?

Steady: I don't know. This was a private project. No one was authorized to give the money but Jack himself.

Well, who's authorized now?

No one, as far as I know. It belongs to the estate.

Miranda's voice rising, with a panic edge. Well, who handles the estate? Who's going to give it to me from the estate?

I don't know if anyone can.

Miranda putting both hands to the sides of her head, squeezing and tugging at her no longer long hair. What are you telling me? Where's my money?

I'm not sure you'll get any money now.

You can't do that. You promised.

Jack Rome promised.

But you made the promise to me. I've come all this way for you, and this is what you do to me?

It depends on whether Jack set the money aside. If he set it aside, you're all right. If he didn't, you're out of luck.

Out of luck. No way. I won't allow it. I've thrown my life away for this. You gave me your solemn promise. If Jack Rome can't give me the money, you find another way. You'll give it to me out of your own funds.

Jane Delaware turned and looked out the window.

You too, Miranda said to you. Yes, you. You're in as thick as she. If she doesn't pay me. Somebody's going to give me the money I was promised.

I don't have forty million dollars.

Tough shit, she said. I'll sue.

Misery growing, organic like a malignancy, feeding on itself, no need for reasons. Miranda next to you in a stew, threatening you, it took your heart away. You were going home. But your memory image of Sharon was hollow like a chocolate egg. A different Jane Delaware, you never thought she could be so cold. Gloomy in the bright ocean afternoon, homeless and loose on the surface of the world with only temporary connections to things more permanent than you. You tried to relax in first class deluxe, the formula of wealth for comfort. Tried to disregard the harsh voice inside you condemning everybody: Jack Rome for crimes, Jane Delaware for desertion, Miranda for gullibility and greed, you for your share in all of these.

After the first class midday dinner—silent and gloomy and upset—Copzik asked Miranda to sit with her for a while. You moved across the aisle while Jane Delaware moved over to the window. She showed some sympathy. The poor girl, she said.

Won't she get her money? you said.

I doubt it. She'll sue for it, you said. No she won't, Delaware said.

Then you ought to tell her and send her straight home. Maybe someone can manage a little something to tide her over, Delaware said. David, maybe. Then she added, You should be prepared, too.

What? To give something to her?

If those fellows go after you. If they want your money back. Be prepared.

Want it back? Explain that.

Nobody has a claim on you, but they might try to make you think so. Stand up for your rights.

That's all you needed. In that moment, without shock or surprise, more like a stupor, you saw it all gone and knew it was fated so from the start.

Meanwhile she reentered her preoccupied silence, and somehow you knew she was out of it too, Jack Rome had left her nothing, and her acquired world was getting ready to expel her. It was that, not grief, she was facing now.

In the dead silence of the midoceanic midafternoon where the clocks themselves refused to advance, you saw beyond the arrested time to the police waiting at the New York airport. You saw them clearly, and though the time barely moved, you strove to slow it down more, to stop it flat if you could. Outside, far above the featureless white cloud cover, with invisible ocean below that, you could imagine it either way: invisible speed, six hundred miles per hour over invisible sea, or absolute stasis, suspended in sky, for there was no perceptible motion to confirm either view. The police would be God's Police, coming for Miranda. Yet as you saw them, they were coming for you too. You rather than Miranda. Nor were they God's Police but true police, authorized by the powers of the law, and Miranda had nothing to do with it. They were waiting to arrest you when you got off. You tried to figure out why you feared this. The customs process perhaps, projecting anxiety. You tried to figure out the anxiety.

Meanwhile from time to time, you heard Miranda and Copzik.

Miranda: It didn't happen every time, if you'd just watched. Mumbo jumbo no.

Miranda: Don't know if they were actually cured.

Miranda: Nobody ever said the people in the wheelchairs were actually.

Copzik: Placebo effect.

Miranda: Daddy said. Everybody who is suffering and ill in this world. Symbols, nobody ever claimed.

Copzik: Your claim to some special spiritual virtue?

Miranda: Devoted members of the Landis Community.

Copzik: Planted in the audience without your knowledge.

Miranda was crying: I know you sympathize.

Once the arrest of time was lifted, you foresaw in the waiting airport beyond the customs line, where the passengers would have to pass through, Sam Indigo. Arrest for sabotage. Murder of Jack Rome. But if Sam Indigo was at the airport, it would be on other business.

Hey Mister, that gal's too young for you, the man said.

What do you know about it?

I know your type. Child killer.

You had a sudden clear and ice cold thought. You were suspected by Sam Indigo of the murder of Jock Hadley. This had never occurred to you before. If by chance you had driven an ice pick through Jock Hadley's skull, neither your suicide in the river, nor your new name, nor Jack Rome's benevolence, nor your marriage to Sharon nor Jane Delaware's irony nor Miranda Landis's dependency, nor your wealth and house, nor Stephen Trace himself, could shield you from Sam Indigo.

Now, if Sam Indigo suspected you, the most urgent question was, Did Peter Gregory, by whom he meant *you*, in fact kill Jock Hadley? Your next clear thought said it was not enough to assume he had not. Was there a possibility he had?

The obvious answer was, No, because you would have remembered. But cold thought said, he could have done it in a blackout, and your memory with its ability to screen things could fail you. Nor could you say he wasn't the kind of person to do such a thing, since *your* whole life as Stephen Trace was based upon a violence, a drastic rejection that set you apart from everybody who leads a natural gradual life. You thought what an irony it would be if irrelevant Jock Hadley could ruin Trace's life as he had tried to ruin Gregory's.

You sat there next to the ruined Jane Delaware, trying to distinguish sanity from perversity masquerading as sanity and unable to tell which was which, trying to settle it by remembering something that could prove one way or the other: he had murdered Jock Hadley or he had not, which mattered because you would have to bear the burden for him if he had done it. Waiting in the park for Florry Gates to drive away after she had put him out of her car. Fragments of the long walk home but most of the walk was blocked out—presumably because his mind had been so busy as you walked. Flashing police lights and the floodlights on the Hadley bungalow and going around the back.

You tried to visualize what he could not remember. You visualized going up to the Hadley door in the dark. Visualized knocking and being admitted. He would have said, What the hell do you want? He could have said, Christ, I thought for a moment you were the Hammer Man. You visualized going around behind him and picking up the table lamp. Hey there, mister. Whatcha doing, mister? Bang, crash, clatter. Would the table lamp be heavy enough? Sam Indigo would know, he could tell you what the murder weapon was. Meanwhile you visualized hurrying out the back door accelerated by the noise. Then the police and the floodlights. You recoiled from your visualizations, repelled, like ripping out your own guts under a local anesthetic. The danger lest visualizing too vividly might create a tumor in the memory you couldn't distinguish from the real. To the point of not knowing whether you had done it or not.

(Copzik: You must seize this opportunity, money or no.

Miranda: Nowhere to go.

Copzik: Spirit of Man, not God. All that emotion people have, all that need, which needs to be directed.

Miranda: Different from animals.

Copzik: Need to select your symbols.

251

Copzik: It is imperative you break free. You need to escape from that environment.

Copzik: Personal growth, evolution. Abused children.)

This state you were in, let's put it clearly. There was a crime once that had nothing to do with you, and you were as sure as you were of anything that you had nothing to do with it. You were sure primarily because you had no memory and no interest and because you had other memories surrounding the time, except for one small gap. However, at that time you occupied a different person, from whom you had later split and whom you had repudiated. Repudiated so thoroughly you were no longer sure what that person was really like or what he might have been able or unable to do. It occurred to you someone, knowing how this former person had detested the old man, might suspect him of killing him. This thought was alarming enough to make you inspect your memory until you began to fear too much looking would shake your faith. You were afraid this would render you incapable of protecting against Sam Indigo's suspicions, confuse you permanently, and even possibly lead you to a false confession. Still, you could resist all that except for the one little gap of possibility, which meant even you could not rule yourself out absolutely as Jock Hadley's murderer.

All the while you knew this was insane, yet this knowledge did not relieve you, because there was always the possibility the sane position was the one you thought insane. The protection of Stephen Trace was vanishing like the emperor's clothes. Sam Indigo was waiting. He did not need the murder of Jock Hadley to send you to jail. If evidence for that were not enough, he could arrest you for Florry Gates's statutory rape charge, which bided still, unmoved by statute of limitations. All it needed was to prove the identity of Peter Gregory upon Stephen Trace and what could be simpler than that? They could put you in jail,

Stephen Trace could not protect you from that. Crimes added up, real and possible, imagined and falsely attributed, all waiting in the person of Sam Indigo, along with the change in Jane Delaware, Miranda's demand, the rumors about Sharon, and the murder of Jack Rome to sink you twice seven miles down through the ocean's bitter surface to the bottom of its deepest part. No wonder you were anxious.

THIRTY THREE

When you landed at three, the sun was as bright as when you had taken off. No policemen noticed you, nor Miranda with her head shaded and eyes concealed. The customs men were indifferent, eager to move the line along. Jane Delaware took a taxi with Copzik, shook your hand and said, Thank you. Memories of a Venetian hotel room lingered in your groin, but her mind was elsewhere.

A taxi driver with Chinese face drove you fifty miles through brutal traffic shifting lane to lane. Routines of familiar life returned, the waterside house took shape, porch, windowed living room, upstairs corridor. Sharon Trace began to materialize. She was not Jane Delaware. Customary feelings, memories coming back strange and pale. In the taxi Miranda sat with mouth clamped shut and hands in little fists.

There was a white van with ladders, parked across the bridge. Scaffolding around the second story windows. You paid your driver and put your bags and Miranda's on the grass waiting for Mr. Jollop or Mrs. Heckel. No one came, so you took them up yourself. Inside with Miranda you stepped on a sheet, the entry way covered by rags. So was the living room. Painters worked on the walls. Miranda looked around. She showed no interest in this new place she had never seen before.

The chief painter's white mustache had blue streaks in it. We was ordered to paint the wakes. Woiks? No one said no one was coming. You asked where's Sharon? The lady? She went away.

This house belong to you? Lady said no one would be here. All tore up. Kinda hard to know what to do about that.

You would need certain rooms. You tried to be angry that someone ordered the house painted without your knowledge. Sharon, of course, but no one could have anticipated Jack Rome would die. Mrs. Heckel, Mr. Jollop, no sign of them either, taking time off, not expecting you. The bedroom was covered with painty rags, likewise Sharon's old guest room. Wet paint in the bathroom and kitchen. Still sullen, Miranda helped you move the heavy rags and clear spaces. You put her in Sharon's old room and yourself in the computer room. You sent out for a pizza.

Speculation about Sharon: she was visiting Mr. and Mrs. Grubbs in Cowland. Or Melly, living with the mother of David Trace and Jack Rome. Don't ask why she wouldn't tell you when she went away. Why Jack Rome was so firm about not letting her go with you. Luigi Pardon in Jane Delaware's gossip, try not to think of schemes and plots.

In the evening, you played Chinese checkers with Miranda among the painty rags, she depressed but less sullen. What had happened was not your fault, she guessed, but it was your responsibility to help her. What she expected of you tomorrow. First you must find out from Mr. Peck what provisions have been made for her. Go all the way to David Trace and Luigi Pardon if necessary. Don't let Jane Delaware get away, either. Make sure everyone knows: if they don't fulfill Mr. Rome's promise, they'll have a lawsuit on their hands. She asked you about lawyers and counted on you to find the best. As the evening advanced, she noticed the silence. A wife should be in the house when her husband comes home, she said. You should be angry and lay down the law. She went to bed early.

The morning news had an update on Jack Rome's death. A body believed to be his had washed up on the Coney beach. It was identified late last night by his grief-stricken wife. Funeral announcements to follow. Though Jane Delaware had called his death a murder, the announcer called it a suicide, he had dived the plane into the sea.

The grief-stricken wife could only be Jane Delaware, unless there were complications of duplication even you had not dreamed of. Conceive the scene in the morgue. The public Jane Delaware versus the secret Venetian one. Imagine her saying, Yes, that's him. It's less easy to see the smiting grief. Wiping her eyes. Still full of Jane Delaware's cool, her ineradicable irony, Stephen Trace wished he could hear in private her description of being the grief-stricken wife in the morgue, naming the cold heavy thing in the plastic bag with the reporters around. Unfortunately, the Venetian Delaware was occluded by the grim ruin over the ocean, ruin that a reporter could easily take for grief.

Mrs. Heckel showed up. She did not recognize Miranda Landis, introduced as Martha Lewis, nor did she know where Sharon was. You went to the office as Stephen Trace, leaving Miranda with Mrs. Heckel, feeling vaguely there were important protective things you ought to do. You postponed them and tried to lead a normal life, not unbalanced by events, sitting at your desk trying to catch up on your fortune. The flag at the Rome Building was at half staff. Your imagination played games with Jack Rome. You took him as remembered, black mustache, thin black socks, in his skyscraper office, and put him into a plastic bag, with reddened bloated arms and puffy drowned blue face. You drove his plane into the sea and broke his neck. Made a suicide out of him, imbued him with guilt and defeat, taught him a lesson before he died, a comedown: hey, I'm not as great as I thought. But your imagination wouldn't cooperate. What the hell, Jack Rome said. The lesson wouldn't take. He would blame it on enemies, jealousy, spite. Fuck you, bastards. Laughing and shaking his gloved fist, ha ha ha. No matter what evil he might be guilty of, you could not make Jack Rome depressed or remorseful. The suicide news was a cover-up.

A high iced white sky, no blue, no life. Heat in the Rome Building could not warm your imagination or Stephen Trace's, anticipating in its hunched shoulders the coming freeze of the city streets. As the long day spread out, Stephen Trace had not done anything for Miranda. You didn't want to, but as you didn't, anxiety grew again like yesterday in the plane, poisoning the ground water, rising up in every spring, a potion creating hallucinations of disaster, which you couldn't stop: if not Sam Indigo, God's Police, if not God's Police, Miranda, if not Miranda, Luigi Pardon and David Trace. Stephen Trace did not want to be questioned about anything. Looking out the office window, down at the rushy shoppers with their coat collars and scarves, you were ashamed of his fears. Why, you could remember like yesterday when there wasn't any Stephen Trace, slogging through countryside with no baggage, fresh from a river, not afraid of anything. That's what you thought.

In the late afternoon, the secretary buzzed, Mr. Pardon to see you. He came in, with a portfolio under his arm and holding out his hand to shake, good to see you again.

First let me present you with this. From his portfolio, a large glossy picture of himself taken twenty years ago, across which he had written in a large hand,

> *To my good friend Steven Trace,*
> *Luigi Pardon*

Too bad about Jack, ain't it? He was grinning like a joke. Not a joke though, his smile was for the camera, not an expression but a logo, trained into his face by years in public, the eyes squeezed tiny in their lids glittery blue. Visible in his eyes was a clear image of his cock. It was a swollen transparent cylinder which contained sparkling martini glasses and scallopini dinners and naked women reclining in luxury hotel suites heaving for joy of the fame jumping out at them through the great star's fly. Meanwhile he talked, winding up one preamble after another like a baseball pitcher. First dispose of Jack, the proper eulogies. Some would say he took the easy way out, some he did the wise and only thing, take your pick, cowardice or courage, who's to say in this life? Only God knows the answer, and Luigi would just as soon not second guess Him, he knew his place, only it did seem such a waste when eternal life was already almost within scientific reach. If Jack had consented to get himself frozen, all problems would pass in a couple hundred years.

You mentioned what Jane Delaware had said. Sabotage. Murder.

Rumors, rumors. May he rest in peace. I bring news, Luigi said. I got good news and bad news. Which you want first?

Give me the bad, it might unblock the anxiety freeze.

Luigi laughed, full of sympathy. Get it over with, right? Well, let me tell you. He began a long mysterious State of the Company speech, full of organization charts, which he took out of the portfolio and spread loosely across the desk. Boxes connected to each other by lines. In his beautiful New York Italianate speech carefully enunciated Luigi Pardon talked about inheritance and lines of succession, all invalid, he said. What was invalid was not clear to Stephen Trace nor why it was necessary to insist on it. Nor where the bad news was. Words about autocracy and tyranny. Overstepped prerogatives. Presumption and arrogance. Luigi Pardon pronounced his big words carefully, conscious of their dangers. He came to the top of the chart. Two boxes side by side with an equal sign between them. It's a duumvirate now, Luigi Pardon said. Doo-um-vuh-rate. Joint rule, equal responsibility, equal authority.

The names in the two boxes were:

$$\boxed{D.\ TRACE} \quad = \quad \boxed{L.\ PARDON}$$

Is this the bad news? Stephen Trace asked.

Luigi Pardon's cocky blue eyes flashed for the sheer pleasure of it. You may wonder why I am going into such detail. The bad news, such as it is, ain't personal. If it was up to Luigi, he'd leave you be. A company decision, and Luigi would like you to know personally he voted against it, but the will of the company comes first. He said it in such a cheerful way, with such a charming heavylipped smile, so full of all the old familiar places where the fundamental things of life go on and a kiss is just a kiss, he could not possibly mean harm.

Luigi Pardon scratched his shiny black hair, scrunched up his face, trying to figure out how to say it. Tell you straight, no beating around. The company wants to investigate Jack's personal manipulations of the company's assets.

Stephen Trace wondered what that had to do with you. (You knew what it had to do with you.)

Jack's loans. Yes? That includes Jack's loan to you.

Beg pardon? (Luigi Pardon liked a guy who could make a joke at a time like this.) No joke intended. What loan are you talking about?

Reading from a piece of paper: The company hopes to recover all assets wrongfully or carelessly disposed of. Will investigate Jack's personal loans. Not that you have anything to fear.

Jack made no loans to me.

No? Well, if he didn't the investigation will find out. The company seems to think he did. (They're mistaken.) Are they really? The company had in mind thirty million bucks loaned to Stephen Trace by Jack Rome plus interest and profits from investments.

That was no loan, that was a grant.

Luigi Pardon looked politely troubled. Is that so? He stroked again his suntanned oiled face, how smooth. His trouble unreal as his troubled grin. He was a melancholy love song, walking alone full of sorrow until I can walk with you, baby. The company wants to be sure the money loaned to you was not taken unfairly from others. Stockholders. Reduced budgets to make way for you. Charitable contributions cut back, the homeless at Christmas.

That money was given to Stephen Trace. Outright. Unconditional.

All Luigi Pardon wanted was peace. All the company wanted—for starters anyway—was a full understanding of the conditions of the loan. To that end, lawyers would be calling on him, and Luigi sure hoped Stephen would cooperate, it would make everything so much easier.

What do the lawyers want?

They want to ask questions. (About what?) About you. Ha ha. He laughed, then took it back, a little. They want to investigate the conditions of your loan, the real reasons for it. They'll want to know all about you, where you came from, what you did to deserve it. Unfortunately, there's nasty rumors going around, you wouldn't want them to be true.

What kind of rumors?

Ah you know, ugly things. Some drunk driving his car the wrong way on the Interstate smashing into a family with kids, killing them all. That kind of thing. Statutory rape, high school teacher with his own student, ain't that disgusting? If something like that proved true, think how it would besmirch the good name of Jack Rome, you wouldn't want that to happen, would you? Makes you wonder how such vicious stories ever get started.

Jack Rome knew everything there was to know about me.

Come on kid, relax. No one knows *everything*. Hopefully it will be routine and you won't lose much. Hopefully you'll cooperate and answer all questions, and it'll be nice for everybody.

The thought of investigation squeezed your heart. What will they do with this investigation?

Well, Luigi said. Hopefully. They want to check if the loan was in the best interests of the company, that sort of thing.

What if it isn't?

Let's hope that's not the case.

Nevertheless, what if it isn't?

Proceedings will begin.

What kind of proceedings?

Proceedings to recover. With the inevitable attendant publicity. Unless you prefer to settle.

I'm not afraid of publicity.

Publicity's incidental. Unavoidable, unfortunately. I don't mean that as a threat. Settling would be better.

Settling for what?

The company will always be willing to settle. If you want to avoid the inconvenience of an investigation.

Challenge him, you thought, ask him to produce an I O U signed by Stephen Trace. On the other hand, he probably has an I O U signed by Stephen Trace.

Luigi Pardon hated to think it would come down to a fight. He wanted to be fair. It wasn't as if Stephen Trace was born rich. It wasn't as if he earned his wealth by hard work or shrewd investment. Naturally it was difficult to think of giving it up without warning, Luigi understood that. But like he said, it wasn't as if Stephen Trace was used to it.

Gather useful words. Treachery. Extortion. Blackmail.

Think it over.

What am I supposed to think over?

The lawyers who'll come to see you. If you want my advice, I'd urge you to settle. The company is not the cold machine you might think. It does have a heart. Even if they foreclose, they won't leave you destitute. They'll be glad to give a person a reasonable allowance, if it's understood they're under no obligation to do so.

How much of an allowance?

The company will decide that after you reach agreement.

How can I agree if I don't know what I'm agreeing to?

Trust them.

Luigi Pardon's smile was fixed. He sang blues in the night and I'll never smile again and love is a many splendored thing and che sera sera. What will be will be, the future's not ours to see.

What kind of business is that? You must be crazy.

You'll want to think it over, that's taken for grant. Only take my advice, be careful. Luigi's eyes narrowed. Just between us. You don't want to get on the bad side of a company like that. The power they have, you wouldn't believe. You wouldn't believe how petty and vicious. It's criminal, pal. They're a bunch of hoods, believe me. There's no depth they could sink, killing people without remorse, I could name you names. I'm on your side, man. I wouldn't cross them if I was you. I'd do whatever they ask me to, I sure would.

Stephen Trace felt warned. He knew what the old songs meant when Luigi Pardon sang them. He wouldn't be stubborn. He just wanted time to reflect and consult his wife.

Your wife? Hey man, that's the good news I came to tell you about.

You have news about my wife?

My wife.

The orchestra stopped, moment of silence. What?

My wife, Luigi said. Sharon.

Sharon who?

Sharon Pardon. Formerly Trace. We got married at last.

Amazing, the good news in Luigi's face which he expected you to enjoy with him.

Who got married?

Me and Sharon. Your ex.

What? Sharon's my wife.

Naw man, that was a mistake.

Since when? Since forever.

You got to your feet, stand up to power face to face, though unfortunately along with his other virtues he was taller and heftier than you. Stop that.

I knew you never understood, Luigi said. It's too bad you didn't. Sharon Trace is my woman and always was, including when she was married to David Trace.

THIRTY FOUR

Two police cars were parked by your island bridge. The police-men arrested you when you went up to the porch. They read your rights and charged you with kidnapping Miranda Landis.

That's ridiculous, you said. Ask her.

She's gone back to her father, they said. The two in front were city policemen. The policemen behind them wore green uniforms with gold insignia: GP/JC. They had mild baggy middle aged faces.

You kidnapped her, you said. You pointed to the God's Police. She didn't want to go back to her father.

We don't know nothing about that, they said.

You went to jail in the Whitfield Municipal Building. They fingerprinted you, making it technically possible to link Stephen Trace to Peter Gregory, drunken highway killer, child seducer, suspect in the Jock Hadley case, false suicide. You made your legal telephone call to Mrs. Heckel, asking her to call Peck and Delaware. The heavy cage bars and lock of your clean tiled cell established your species kinship to lions and wolves. They also forced together the mutually repellent identities of Gregory and Trace.

It was David Trace who delivered you, big with his beard and concealed tiny ice blue eyes in the police office when you came out. This is stupid, he said. Your lawyers will fix it.

He drove you to your house. Mrs. Heckel gave a vivid description of the men in the green uniforms with brass crosses who took the girl away (Mr. Trace, you should have told me she was Miranda Landis). Who went quietly, not fighting or weeping, though disappointed, as if she knew her dreams were foolish and her destiny unique.

In which case, David Trace said, you won't get much support from her. He sat on your porch, giving advice in his once booming voice, quieted now for conspiracy purposes. Said he heard from Peck and came out to see were they pulling tricks on you already. Not so, this is only Landis. Landis you can deal with. He'll make a stink, but Fitch can handle it. What I came about is the others, the Rome folks, if you start hearing from them.

Maybe you'd heard from them already.

Luigi Pardon, eh? They'll try to intimidate you. Ignore them. They'll talk about claims, rights, dig up your past. Don't listen to them. You can't be blackmailed unless you want to be. They'll try to make you think they have criminal enforcers, ambushers around street corners, snipers watching your lighted windows. Disregard. Walk down the middle of the street, they can't do anything unless you react.

Repeat: They have no legal claim. See Fitch. There's nothing they can do you don't let them do.

You asked how to get Sharon back.

Sharon unfortunately is different. With Sharon it's not you versus Luigi, it's you versus Sharon. If she prefers Luigi, too bad.

She gave you no warning. Not a hint.

Like your marriage, right? No woo, no hard choice, no push and pull. Sharon was your geisha girl. Off she goes.

You were married to her once yourself.

So I was. One tends to forget one's marriages to Sharon.

Even if it was ephemeral it wasn't very considerate of her to disappear like that, leaving it up to Luigi to tell me.

He's trying to spook you. You're not totally unfamiliar with that principle yourself.

What will happen to Jane Delaware?

They'll try to scare her out too. But she'll fight back. I might marry her, myself. Why not? Political, consolidate power. Keep watching, it could be interesting the next few months.

I thought you were a socialist.

That's in the past, pal.

You went bravely to Jack Rome's funeral to stand up for yourself, as David Trace said. Stephen Trace put on his dark suit, rich for mourning, shined shoes like steel, weighing Anonymous swimming the sidestroke against Nobodyatall feeling a bullet between his shoulder blades. Looking for the place, a small church in Westchester, hard to find, afraid he would be late. All the parked Rolls Royces and limousines blocking up the residential streets in front of the tudor houses with their leaded windows: he walked under the wintry bare shade trees expecting ambush from behind a child's tricycle in a garage door. David Trace's advice had missed its effect, something else had slipped through the current of his words. At the church, people in funeral clothes, handkerchiefs in breast pockets, no one noticed Stephen Trace. Through the open doors between groups of people who looked at him as they made way, he felt his muscles contract against bullets from behind. Inside, the church opened up, the high stone arches, the modern stained windows depicting saints and children in colored sunlight. A fine new painting of Christ at ease upon his cross. Carved wood pulpit and candles and glinting brass and red velvet and gold. The church was full of prosperity, a clean modern incarnation of tradition. Trusting not even Jack Rome revolutionaries would shatter a bullet in this sanctuary air, he sat not too far forward and let himself rest too. The enclosed air heard the people coming in, converting their feet on the pavement, their whispers, into an uncategorized hiss. Then organ music, dreaming listlessly through hollow tubes. You heard your journey echoing and fading in the tubes all the way back to the river.

After a while a racket in the back. Coffin covered in an American flag trundling on wheels down the aisle, followed by privileged mourners. There's Jack, processed and packed: you tried to x-ray into the box—still not convinced this was not a trick, Jack alive hidden away somewhere getting ready for a different name, a new life. There was Luigi Pardon in a black suit with a veiled woman in black clutching his arm. Behind Luigi another woman also in black next to a big man with a beard. That was David Trace, dressed up like a president with a heavy executive front. The woman with Luigi was Sharon. Stare, project, make thought heard: Sharon! Look over here. They were watching the coffin, making sure what was inside did not get out.

Stephen Trace lived through the funeral. Speeches and music, rising and sitting. That great heavy flag-covered thing and the black hats of Jane Delaware and Sharon Trace in the front row. The stained glass windows which brightened and faded as the clouds moved. It was a chamber of silence, in which silence ate everything up. It ate up the speeches and music. It ate up the great rush of catastrophe. It ate up the crash of Jack Rome's plane in the sea. It ate up Luigi Pardon's threats, the jail cell, God's Police, the disappeared wife. It ate up the skyscraper office and the check for thirty million and the great stone house on the edge of the Sound. It ate up, in fact, Stephen Trace's whole life and that of his forebears and ancestors from the time they first scrambled out of the sea.

They trundled the squeaky coffin out again, and the people followed crowding down the aisles, Stephen Trace among them.

Keeping inconspicuous. He wanted to see Sharon or Jane Delaware. The person closest to him in this life, the one he could trust most—either one would do. In the chilly outside sunshine, waiting at the sidewalk for the row of pennanted limousines to take them to the cemetery, they stood together in their black dresses and veils while their escorts at the curb signaled the drivers. Stephen Trace went forward, he went direct to Sharon: Sharon, my Sharon.

You got a little smile out of her, a glance up at Luigi, who was peering around over heads, then suddenly a big overt shrug, hands out palms up, and a half-amused grimace with plain meaning, What else could I do? That was her goodbye, after which she turned under Luigi's arm and got into the car. The next moment Jane Delaware, who had seen that. Her smile was sardonic, with her own kind of shrug (That's life), followed by a little fist no higher than her chin, which meant something or other, before she too was gone.

Someone at your side, looming close whispering, David Trace: Notice how light the coffin looked when they lifted it into the hearse?

What?

His eyes twinkled merrily like Santa Claus through his beard.

What do you mean?

What do you think? He was gone. You tried to follow but he vanished in the crowd.

Left alone among strangers, you noticed by the church door a tall man with a bald head, back turned, who you were quite sure had been looking at you. You stared, but he refused to turn again, disguising himself by shaking hands with people he couldn't know. You drove off quaking, caught between wondering what had brought Sam Indigo back and what had happened to Jack Rome's body, if David Trace were right. You heard definite words in your head: This is the end. I don't mean you actually thought it was the end. I just mean you heard words saying it was.

Two views of the same events. In one, everything is logical, decisions are made after thinking things through. In the other, it is a flight of panic.

Logical panic. In the car after the funeral, logical and calm, you thought seriously about moving away. Not to fight Luigi Pardon as David Trace suggested; you'll resist if he attacks, but if they don't want you here, you had no reason to stay. The plan was to see Mr. Fitch, line him up, and then perhaps an automobile trip to scout homes, San Francisco, Seattle, New Orleans. You could do it, you had done it before, you were expert in starting over.

Then there was the diversion of your course from the funeral back to the house: you came within sight of the house across the little bridge and quite suddenly decided to go to the apartment instead, which was perfectly logical since the house was still full of painty rags—except for the non-logical images of police cars and kidnapped women and bald detectives. So you headed for the city, thinking sanely this will be more convenient for seeing Mr. Fitch tomorrow, and maybe you don't want to keep the house anyway if you intend to start a new life.

Yet thinking while driving into the city, if the apartment was booby trapped. As he turned into his elegant street, drove into the private garage, walked flinching on the sidewalk, greeted the old doorman his friend, stepped flinching into the elevator, unlocked flinching the possibly wired door, stepped in with hunched shoulders, looked cautiously around in his own flat, your Stephen Trace was bolstering himself with Hamlet thoughts: if it be now, 'tis not to come; if it be not to come, it will be now;

if it be not now, yet it will come. You chose not to go out again that day. When it got dark you pulled the blinds. You kept the volume of the television low.

Now you think of it, perhaps there were three levels of rationality. Between the calm plans at the top and the visions of crazy fright at the bottom, was another motive for what you were going to do, mysterious, rational and irrational, which you remember knowing without knowing you knew, never quite clear but reasonable in its own way.

You packed as if planning a trip. You were planning a trip, but may not have realized it until you found yourself packing. This was the trip you would take after seeing Mr. Fitch. You would drive to other cities, live in hotels, and talk to real estate agents. You started to pack your suitcase, but something said a suitcase would be inappropriate. You packed your backpack instead. Perhaps you didn't know why a suitcase would be inappropriate, for you were stuck a while trying to decide between suitcase and backpack. Whatever reasons you had either way were overridden by feelings of inappropriateness based on thoughts you couldn't remember, which you would have to recover if you were to judge the question properly. When the backpack won, you weren't sure why, but in the morning since you had packed it, you dressed for it—heavy sweater, mountaineering jacket, jeans—without reviewing the reasons, since you had already made the decision and didn't want to go through it again.

You looked in your wallet and counted your cash, about two hundred dollars. With Stephen Trace's credit cards, you wouldn't have needed more cash, yet you intended to go to the Rome Building anyway, to see Mr. Peck about something or other. Unless you were confusing him with Mr. Fitch. You may have been supposing, at the level of fears, that Luigi Pardon would freeze your assets before you could stop him, and therefore you should get cash while you could. Whatever it was, you suddenly decided not to see either Mr. Peck or Mr. Fitch, the given reason being that you weren't properly dressed. A backpack was inappropriate for the Rome Building. You had also shaved off Trace's beard in the night and might not be recognized.

Why you decided not to take the car is harder to reconstruct. It was suspicion of the garage attendant, his paranoid links to Luigi Pardon. No, you're forgetting the logical step in between which gave it sense. You didn't take the car because you were going to the Rome Building to see Mr. Fitch or Mr. Peck, and it was more convenient to take a taxi than to park your car in midtown Manhattan. That was why you didn't take the car, a reason disconnected from the fact you had just decided not to see Mr. Fitch or Mr. Peck, there being no need until you got back.

You were going in search of something, that much was clear. Presumably a new place to live—as we have seen—unless it was something else, information you could bring back to Mr. Fitch or Mr. Peck or some appropriate person.

In any case, you couldn't sit around forever postponing your departure. It took a gut of courage to go out finally with the backpack and the keys in your pocket.

If there had been a man in the corridor watching, he was gone now. The doorman said, Going on a trace, Mr. Trip? The man on the bench was reading *Hustler Magazine*. You walked fast to the corner. No one shot you in the back. You went past the parking garage, not looking at Pardon's accomplice. Around the corner and down into the subway. You waited up against the wall for the train. The tracks below the platform like a river, you had a certain fear of falling in. The train came soon.

In retrospect it looks like you simply scrammed out of there. You left Stephen Trace behind. Also his house and his apartment along with furniture, silverware, clothes. Left to rats and vultures.

Also money, securities, certificates, if anyone who wanted possession could forge his signature. People too, with names like Jollop and Heckel, if not Trace and Delaware who had abandoned him, without even a note this time to throw them off the track. Scrammed out of there, heading West.

But that ignores the fact you had a purpose and did not think, at least at the start, you weren't coming back. You took the subway because you felt it inconvenient and awkward just then to encounter the Mafia attendant—and perhaps backed by a secondary reason, such as that it would be more modest for you to accomplish your mission on foot, without the ostentatious protection of an expensive car. Next, you took the bus because it was easier and less ostentatious than going all the way out to LaGuardia for a flight.

You remember that. You remember also later, head leaning, jiggling, against the pale green window of the bus as a dawn light began to distinguish brown fields, rolling slopes, dark shadowy barns, roaring along the turnpike, everything dim and obscure through the dirty glass. You saw the green light in the sky. Soon they would wonder what happened to Stephen Trace—you wondered how long it would take them to notice. They would poke into his apartment and house, getting permission if needed, or not getting permission, looking for a way to get around having him declared legally dead or a way to have him so declared. You remember thinking about that, though you had no intention then, as far as you knew, not to return as planned. Thinking, just because Jack Rome died is no reason for Stephen Trace to die too.

Prester Truitt. Gulley Hamilton.

Saying, My name is Stephen Trace, millionaire. I'm not running away. I'll be back. Just a little trip to settle my stomach. Saying this to combat the feeling of ugly familiarity in the world you had forgotten. No one, looking at this man in his expensive jeans, with his well-stocked pack, could guess the variety in his diversified life. Arnold Pettigross.

Lack of sleep. Birthpangs with stress. You remember getting off the bus at noon in a small town, avoiding the bus's destination. Impulse, no good reason. Arthur Gratis. Questions faded under heavy eyelids in the mid afternoon sun, as you sat on a bench at a truck stop.

The following incident is worth mentioning. You stood by the highway with your pack on your back. A car stopped with three young men. Brakes squealing, they grinned, you didn't like their looks. You tried to wave them on: Thanks anyway.

What's the matter, don't you want a ride? So you changed your mind, you got into the car, sat in the back seat, next to a guy with blond hair, the other two in front. You noticed the adams apple of the guy next to you. They drove fast.

Don't you like our car? It's a fine car.

I like your pack. Let me see it.

You held the pack in your lap. What's the matter, don't you trust us? You handed the pack over to the guy in front. He opened it and went through it, while the blond guy in back leaned over to watch. Hey you, cut that out.

Look at these clothes. Wish I had shoes like that.

What? Give them to me. They're mine, I need them. You don't need them.

Say mister, what's your name?

Mitchell Grape.

Mitchell Grape, ha ha. How much money you got? Not much. Let's see your idea of not much.

I don't have much. You said that. You showed your wallet with a hundred and fifty dollars left. The man with the adams apple took the hundred and fifty. Hey I need that, it's all I've got.

Give him a percentage. The guy with the adams apple gave you back a twenty. Thanks. Now we'll let you out here.

The car stopped. Can I have my pack please?

The man in front held the pack out the window. Come round and get it. You hesitated, not wanting to step out of the car without it. The man behind nudged you, and you stepped out. You went to the front window, and the motor roared. The car leapt ahead and sped down the road. You saw the man in front waving your pack at you through the front window as they went. You tried to remember the license plate.

PART FOUR

Brown and Beyond

THIRTY FIVE

On fine days from your basement room you saw across the rooftops and over the Sound (a different Sound) the mountains to the west, snowy and hazy in the clouds. Container ships moved toward the sea. Big green ferries slid into the harbor, to the docks colorful with glass and shops and flags, walkways and entertainments and places to sit. Your cab climbed the city hills, the steep residential streets, with sudden views, the sudden blue of the Sound or lake, sudden snow extricating from the sunny clouds on distant slopes. You knew your way, the necessary turns, the streets that will take you through. Each day you sewed the city together again, from the flaglined wharves to the city center, the space tower, zoo and rose garden, the hills, houses, and hotels.

From the bed you looked out at the distance of the night. You shared the apartment with Bonnie Brown, who refused to believe your life. She called you Mitch.

There was a name, won with some difficulty, on your cab driver's license, as also on the certificate posted for the passengers with your picture. The same name was on your mailbox and voter's registration card and in the telephone book. As for Bonnie living with you in the furnished flat, she had a nice round face and short black hair and sharp black eyes. You met her when she asked you as a taxi driver to carry some boxes into her apartment. She was a solicitor for the World Organization of Good People, a small charitable outfit that contracted with other agencies to collect money in the neighborhoods for good causes. She went out afternoons and evenings persuading people in houses to give.

She didn't believe your life, though she expected you to believe hers, her lovers and former husband. About Jay, with whom she had recently broken, who had been her whole world. You met her parents, looked at her albums, discussed her grandparents. But though you tried to be as candid as she, she thought everything you told her was a joke.

The first night in her apartment, after the passionate part, you told about the river and hitchhiking without a name. Lying on her stomach without clothes, sucking on a piece of candy, she grinned and said, Come on now, tell me the *truth*.

It is the truth.

She moved into your apartment anyway. It may be the mistake of my life, she said. You're probably a con man, but you only seem to be you. It will save rent. She was a little chubby, warm and sturdy and somewhat brisk. She went around the apartment with nothing under her bathrobe and got a bang out of sex without lingering over it.

No longer as afraid of your former lives as you used to be, you said all she need do is call the Uptown High School in Cincinnati and ask about Peter Gregory. She looked at you with her realistic eyes. So I'll find out Peter Gregory drowned in the river, she said. It won't prove a thing.

When you told her about Jack Rome and about Stephen Trace's house on the water, she laughed outright. That's too much. You expect me to believe he gave you thirty million bucks, and you lost it?

You didn't lose it. As far as you knew you still had it.

Wow. Why are you driving a cab, for heaven's sakes?

As far as you knew (explaining this, you yourself were shocked, as if you had been asleep while the house burned down), you still had title to Stephen Trace's wealth and were free to reclaim it any time.

Well goodness gracious, she said, throwing her arms around you. We sure could use a few million around here.

So why don't you believe me?

It doesn't fit, Mitch, it's not you. The you in your story is bold, romantic, antisocial, selfish. The you I know is ordinary, cautious, decent, human. Why would someone like you jump into the river? And why would you abandon all that money without a fight?

You jumped because you were ashamed, and you ran because you were scared. You saw the shadow on her good natured face, wondering what kind of crazy she was stuck with. She objected to your women. People like Sharon Trace don't exist. Women like Jane Delaware don't jump into bed with timorous men like you. If they do exist, she disapproves.

You exist, you said.

Of course I exist, I should say I exist, indeed I do.

The obvious way to prove yourself would be to get Mr. Peck to send you a check, but you postponed that. (That's because you were still afraid, rightly, of being pursued.) To make Gregory's jump more plausible, you told her about the Sebastian accident. But she looked so hard and doubtful that you couldn't develop it. You couldn't tell her how it felt or what harried you, because her stare made you too conscious of your words trying to tell.

She said, You're too wrapped up in yourself. You live in yourself like a cage, a captured bird, you drive around in your taxi and think about yourself. You need to get out and do something constructive. Live for others. Face up to the miseries of the world. Hold up your head and say, I'm doing my bit.

She read you things from the newspapers in the evening to convince you of the miseries of the world. There was always something. War in Yugoslavia, war crimes, atrocities. Gang wars in Los Angeles. How hard for a black boy growing up in the city to make it to adulthood. Homeless people under the bridge, with signs, I'll Work for Food, people who used to be like you or me. To please her you joined the World Organization of Good People. Go out and persuade. Touch people's consciences. You went soliciting for starving people in Africa. You did this on weekends and when you weren't driving a cab.

You had pictures of starving black children, lying on the sand with mantis legs. A haggard woman, wrapping a dead child in a white cloth. To the other woman who stood listening inside her screen door, you said, It's happening this chronological minute in this contiguous world. Real people are burying each other because they don't have enough to eat.

Don't preach to me, the woman said. I have to pick and choose, I can't give to everything. She asked what you were doing for the drugged youth in this country. Can you believe, while you're trying to squeeze money out of me, in our own downtown ten blocks from here, doomed young men and women are lying in the park in a stupor?

A man said, Your cause is good and so is mine. Too many people, he said. Waste and poison everywhere. The rain forests are dying that take the carbon dioxide out of the air and restore the sweet oxygen by which we live. Our stinky machine breath infects the upper atmosphere. It used to be a lovely world. Let me take your name, a small check will do.

You went out with Bonnie in her car to assigned neighborhoods. Park the car and take the street, she on one side, you the other. With documents to show, horror pictures, your clipboard for signing membership forms. You rang the doorbell, and when the woman came, you spoke politely, identified the Organization and gave your spiel. Yes ma'am you live a modest living, we all do, which makes it hard to realize how rich we are compared to the rest of the world. We look over the world like a skyscraper not seeing the people in the streets. We feel guilty, yes ma'am, that's what I want to talk about. You don't need give much, but if you do, you'll feel a lot better, you will.

Bonnie used the same line on you. Don't you feel better? she said. Certainly better than in your imaginary mansion on Long Island Sound.

It wasn't imaginary.

All the better better.

Unfortunately, you had trouble imagining what you were trying to make other people imagine. You tried to feel the outrage you wanted them to feel. The pictures were too familiar, the words too routine. While you were trying to convince the woman at the screen door of the reality of starving people, you saw the reality of the screen door, the peeling paint on the door frame, the woman listening inside a little scared, on the edge of dangerous anger, a tense and touchy moment while you tried to talk fast enough to prevent her from slamming the door in your face and giving you another existential shock.

You were waiting in your taxicab by the hotel, and this large man with a beard got in, going to the airport. He reminded you of somebody, but you didn't get a good look, the big body, light brown beard, small shaded eyes. David Trace? You tried to get a better look at the gate while he counted his change. He glanced at you and then you were sure, yet he gave no sign, which made you doubt. The mysterious magic of recognition, so intuitive and sure, faltered into reason and inquest.

But then this man, after giving you your tip (which was large) tossed his newspaper onto the seat beside you. "Read this," he said and hurried off through the door.

Why should you? It was open to an inside page of a New York paper, where you saw:

ROME ASSOCIATE SLAIN IN STREET

A man identified as Stephen Trace, 36, of Whitfield, Conn., was shot to death early this morning as he was leaving the Giovanni Siciliani Restaurant on 14th Street.

Stop there, read no more until you find the strangeness of this news. Who was Stephen Trace? When you remembered, you read the rest:

According to police the killing appears to have been a gangland execution. The victim had residences in Manhattan and Whitfield. He was reportedly a friend of the late Jack Rome and was said to have left behind a considerable estate.

According to police spokesperson Amanda Maynard, Trace left the restaurant about 12:30. Shots were heard in the street a few moments later, and his body was found on the sidewalk. Police believe he was shot from a passing car. No witnesses have come forward.

The body was identified tentatively on the basis of documents found on it. Identification was confirmed at the morgue by Mrs. Luigi Pardon, who had been previously married to Mr. Trace, and by Jane Delaware, widow of Mr. Rome. Little is known at this time about his life, though records show he was born in Brooklyn, and according to his wife he earned a degree at Harvard University.

This news stayed on the seat beside you through the day while you tried to understand. You had bifurcated and left behind a mortal residue. Your soul was a traveler from one body to another, with an inadequate memory seal. You were dead, and all this was but hallucination of the taking off.

In the reality of city traffic, red lights, stops and starts, with real passengers and their moods, rudeness, politeness, you seemed alive and real enough yourself, but your memory was insane—or not your own. If it wasn't yours, how did it get into your head? The question infuriated you. As you coped with customers' travel needs, you tested your memory whenever you could, measuring its solidity, wondering what solidity was. The present was solid. The woman behind the screen door, shutting the main door in your face, was solid. The starving children in Africa were not. Your house on Long Island Sound had been solid but now you weren't so sure. There was a difference between solidity and reality: the taxicab and the streets were solid, but your own solidity in the cab as you drove was unreal since a small deviation could crash everything into metal and glass.

After a while you realized that the death of Stephen Trace was an invention of high officials in the Rome empire. With a special effort by David Trace to make sure the story reached you. The reason for this invention was mysterious, but before evening you figured that out too.

You showed the paper to Bonnie. Here, you said, you don't believe me, read this.

But Mitch dear, she said, this doesn't prove you were Stephen Trace, it proves you weren't.

What could you say? You remembered Jane Delaware wondering who they had really killed under the name of Angelo Firenze. But try telling Bonnie Stephen Trace's death was faked.

Try making her believe someone else had been killed and then named, falsely and for definite purposes, after you.

She laughed.

Explain it again. After death, assets freeze, rigor mortis, legal procedures. Stephen Trace died carelessly without a will, no relatives; the Rome empire has found a way to get it back.

Sardonic Bonnie: You're off the hook. Now you don't have to come up with the money.

She didn't understand the world. Someone had died for you: some poor jerk whose anonymous death was doubtless serving a double purpose. Your two women, whatever their motives, had cooperated. You could say they killed you, for Stephen Trace could never return alive. Equally, they saved you, letting the poor hoodlum be sacrificed out of Giovanni's Siciliani Restaurant so you could escape. A man had died. That was serious and real, leaving no reason to suppose they would choose a second surrogate if Stephen Trace refused to accept the first.

To Bonnie you said, Why can't you believe what I tell you? Because, she said, you're Mitchell Grape to me, with a small chin and half balding curly yellow hair and squinting eyes, and I can't convert you into Peter Gregory or Murry Bree or Stephen White or Stephen Trace. None of those names fits.

You stopped telling Bonnie about your life, but she didn't notice. Talking to herself as much as to you, she would say, it's not normal to chop up your life like that. Mitch dear. She couldn't imagine being you. How can you bear the losses? she would say. In her life everything that happened was precious, even the bad things. She kept albums and scrapbooks and an uninterrupted diary from the age of eight because she couldn't bear to lose anything. Whereas you just cast things off. How can you live with yourself? she would ask.

She decided you had escaped from a mental institution. It took hold of her, she believed it for a while, pretending she didn't mind. With great sympathy, she played her part making life comfortable for you, with smiling and wheedling eyes, conspiratorial, on your side against the cold sane doctors and the jailer nurses. She would catch you when you were most relaxed, after sex in bed, whispering in your ear, it's all right, there there. Dark, her head nuzzled close, her hair on your neck, it's nothing to be ashamed of. That soft hair on your shoulder, warmth of the body close, how could anyone be sure he was not insane, that everything in life was not an illusion, the universe a dream? What you had told her was what you knew, but how could you know what you knew was true? If it was hallucination, you wouldn't know.

With time passing and getting used to you, she gave you more credit. A better effort to understand. She projected her imagination into the Gregory soul after the Sebastian accident. How you must have felt. She could imagine it, yes, the shame, the problem of waking up and finding this thing you had done which wouldn't go away, stuck permanently to your conscience. The horror of not being able to escape from yourself. She was full of sympathy, except that there was always a *but* or a *nevertheless* coming while she spoke, and you waited for it. *But.* Time has passed, she would say, events have run their course, it's over. You paid the price, Gregory or somebody. You have proven your capacity for shame, demonstrated you're no villain. Sebastians have done. Florry Gates has gone on to other things. The children of Peter Gregory are growing up. No one cares what you did.

Out of the newspapers she picked up the importance of *integrating* the personality. Got it from the psycho columns, the advice and medical people. Bring those conflicting parts of yourself together. Mental health, she said, when all your parts work together as one. She had something in mind. Action, maybe, radical. You wondered what it was. It made you nervous. You didn't want to know, you were afraid to ask.

In the corridor of a slummy apartment building with a urine smell, this happened. You were canvassing alone, and you had worked up to the top and back to the main floor by the mailboxes and were about to go out when this kid came behind you.

Get much? he asked.

No, you said.

What's it for?

Starving children in Africa.

I'm starving too, the kid said. You looked at him. He was big, olive skinned, he had a smile and a wool cap, his cheeks smooth and plump.

You look pretty healthy to me.

Fuck you. He grabbed your arm and pinned it behind your back. Another kid came out from under the stairs.

Give it over, one said.

It's for the starving children in Africa.

Give it over to the starving children in America. They took the bag out of your hand and threw your papers on the floor. Pinned you against the wall and took your wallet. Laughed.

Dragged you into the back, through a door. You struggled, tried to break loose. They held you, pinned you, unbalanced you. Down back steps out to a frozen yard inside a fence. Kicked in a basement door into the room below, clotheslines, stick chairs, cement floor, cold.

Knocked you to the ground, pinned you by the knees, two of them, big greenish faces looking down at you, eyes full of spite.

Spy, one said.

What do you mean?

You're a fucking spy. Poking around trying to find none of your business. Who sent you?

Nobody sent me. I'm collecting for the Organization.

What organization? They sent you, snoop around, sneak into our houses. You stay out of here, see?

Give you something to remember us by. Whack him one.

Kicked the side of the head. Kicked in the ribs.

Cut it out, I didn't do anything to you.

Whack him again for that. Keep out of here. Nobody wants you around here.

The starving children of Africa.

Ain't no starving children in Africa, it's the starving children in America. It's the starving children of America kicking the shit out of you. Don't come around here no more, okay?

I have no intention.

Don't tell no one neither. Got your name and address. Mitchell Grape. You tell anyone, we come round and kill you. Kill you dead. Got that, Mitchell Grape?

Got it.

You worthless, see? The world's a hateful place, no room for you. Hateful, don't forget.

I won't.

Say it after me, The world's a hateful place.

The world's a hateful place.

You staggered back into the alley, around front, Bonnie's car, home, the doctor and pain killer and a slow easing back to normal, with deep injury inside, which gradually healed, slowly as these things so far always had, but eventually would not.

You wanted to quit the organization, but Bonnie said it was important to stick with it like getting back on the horse to restore your confidence.

*

One day she said that if you were really Peter Gregory (and by now she almost believed it), you should go home and clear up your accounts. As if your whole effort since the river were a mistake. She talked on. Time to think about your life, she said. You had a wife, you had children. They meant something to you. People can't live divided from themselves. You need to heal yourself. Close your wounds. Bring your divided selves together. A reunion.

She was inspired, and you tried to cooperate, a little inspired too. Something was happening. A nostalgic sadness crept into her tone, elegiacal. You thought it was rhetoric, for she was always a little melodramatic, but it caught your attention just the same. You must go back to where you began. Look up Peter Gregory—that's how she put it—tell him he's forgiven. See his wife, tell her too, even if she is married to Louis the Lover. Don't interfere, just let her know. And the children, you must bring them back into your scope. They'll have some forgiving to do, but that's what you need. You need an ordeal.

It had not occurred to you that it was possible. The idea was exhilarating. Why not? Go clean up the woods, then return and marry Bonnie. You saw boundaries falling down between everybody, Gregory and Grape and Trace. If you could reclaim Gregory, perhaps you could also reclaim a little of Trace's money, despite his death. A little courage, a little assertion. All that you had feared, that had driven you into the river and out, into disguises and shields, had vanished in the simple passage of time. The Sebastian case was over, paid for by Murry Bree and Stephen Trace and Mitchell Grape. Florry Gates had her life to lead. So did Linda.

It would have been more exhilarating if she hadn't sounded so sad and religious. How lingeringly she looked at you. You reassured her. I'll go, you said, but I'll be back. I'll pay my respects, mend my fences, come right back to you. She kissed you and said nothing.

Keeping herself to herself—you never suspected, never dreamed. You came back from your taxi rounds the very next day, just when you were most invigorated by confidence in her support for you to do this life-changing thing—you came back at that moment and found the apartment stripped. The place was bare, as if to be redecorated. Everything of hers was gone except her bathrobe forgotten on the hook of the bathroom door, and nothing belonged to you. For a second time you had returned unwarned to an emptied house, cold and terrifying. And a note.

She had gone back to Jay. Nobody was more important to her than Jay. He wanted her back, and she had no resistance. It was fun living with you, she said. I never knew what crazy thing you'd tell me next. But I don't know who you are, and you can't expect me to stay when Jay wants me.

You had a reaction. Revulsion like a storm out of the west, tearing up ground. Loathing. The city, your life in this apartment and around, hateful. Driving a cab, vile. Detest the Organization and soliciting to alleviate the world's misery. Revulsion against Bonnie and being good, and integrating yourself. Disgust with skepticism. Revulsion against doubt and every thing that set itself up to be doubted. Hatred of every criticism and objection one person might make to anything else. You despised contempt and all kinds of dislike, whatever they were. Abhorred divisions, every separation, every distinction between one thing and another. You loathed the necessity of naming because every name made a distinction between one thing and the rest, and you hated distinctions. Your own names and all names. Hated the distance that separated places, distances you would have to travel again, as you hated the differences in time that placed one day before another and put everything that had happened out of reach. You hated the distinction between life and death and between male and female and between young and old and between good and bad. You hated the thought process that kept isolating everything by putting it into words, words that never satisfied or soothed but only stirred you up and agitated and riled you with the implication that there were other words around that could do better if you could only find them.

All this converged into a peculiarly overwhelming hatred of this room, the blank window by your bed that looked out in daytime over housetops to mountains across water but now on a rainy night showed nothing but black. You hated it and its walls and the flimsy pictures you and Bonnie had clipped from magazines to hang on those walls.

Then suddenly as if it were all the same, revulsion was identical to euphoria, as you realized what was open to you. I've got to go, you said. Where? you asked. Ah, that's a secret. But you felt it like force, the place you had to go next, waiting for you. You'd recognize it when you got there.

THIRTY SIX

Mean and cold, November. The long bus ride is no fun. The fields full of dead sticks, the hills gray, night villages with premature Christmas lights, false cheer for nomads in the shortening days, lowering sun, dimming light. The bus grinds across the desert, through burned-out mountains, across bad lands and flat lands and exhausted prairies waiting for snow in the sky. The sky follows the bus, glooming down on it.

In the early afternoon, day before Thanksgiving, Peter Gregory struggles into the bus station of the city where he used to live. Wearing a heavy plaid jacket, with a small bag of minimal belongings. The day is sunny, but the light is cold, ice at high altitudes. The bus station is at the edge of downtown, with a view of the downtown skyscrapers across the parking lots.

All the way Peter Gregory has been trying to decide what to do when he arrives, and he still doesn't know. This once home town of his has no center now. The apartment where he last lived, hateful to remember. The house he shared with his Gregory family, are they still there? Linda and his disinherited children, would they be happy to see him?

He finds a telephone book in the bus station. Trembling with courage, he looks up Gregory, Peter. Not listed. Okay, the surprise would have been if it were. No Mrs. either. Nor Linda. Several Gregory, L, with wrong middle initials. It means they've gone. Dispersed into the United States of America, where they dissolve. Not necessarily yet, though. He tries Louis the Lover.

Here's news: Hamilton, Louis, is also missing. That's a surprise. Louis the Lover has left town—unless he has died or taken an unlisted number. More than ever putting them out of reach. The forlorn feeling is less than the relief, such a relief he wonders, maybe he didn't come to see them after all.

Taxi now? Where to? Alternative destinations occur to him vaguely, none satisfactory. Skip the taxi, he'll walk, though he'd never have walked when he lived here. Walk where? Uptown High School? Though not friendly, it's the only sure place, decide the rest when he gets there. Uptown then.

How long, two and a half years? What he sees shapes his memory. The city has returned to mind, but the real view changes everything slightly. More sky, that's it. He walks into the upper downtown, past the granite courthouse, the Catholic Church, across Central Parkway, up Vine through the slum part with the old architecturally interesting but shabby buildings, clutter in the streets and broken windows. Up the long hill toward the school, passed by laboring cars and buses.

With always the chance someone will see him and reconstruct his disappearance. Peter Gregory is ready for that, he knows what he'll do: accept the surprise, respond to the greeting, make to the old friend or acquaintance the necessary confession, here I am, I misled you. Such a confession was not his purpose, but it was an implicit consequence of resuming his name.

When someone finally recognizes him, it will start a chain: the first surprise, the puzzled greetings, then a campaign to spread the news. He could imagine former friends and colleagues coming in a line to shake his hand. It was possible the chain had already started. Someone already might have seen him from a car and sent word, so they'd be waiting when he got to school.

Near the top, he comes within a block of the apartment he never thought of as home. He detours to see what the hateful old place looks like. The street answers his memory except, like the rest of the town, for the increased openness, the magnifying sky. Approaching, remembering Mrs. Gumbert the landlady, he feels old guilts gathering and hunches his shoulders to weather the abuse from Jock Hadley on his porch across the street. But Jock Hadley is dead, and Peter Gregory can't find his house, lost in the configuration of this block, strange absence in the heart of the familiar, a gap in the gestalt. It takes a while to understand the house is truly gone, replaced by a yard with a dog kennel.

Still he meets no one, and in a few moments he passes the edge of the university campus on the familiar route he used to take to school. Past the bookstore and the college tavern, not many people here this last day before Thanksgiving, when college students cut classes to extend their holiday. Across to the Uptown High School opposite the campus like a medieval castle, turrets and arches. All the classroom windows are lit although school is out for the day. The small groups of students around the door and on the walks are a new generation, unlikely to recognize him. Inside, his former colleagues are still at their desks, finishing up for the day and holiday, but Gregory is not going in there. If there is any sure way to begin recognition, surprise, greeting, unroll the chain, it would be to go inside and present himself, but he won't do that. He waits for the recognition, he walks about expecting it, but he won't force it. That's his plan, not to force but wait and let it happen, as it surely will.

So he walks by the main door of the High School and below what used to be his classroom windows, with lights for the gray afternoon and someone hired in his place, but no one is looking out, and he is past. Then like the crisis after another goal achieved, again the vacant feeling, What next? and recognizing his next ordeal he descends behind the school to the most familiar of abandoned residential streets on the slope, all the while again trembling with courage. He rounds the corner and looks where the street goes down to the busy avenue, and sees the house third on the right, just as if no time had passed. Heart clutching now but still driving himself, he moves on down the opposite sidewalk, looking at it. Lights upstairs. There are many possible reasons why it is not in the telephone book. She could have married someone, if not Louis the Lover someone else. She could have taken an unlisted number. There's a car he does not recognize in the driveway. She could have bought a new car in the interim and very likely did. He stands opposite, looking up, where the house stands a few steps above the street. He imagines someone looking out at him or looking at him from somewhere else, but he sees no one. He waits, no one appears, no one comes, though the light upstairs and another in the back, in the kitchen, continue to burn. If she's back there, as she normally would be at this time. Then he notices an infant tricycle on the front stoop, a stuffed goose, small child equipment, full of implication, inviting inference. His heart lifts and sinks. Again he must choose. To go up to the door and inquire—or expose himself. He waits, undecided. Nothing happens. He waits long enough to be afraid someone might notice and call the police. He's waited enough, he says, turns around and goes back up to the corner, thinking with a deepening disappointment and relief what the toys prove without his having to ask. He's tried, he says, he's done the best he can.

Again the vacant feeling, What next? and now he ascends the hill and enters the university campus on his way to the campus McDonald's. The gateman, the same old black man to whom he used to nod, nods again as he passes, not realizing he has not seen this face for a while. He passes the library, the administration building, where the dead lawn spreads down to the street and fraternity houses below, a few stragglers on the walk, and some playing frisbee on the lawn, all the trite old views. In McDonald's, almost empty, he gets a hamburger and sits, just as he sat long ago at the picnic table, for as long as he can stand it, letting the time pass. No one speaks to him except one familiar-looking educational face going by his table, who says "Hello" without surprise to his own familiar-looking educational face. Gradually as the afternoon tilts toward evening, he realizes that it was not for this he came, but for the evening, that his purpose is gathered in the night, though he does not yet know what it is. Around five o'clock, he gets up from his McDonald's table and finds another telephone book in the student union, where he looks up more names. Sebastian, Thomas, still lives bereaved (unless remarried) in his house on Lafayette. Gates, Magnus, has not moved, and the telephone book still does not tell you whether Florry lives there or somewhere else. Long, AJ, is where she always was. All these numbers not to call, these reasons not to have returned. Another idea comes to him, an impulse to find a name he never looked for before: Indigo, Sam. He too is listed, on a street close by in the university neighborhood. In a few minutes Gregory is there, looking for the number. Again, it is not a question of forcing recognition, only of exposing himself to the possibility. He identifies the house as he approaches, and looking ahead sees this time he will not escape so easily.

Though by now it is almost dark, the man is in front, working on his car, the man himself, though all Gregory sees are his legs from behind as he bends over the engine under the hood. Now he regrets and crosses to the other side, wondering whether to retreat, but that too would be against his plan—while the man straightens up and shows himself, lean body, stooped shoulders, almost bald head, wiping his hands on his jeans. Unable to turn back now, Peter Gregory walks on, seriously hoping the man won't notice him, but you can see the pause in Indigo's look, the memory interrogation preceding positive recognition before he speaks: Hey there, pal. How're you doing?

There's a momentary stop in time, Peter Gregory wondering for a few seconds if this is actually his trip's objective, and they stare at each other across the street. But when Sam Indigo starts to cross over, Gregory turns away, with a quick wave not to be rude, and not running but walking fast, not looking back, down the block and over to the avenue, not knowing if Indigo is following but hearing no footsteps.

He waits at a bus stop. The bus takes him downtown where he has dinner at another quick food restaurant. With another long stay at his table after dinner, waiting for whatever it is.

At nine o'clock that night, Peter Gregory leaves the downtown Wendy's, finds a taxicab and asks the driver to take him to the park. The driver thinks he's crazy, why anyone would go to the park alone at nine o'clock on a cold November night, but he takes him and leaves him by the playground. Park closes at ten, he says. Gregory watches him drive off, the headlights disappearing behind the trees like Florry Gates's when he refused to come out after she came back in remorse to pick him up having thrown him out.

As a result of which, we shall now walk again the walk we walked before, down the wooded hill, across the bridge over the industrial valley, up the long residential street back to the university district, to the apartment where we lived. A strenuous long walk, not quite so bad this time as the landmarks pass more quickly, aided by a sense of purpose lacking then. A sense of purpose—not the same as an actual purpose. The walk recalls the other indignation, angry thoughts, inner speeches and shame, ranging from Florry Gates to her father and to Anita Long, long gone, to Linda and Louis the Lover and the principal of the high school and the other teachers and coming to rest in the misery of an automobile crash and the righteous judge and the righteous reporters and all his lousy earlier life, reanimated in the mixed assortment of landmarks in the dark, streets and houses and bridges and shops, lights in homes protecting people from the chill, a chill which was abating then in the advance of spring and is intensifying now in the acceleration of winter.

He passes the corner of the street where he knows the Sebastian family used to live before he killed them, and obeys a masochistic impulse to look at that house which in the old days he never dared to see. He recognizes it by its number, sees it, unexpectedly large, windows blazing with light downstairs and up, a virtual mansion with a large lawn and a semicircular driveway, occupied by the rich. Yet remembering from the telephone book that Thomas Sebastian whom he bereaved is still living there, he can conclude, with another slight drawing of relieved breath, that Sebastian has made a new life. No doubt that entails no forgiveness, but it's something anyway.

He returns to his route. This time there will be no warm though dreary room to shelter him at the end of the walk, but neither will there be the flashing police lights and floodlights all over the street as he enters the last block. His heart clutches with remembered dread as he approaches this scene, anticipating surprise: what? The tall bald figure of Sam Indigo, perhaps, sitting on the porch waiting for him? He remembers now keenly the flashing colors and white floodlights on the Hadley house, which caused him to change course, avoid this street altogether, and go around the back to his apartment. He remembers his inability to believe it only a coincidence or to avoid believing the real purpose of the lights was to illuminate his predicament with Florry Gates, to publicize that and all his other troubles so brightly as to obliterate distinctions and make him suspect in all the crimes which police lights announce. He turns the corner. The street is empty, peaceful, innocent with its spaced streetlamps and lighted windows. He stops. He remembers the strange fear that seized him last year in the airplane at the time his Trace fortunes were just beginning to collapse, the strange crazy fear that he might have been the murderer of Jock Hadley in a deed obliterated from memory. He had forgotten about the fear itself in his subsequent adventures, but remembers it now as this simple realization erases all its grounds: since the floodlights were already on Jock Hadley's house when Peter Gregory returned from his walk, Jock Hadley must have been already killed, with time enough to be discovered and the police called. Therefore it was impossible for Peter Gregory to be involved, as he really did know all along.

He remembers a conversation earlier that evening when Florry Gates came for him in her car. It was Jock Hadley calling him across the street, Hey Mister. That gal's too young for you.

Ignore him.

I know your type.

Who's *that*? Florry Gates said. Then, in a loud voice, clear and young and virginal: Shut the fuck up, you old fart.

No one knew there was a boundary near in Hadley's historical time, these possibly the last words his ears would hear if the murderer, coming in less than an hour, did his work without speech.

He takes a breath, grasps his courage, and enters the street. He goes by the quiet lot with doghouse and dog which does not bark: where the illuminated bungalow with its mean and nasty voice used to be. He approaches his apartment, where Sam Indigo once asked him innocent questions. Another simple realization occurs to him: at the time of the lights, Peter Gregory did not know what they meant. He did not learn of the murder until the next morning. It was only his memory that mixed things up, confusing before and after, transferring shames, one for another, making all his fears both screens for others and screened by them, so that everything was merely a screen for something else.

When he is past there's another crisis of transition, What next? but this is evidently a false crisis because he keeps going as if he knows. He is going downtown. A dark destination at the downest part of downtown. Now it occurs to him with a thrill for the drama of it: I am re-enacting. I am acting out so as to remember what I rejected and thereby rediscover the connection between the old Peter Gregory and whoever I have become since. As he walks the memory grows clearer, while his feet carry downward, down the long hill he had climbed in the afternoon, through the slum, beyond to the shops, the hotels.

He constructs a chronology, like this:

Sunday evening: Florry Gates drove him to the park, and there, after a dispute, she made him get out of the car and when she changed her mind and invited him back in, he escaped and walked home by himself. When he arrived, there were police lights in front of Jock Hadley's house, the meaning of which he did not learn until the next morning.

Monday: in the morning, Sam Indigo, gathering information, called on Peter Gregory, just as he was about to go to school. He asked him what he might have seen or heard. He knew this

Sam Indigo, who had questioned him once before, after the Sebastian accident. Why the homicide detective, if that's what he was, was involved in the accident case, he did not know. He remembered him both times mild and sad, as if not knowing what he wanted to find out. In this interview, Gregory, afraid of the scandal of Florry Gates, said he was in all evening and heard nothing. A little later, from his classroom window, he saw Sam Indigo outside coming into the building. To question him again? It occurred to Gregory that Indigo must have realized he had not told the truth about last night. A lie: that was the lie he had tried so hard later to remember. Not having a class in this period, Gregory decided to leave. He went out to the faculty parking lot and got his car. Drove out on the Interstate to a shopping mall, cruised around a parking lot, went on to another mall. He had lunch at a cafeteria there. He doesn't remember what he was thinking, whether it was Florry Gates or Jock Hadley or the career of Peter Gregory and Linda, and doesn't know if he knew he was being irrational, nor if he was making excuses, nor if he had any purpose in mind. In the afternoon he returned to the school, went to his classroom and realized—he does remember the shock of this—that he had missed all his classes.

This gave him the idea he was going through a crisis and was therefore free to act in an appropriate way. He went home without speaking to anyone. That night he turned off the lights in his apartment, so he could revel in the sensation of being hunted. His burrow, hutch, lair, cave, Peter Rabbit and the goshawk. This is really irrational, Peter Gregory remembers telling Peter Rabbit. Play acting. There was play acting in everything he did, then and always, long before, and now. Drama, tragedy, comedy, before the imagined audience judging, wondering, appalled.

Tuesday: He woke up refreshed, feeling fine. Good, he said, a crazy interlude, now I can get back to work. Then the telephone rang, and everything resolved was unresolved again. The ringing telephone was the lawyer for Mr. Gates. Friendly and respectful, meet you in the principal's office at ten.

He remembers packing his suitcase—two suitcases, cramming the stuff in, everything he could stuff. He remembers at the same time remembering everything bad he had done in his life. Now (walking) he does not remember those bad things, only the act of remembering. All that stupidity, cowardice, lust, self-deception, things like that. With a certain exhilaration in so much shame, for the justifications it might give.

He can't remember where he meant to go with his packed luggage (now: having passed the struggle of the migrated mountain folk trying to make new lives in the city, he is in the midst of the downtown hotel district, by dimly lit closed airlines offices, luggage and computer shops). He got into the car, leaving his packed luggage in the apartment. He went downtown, ate lunch, went to a movie which he doesn't remember, coming out into a wash of white reality in the late afternoon. Another meal. Couldn't go home because of the packed luggage he had left there. So he went to a motel. Went into the motel room, but couldn't go to bed because he had no luggage.

He wrote the suicide note in the motel. You would think, as Peter Gregory in fact did think until *this* moment (now: going down from the downtown center past the garages and warehouses), that writing the suicide note implied an intention to act, that in the motel room he must have reached the bottom of depression and misery. But now (the public landing coming into view, darkly ahead) he remembers the suicide note as another theatrical experiment. To see what it was like to write one. Because the real Peter Gregory was too domesticated, ritualized,

301

civilized, pasteurized, intellectual, skeptical, multisided, for anything so consequential, and all he could do was pretend to be different, pretend to be crazy and full of despair, concocting a note like an actor, and by such imaginative projection to stand for a moment on the edge of himself and get a glimpse of the animals inside.

He remembers this now, as his walk finally breaks out on the public landing itself: he never intended to kill himself. That was not the idea at all. Writing the suicide note was a game, a gesture. Writing the suicide note was exciting and fun.

THIRTY SEVEN

The public landing is a large concrete plane sloping down to the river. There's a little theater in a barge moored at one end. In the daytime the slope is full of cars parked at an angle. Now in the night it is a black hole below which the water trembles with snaky light. Behind and above are the concrete struts of highway ramps leading to the bridge, and the great circular void of a coliseum which on that other night contained, unheard outside, the spiritual noise of Osgood Landis and his daughter the Virgin Miranda.

The landing slopes down from Gregory's feet to death at the bottom. Real death, simpler than his imagination, tugging with a slight but definite force. He holds back, not wanting to let the magnetism or gravity get stronger, while an internal argument goes on, challenging the notion his suicide note was phony. That charge was disproved, so the argument goes, by the fact that he went into the river. He really did.

He feels the pull of the slope in his feet, in the obtuse angle to which his ankle is stretched. The other time he had the car. The least he can do now is go on foot half way down, to where he left it then. The pull of the slope is not too great for that: he walks easily and still feels relatively safe.

Yet the danger is palpable, unless it is only memory of the first time. He has reached the crystal point of his mission, from which looking back he sees what a long and postponed mission it has been: from the far point of his eastern trajectory in a

Venetian hotel room, the rebound seeking to reverse that trajectory, flung back to the west with such acceleration that he missed the river and landed in Seattle. Now that he has found his way back it would be criminal not to finish it.

What does that mean?

He goes down to the edge.

The pull is there but it's resistible. An attraction but not a longing, rather a fear that he will go against his desires. His desires are with Bonnie Brown back in Seattle, who unfortunately went back to Jay.

And there is all the alertness and clarity of simple thought, neither hypnotized nor confused, which denies any reason to go into the river and cannot remember any plausible reason why he went in before. Hank Gummer, who leaped down the stairwell, also had no reason, they said.

So the mystery remains right to the water's edge. It's at his feet. He looks down at it. The waves on the concrete go slurp, they slobber, they lip their tongues, they slosh and splash, vulgar sounds like drinking soup, slopping at him like a lover.

Peter Gregory standing here at the threshold can't remember what he wants to know.

Someone is watching him. He knows before he has evidence, no sound, nothing visible in the dark. He knows because of some memory in the river's flood, leaking through the locks. It makes him stumble, almost fall, touch the pavement with his fingers to regain balance.

Over to the right somewhere, he hears the footsteps, sees the shadow in the shadows, too fast to be casual, hurrying down the slope near the bridge.

He steps back, slips, his foot skids on suddenly slippery pavement like a coat of slime, he topples and as he rights himself he slides into the water. He steps back a little more to regain his footing, and there is no footing. Submerged for a second, thrashing in the powerful November current, cold. Damn it.

While his busy mind says, Don't panic, you can manage this, another busy part notices the familiarity. So that's how it was. Water sloshing in the nose, the primal scene again. Drifting fast, he treads water off shore, keeping his head above the waves watching for the prowling figure.

He notices the gap between himself and the shore widening fast, is it faster than he can swim? which shocks him into urgency: watch out, get busy, you'll drown. The water is real closing over him, whistling cold and black, tasting of mud, his clothes dragging him down, while he thinks, Stupid stupid, have I gone and lost it because my foot slipped?

Stupid and triple stupid, the elephantine ego needing to know at all cost, even though the only knowledge is trivial knowledge, stupid knowledge, and the cost is drowning. He sinks. Then there's a fight in the river, Peter Gregory resisting death. He did not know death could be so violent. First a blow on the back of his head, heavy splashing, then a blow to his jaw, hard as wood. Then death clutches him around the throat, pulling his head back into the water. He struggles and regains the air, but death won't release him, holding him still around the throat, with the waves sloshing into his mouth, choking him down.

Something pushes him. His hands scrape the pavement, he pulls himself up on hands and knees and flops down on the surface. He spits and coughs and breathes. He watches Death climb out of the river behind him, out of breath too, and both are soaking wet in their clothes.

Sam Indigo says, What the hell's the matter with you?

It was an accident. I fell in.

Some accident.

Peter Gregory is too wet to argue. Sam Indigo is Death, Sam Indigo saved his life. He realizes this with surprise: You saved my life.

Hell, man, what's wrong with Long Island Sound?

I don't live there anymore.

You don't live here neither.

Sam Indigo sitting there on his haunches, dripping ice water, shivering and looking at him. Gregory is freezing too, wet clothes on his skin like ice. The difference between this and the other time is between November and May. Gregory notices how carefully Indigo watches him.

And you with all that money, too.

What money? It takes Peter Gregory a moment to remember his money. I lost that.

Lost? The big house, the fortune, the fancy cars? How did you accomplish that?

Embarrassed as if he had failed at a job. I can't remember, he says.

Gregory squirms in his wet clothes. The movement incites a quick start on Indigo's part, as quickly restrained. Watching me, Gregory thinks, ready to jump me. He looks at Indigo, hard, and Indigo stares back. Meaning is exchanged, though Gregory is not sure what.

So he says, What?

Don't you move like that, Indigo says. I'll conk you so you'll really want to die.

Gregory incredulous. You think I want to jump in that? I'm not that crazy.

Sam Indigo gets to his feet. Sheds his jacket, rips off his shirt in the cold air. What are you doing? It's too damned freezing. Come up to the car.

Gregory doesn't move. Takes a breath and asks: Why do you keep following me?

Hell, man, why are you following *me*?

I'm not following you.

You found my house this afternoon, and you walked by it tonight. Lucky I saw you. I could have been watching TV. Everything he says comes shivering and trembling in the November air.

You followed me to New York. You followed me to Jack Rome's funeral. You followed me here.

Whose funeral?

Jack Rome's. I saw you there.

You're imagining. I never went to no Jack Rome funeral.

Shivering there, halted, barechested in the cold with his shirt in his hands, stamping his feet with impatience. Hell, man I followed you here because of your known propensity for suicide, and it's a good thing I did because look at you. Now you come up to the car so I can get warmed up. Let's go, don't make me freeze here like an idiot.

Peter Gregory pulls himself up heavily. His clothes would dry in time, settle on his body like a cold crust, he knows that from experience. The shirtless man's shivering body emanates a faint freezing mist. He bounces on his feet, double time, swinging his arms, while Gregory trudges behind. I'm going to change clothes, Indigo says. I've got a blanket for you if you want it.

Lagging behind, Gregory is distracted by a confusion, blending this November dowsing with the original May one. He is fixed on a familiarity noticed in the water, which has now become a familiarity of more than what water feels like when you're drowning. A similar furtive feeling the other time, a similar desire to escape, a similar shadow slinking down behind him. As this familiarity articulates it becomes a memory never recalled during the non-Gregory years but too real to be invented, namely, that Sam Indigo pursued him the first time too, and that Gregory, never intending death but enacting the part of someone in extremity, slipped into the water as he tried to escape, then as now. It was only later, looking back at the evidence, that he supposed he had been trying to drown.

If this was true, he says to himself gasping in the cold, the great change in his life was the result of nothing more than an accident, which means, thinking about the names he had adopted, his whole life was accidental. He had renamed himself for one accident after another, supposing in each case an important choice had been made. What an astonishing thought, he says to himself, what an interesting idea.

Meanwhile Sam Indigo after stripping himself naked (stark, skeletal in the November night) has covered himself with baggy pants and a heavy sweatshirt from the car and tossed Gregory a blanket. Don't know if that'll warm you or not. While Gregory already is reconsidering his astonishing thought, suspecting it's old stuff he has always known, Sam Indigo talks, saying: Listen man, you've got no reason to kill yourself. I got no patience with that. Life is good, man. I mean your basic, material life, the original thing. You got troubles, lots of people got worse. You and me, walking around in good health, it's a crime to kill ourselves, don't you know that?

Peter Gregory ignores his irritation and says, The other time when I went into the river, did you follow me then, too?

Hell, man, how paranoid can you get?

You didn't?

Why should I?

(It could have been someone else, a stranger, a bum looking for a place to sleep, a fanatic escaped from Landis in the Coliseum.)

You didn't come to my house in New York to blackmail me?

Goddamn, did I blackmail you? Did I threaten? Did I ask for anything?

Why did you come then?

I told you then, you don't believe me. Can't a guy pay a friendly call once in a life? I was in New York, I had business, I knew you was there, I was interested. You were an interesting case, don't you know that? Interesting. It had nothing to do with you.

Peter Gregory, ashamed to be thought paranoid and groping for warmth, feels safe enough to ask. Do you think I killed Jock Hadley?

What?

Sam Indigo stands there. He squats down, slowly, near Gregory, looking again. Studying him. Saying, finally, Did you?

I don't think so. Alarmed by the physical symptoms in his body, accelerated pulse, pounding, shivering.

What do you mean, You don't think so? Did you have something to do with it?

Not to my knowledge.

Then why do you ask?

I just wondered if you suspected me.

Two men squatting on their haunches in the dark near the detective's car, above the cold flowing river, one in wet clothes, the other dry, trying to figure each other out, while the wet man in accidental alarm wonders if he has already begun a new life as a penitentiary inmate. The dry man says, What's your connection?

None. I was out with a girl. Then I walked home. When I got home I saw the police lights. You have no grounds to suspect me.

That's what I thought until you brought it up.

A silence for a while except the rushing floody river.

I believe I brought it up because I didn't like the man, and when I heard he'd been killed, I was glad.

Is that all?

To the best of my knowledge.

Why do you keep saying, "To the best of your knowledge"?

What else should I say?

Say you didn't do it.

I didn't do it. I have no memory of doing it.

Memory blackout?

If I had a memory lapse, there would be a hiatus, right? I was out with Florry Gates, a horrible evening with no hiatus anywhere. I couldn't have done it. It's not the kind of thing I do.

You sure of that? I have a standing principle which is, Never be a character witness. If you didn't do something, you shouldn't go around asking people why they didn't suspect you. Lucky for you, we caught the Hammer Man two years ago.

Glad to hear it.

The one you killed was the Sebastian folks. That's the one you killed.

That's right, Peter Gregory said, angry and disappointed all over again.

Can't get away from it, huh?

I got away from it. I got away from it three times.

So you did. And here you are again.

Peter Gregory was beginning to warm. Do you know why I came back? he says.

Not yet.

I'm living in Seattle now. Had a friend living with me, best ever in my life, and I changed my name to Mitchell Grape.

A fine name. You like that better?

I liked it fine. I was doing good for the world. Canvassing for the starving children in Africa. It does you good to do good for the world. Do you know about that?

I did good for the world before I retired. I caught crooks.

It's good to do good.

Guess so, if you say so.

Only it didn't last.

How come?

She left me. I keep forgetting she left me. She gave me advice before she left, integrate yourself. So here I am.

Integrating yourself.

Don't laugh.

Who's laughing? So do you feel integrated?

I discovered I fell into the river by accident. Makes me look like a fool.

Nothing's an accident, man. Don't you know that?

Is that so? Now I don't know what to do.

What more do you want? Go back to Seattle.

She left, I told you.

Stay here then. The old home town.

What can I do?

Put up a sign: Peter Gregory has returned. All questions answered for a fee.

You're not taking me seriously.

Sorry.

If I came back here, I'd need to know what's happened in my absence.

Lots, lots. The world has turned upside down in your absence.

Come, tell me. I couldn't find my wife in the phone book. Nor her lover either.

Sorry, I have no information about that.

What did the high school do when I disappeared?

They made a fuss and replaced you and hushed it up.

They wouldn't like me back. There was a man named Gates who was going to charge me with statutory rape.

Never heard of that. I guess he'd be satisfied to have you commit suicide.

Would he still be satisfied if I came back?

Hell man, how would I know? Go back to New York, then. Look up your rich friends.

Impossible. They threatened to kill me.

Well, maybe you should jump in the river after all.

There was a silence.

Maybe I should start over.

No kidding?

Make a fresh start in some new place.

With a new name?

That would liberate me.

You have some experience with that kind of thing.

Where would you suggest?

How about the South?

The South, yes. New Orleans, could I go to New Orleans?

You could go by bus.

I could hitchhike.

You have some skill at that too.

Yes, I know what to expect.

You know how to do it, all right.

You felt a rustling, rousing, coming back to life, as if you had been buried a while, like in a ditch under leaves.

The whole world would be open to me, I could try anything if I wanted to.

Just like always.

Something always went wrong before.

This time you'll get it straight.

You squinted at him, unable to determine his expression in the dark. You were thinking of the life ahead, and the old lonely fears began to arise. You remembered the renounced loneliness of your previous lives, which you were not allowed to think about in the harsh discipline of your names. You remembered prohibited mourning for children whom you could not acknowledge, and for thoughts you were not permitted to indulge. How surreptitiously, guiltily, you allowed your memory to play, illegally opening up the tomb where once, once, a gentle mother sang to you—*you*—in a time of no time, breathing love into you, planting it so it would grow, and a gentle humorous father secured it with quiet jokes. You longed to grieve, for the luxury and comfort of grieving, that useless nostalgia not allowed in the forward busy lives of people like Stephen White and Stephen Trace, Mitchell Grape, and Murry Bree. Lives full of boundaries, barbed wire and chain link fences. How wasteful, how bleak. You said, Do I have to go through all this again?

Find someone, he said. You've done it before. Tell her your story. Tell her you fell in the river. If she don't believe you, tell her the meaning is too deep for words.

Eventually she'll leave me.

Or die. Or you'll die and leave her. It happens all the time. Take me, Indigo said. My wife died. My kids off and married. I'm writing my memoirs.

Ah.

You could do the same. You got the material. Come, he said, You're freezing to death. I'll take you to a hotel.

Where's my luggage?

What happened to your bag?

My God. Peter Gregory looks at the river, a vast invisible black gap of turmoil downstream, across which light bobs and shakes from the lines of one shadowy bridge to another, exposing now and then an impurity, fragment, floating object for a moment before gone. Well, he says, it must have slipped out of my hands.

Sam Indigo laughs. By accident escaping from me? Looks like I'll have to lend you something. You can pay it back from New Orleans. Will you remember?

Sure I will. You can trust me.

THIRTY EIGHT

You followed the retired detective's suggestion and began to write. From now on, wherever you went, hitchhiking or by bus or plane, in style or threadbare, you had a text in your luggage. It had weight. Your name was written in it, typed on the first page: by So-And-So.

No longer were you a mere first person trying to articulate in no particular medium or the evanescent air an identity different from the third person name you happened to carry. Instead you lived in the word *you* written into page after page, a fixative for memories turned into adventures. Evening by evening this written *you* accumulated, pages on pages in the distillation of a name, creating (if you could avoid the dangers of fire and loss) an imitation of permanence.

You came into being in the river twice. The second time you completed your birth in a motel two nights later. By then you had hitchhiked three hundred miles south, thinking all the way what to write. Already the climate was warmer, pleasanter, more comfortable. Let off at a town square in a village in Georgia among the Southern speakers, you found a motel room and went to the drugstore for paper and pen. You had supper in a café on the square across from a Confederate monument and afterwards went directly back to your motel to begin. The motel was chilly, but once you started you didn't notice. It was like every motel room. There was a heavy drape across the room-wide window, a small table and a stiff hard chair. You leaned over the table and wrote by hand, getting into it, lubricating yourself by describing where you were. The light was dim. There was a hum of machine noise, which must have been a heater since it wouldn't be the air-conditioner at that time of year. There was muffled television, voices and an audience laughing in some near room, and the sound of a slamming door, and a can dropping into the slot in the Coke machine outside. You wrote it down. The next day you moved on, and thereafter what you did in the day made it possible to write at night. You wrote and wrote. You wrote this story you had previously tried to tell in the disappearing air like oral history to disappearing listeners. You got it down where the words would remain the same and anyone could appreciate it as much as anyone else.

You didn't get a typewriter until later. Then you retyped everything you had written so far and went on from there. Writing added mass to your travels. The computer came after you had settled down and had some money. Now a year later there's a study and a desk with manuals and containers for disks, and a view through the curtains of bare December trees with sparrows scrounging for berries and dried seeds, while you looking back remember the origins in the motel. You read back over what you wrote and remember the seasons and places and what was happening as you wrote all mixed together.

When you started you wondered who would read it. Consistent with the notion not quite abandoned yet that you were integrating Gregory, you thought of your reader as his wife Linda. You imagined what to do when you finished, thinking you would seek her out and find her by placing personal ads in newspapers around the country. You'd send these ads to all the cities, the major papers. It would take a while, but you could wait, for you had found your vocation.

The ads you imagined would address her by name: LINDA GREGORY. To make it more certain, add the children: ALSO JEFF GREGORY, PATTY GREGORY. And you would spell the original of all your names, no longer taboo:

Peter Gregory your once husband and father is alive and well and has a story for you. Please write or call.

You thought how courageous and emotional this was, this return to your first name. With an appropriate element of chance: you did not know the odds on your success, which might be for you or against you. Probability would decide—or be violated. Chance would determine what you deserved or did not deserve. There was a problem in that Linda Gregory never looked at personals. If she didn't look, you wouldn't find her, no matter how many cities you canvassed. But other people read them, which improved the odds, for any friend or acquaintance seeing such a notice would surely tell her. So you reasoned while you worked, full of the patience of the long term, postponing a closer look. You could wait. As long as you were writing you could wait.

Your narrative moved on, rediscovering Amy and Joe, and Hank Gummer, and Jack Rome. Then something happened. You got used to writing, it became a habit. You went on without realizing the consequences, until this recent crisis when you arrived at the point where you had expected to end. This was to be the moment in the preceding chapter where Sam Indigo suggests you write it down. And look—already you've gone beyond.

You're faced with the crisis of stopping. Perhaps in the beginning you did not expect to get this far. But here you are, and here come the problems. If this is the end, it's time to place the personals that will find Linda. But things have changed since you made that plan. How far away she seems now, and how far you have come. Perhaps she is not your audience after all, perhaps she never was. She wouldn't want you anyway. How upset she would be to discover you're not dead. Nor do you need her now that you have Dorothy. There was no Dorothy when you began, so how could you have known? While you write, Dorothy studies her lines, preparing her next role, which opens in six weeks. What would Dorothy say about Linda's return?

The more you write, the more independent you become, standing by yourself, the less a pronoun standing for another name. You, all of you, just you and only you. You did not foresee that you might not want to stop. You have developed this good writing habit along with the accouterments and auxiliary pleasures, including rewriting, and editing, and polishing, and reorganizing, and restating, all that tinkering and fiddling with words, making things sharper, clearer, more incisive, funnier, sadder, deeper, shallower. You didn't realize how much you would enjoy it. These supplements to the raw truth of story are to your new name what riches were to Stephen Trace, freedom to Murry Bree, goodness to Mitchell Grape.

Consider the possibility of not stopping. You could carry on the story into the period of writing chasing your tail like Tristram Shandy. You could postpone indefinitely, an endless deferral, digging more and more minutely into time, draining your substance away.

No, you must stop. The plot requires it. Call it a book, you can always write another. If not Linda, let everybody read, Sharon, Jane, Bonnie, Dorothy, Jack, David, Luigi, Sam, all the first names, those who knew you, those who didn't. Which is to say, publish. That will solidify your name and convert you into the first person, full of ego. Readings and talk shows. And what will you do next? Your name propels another book. Continuing where this leaves off, filling the gaps unfilled in the present chapter. After that, again, What next? By then perhaps you'll know how to tell the story in a different way, with other symbols.

But for now, time to stop, with good wishes and thanks to all of you who generously shared your second person with me. Are there loose ends that need to be tied up?

Here's one. If you really wanted to find Linda Gregory and her children, you wouldn't need to place personals around the country. A simple letter to the university, Department of Romance Languages, where she used to work, would suffice. They'd know where she went.

Another loose end: the rumors about Jack Rome. You hear them still, whispers that he did not die, the plane crash faked or rigged. The latest (you got this from the mechanic who was working on your BMW) was that he sails a fishing boat on either the East coast or the West coast, or else it's the Gulf coast or if not that the Great Lakes, having the time of his life under an assumed name. A rumor like any dead rock star who refuses to die, you know.

This suggests another line of activity if you run out of writing or find yourself reduced to metafiction: become a detective like Sam Indigo. Make it your business to track down Jack Rome. Not to expose him but to join him. Go fishing with him. You could have the time of your life with him and Dorothy, incognito at sea, like your Uncle Phil.